SECRETS

of OUR

HOUSE

ALSO BY REA FREY

Until I Find You
Because You're Mine
Not Her Daughter

SECRETS

of OUR

HOUSE

A Novel

Rea Frey

ST. MARTIN'S GRIFFIN
NEW YORK

First published in the United States by St. Martin's Griffin, an imprint of St. Martin's Publishing Group

www.stmartins.com

Designed by Gabriel Guma

Library of Congress Cataloging-in-Publication Data

Names: Frey, Rea, author.
Title: Secrets of our house : a novel / Rea Frey.
Description: First edition. | New York : St. Martin's Griffin, 2022
Identifiers: LCCN 2021039185 | ISBN 9781250241603
   (trade paperback) | ISBN 9781250241610 (ebook)
Subjects: LCGFT: Novels.
Classification: LCC PS3606.R4885 S43 2022 | DDC 813/.6—dc23
LC record available at https://lccn.loc.gov/2021039185

Our books may be purchased in bulk for promotional, educational, or business use. Please contact your local bookseller or the Macmillan Corporate and Premium Sales Department at 1-800-221-7945, extension 5442, or by email at MacmillanSpecialMarkets@macmillan.com.

First Edition: 2022

10 9 8 7 6 5 4 3 2 1

For Alex,
the very best secret keeper

NOTHING BURNS LIKE THE COLD.

—GEORGE R. R. MARTIN

SUMMER

1

Desi

DESI woke from a jarring nightmare and sat up.

Beside her, Peter's side of the bed was still intact, the sheets crisp and untouched. She smoothed a hand over the duvet, conjuring her nightmare.

In it, she'd been chasing Jules and Peter. Peter had stepped onto their frozen pool. A spiderweb crack formed under his boot, then fanned across the entire surface. Before anyone could move, his right foot broke through. One moment, he was smiling. The next, he was gone. The other details faded before she could dissect the dream's possible meaning.

She pulled on her robe and brushed her teeth. Her reflection mocked her. She assessed the sharp bones of her face, the cups of her eye sockets, the violent tips of her clavicle, the sunken ball and socket of her pointy hips. Where she was once soft, bright, and healthy, she now appeared to have been hollowed with a spoon. She knew it was from stress—the stress of being away from the office for three months, stress from her flailing marriage, stress about her child leaving for college, stress from . . .

No.

She spit into the sink and tidied the counter. Peter's toiletries sat, unused. He must have slept in the guest room again. Though they had agreed to spend the entire summer here to make one last-ditch effort to save their marriage, so far Peter was showing little interest.

He blamed the distance on staying up late, on working on the shelter in the forest, but she knew he craved space. He wouldn't dare come out and say it, or disrespect her in front of Jules, but his continuous silence tormented her. The way he'd sit across from her, chewing the food she'd prepared and not offer a word. The way he'd purposefully let her fall asleep alone in their bed and wake up just the same. The way his eyes burned into her, as if he *knew*.

She stashed away that thought and glanced out the bathroom window. The morning glittered under the protective cover of pines. It had only been a month ago that they'd arrived for their summer vacation at The Black House, which stretched like an ink stain on the crest of a bulbous mountaintop, blotting out almost an acre of land.

It was Desi's greatest professional accomplishment—a giant ebony compound that had been flattened and resurrected with endless panes of heavy floor-to-ceiling glass; solar panels; a cavernous, vaulted ceiling; massive bedrooms with steam showers; a sauna, gym, and other modern, high-tech touches. Acres of sugar maple, American beech, eastern hemlock, and Virginia pine cut them off from the rest of the world thousands of feet below, casting The Black House in shadow.

Now, Desi padded down the hall, releasing the viselike grip on her foolish beliefs that a house could save her marriage or keep her daughter from growing up. She grabbed a cup of coffee from the freshly brewed pot and eased outside by the pool, where Jules and Peter were already swimming. It was still early, but she wasn't surprised. Peter and Jules had always been such early risers.

Peter splashed and tossed a football to Jules. Her daughter jumped straight out of the water, the spray gliding off her athletic body. She palmed the ball and crashed back into the deep end. Peter hoisted his hands in victory and Jules threw it back with ease. How odd to see her glistening, confident husband, when she'd just seen his feet crack through the ice and disappear in her dream. She buried the image and told them both good morning.

"Coming in?" Jules asked. She wrung out her hair and waded to the edge of the pool.

Desi laughed. "Priorities first." She hoisted her favorite mug in the air.

"That stuff will kill you," Jules commented before diving underneath the water and swimming end to end without breaking for air.

Desi rolled her eyes and admired her daughter's smooth strokes. When she surfaced, Desi hesitated. Finally, she asked: "Why did you quit swim team again?"

First it had been cross country, then swimming. Jules had given them up on a whim, when she could have received college scholarships for both. Instead, she'd chosen Columbia due to her deep interest in art. After some gentle prodding at Desi's insistence, she'd now be studying biomedical science in the fall. Jules floated to her back, turned, flipped underwater, and expertly eased off the wall.

Jules was one of those rare breeds who was good at everything: she was artistic, kind, self-sufficient, smart. She could have easily trained to be an Olympic swimmer, a track star, or even a model, but she wore her disinterest for those natural abilities like a badge. While she was insanely talented, she often started and stopped things or seemed to pivot just when she could really make something of herself. Perhaps it was her age, or maybe that's just who she was.

But Jules maintained other interests that never seemed to fade. She was a total survivalist. Peter, an ex-Marine, taught Jules environmental navigation, how to handle a Kukri long-blade knife, how to collect rainwater, how to spear and clean a fish, how to start a fire, how to sew wounds, how to fend off an attack, how to assemble and disassemble weapons, and how to put someone to sleep using only a lapel. She thrived on building her survivalist skills, though Desi often joked that she'd need a different set of skills to survive New York.

In just a few months, Jules would move to the city and begin an entirely new chapter without them. Desi wasn't ready for her to move out, but was thrilled with her choice of school and the bright future that awaited.

When Jules finally stopped swimming, she addressed her mother's question, never one to leave someone hanging. "I outgrew it," she said, pulling her lithe body out of the pool.

This summer had changed her daughter. She'd met a boy the very first week in River Falls, for starters—Will. Jules worked so hard *not* to be a stereotypical teenager, avoiding anything that screamed teenage girl. And yet, here she was, involved in her own whirlwind summer romance.

Desi adjusted her sunglasses and took a sip of the medium roast. She could practically chew the coffee, it was so thick. Peter always made the best coffee. She sighed and tipped her head back. She liked to think it was a peace offering of sorts. *Sorry our marriage sucks! Have some amazing coffee!*

Funny how a marriage could sway like that. The good days used to carry her for weeks, those rare moments when they'd share a laugh, physically reconnect, or just let go of logistics and meet each other as equals. However, those moments were flanked more frequently by bitter, silent ones. By the time she'd scaled her own interior design business, managed to pay all four years of Jules's private high school tuition, sustained a thriving city life and social circle, and built The Black House for her family, her marriage seemed too far gone, the last lonely item on a very long list of priorities.

"Great coffee," she offered. Peter adjusted his goggles and dropped into an effortless freestyle. She wasn't sure if he was ignoring her or if he just hadn't heard. She wasn't sure of anything anymore. She closed her eyes again, forced her thoughts to settle. The slap of Peter's palms and his steady breathing gashed the surface of the pool. Jules dove in to join him, a tandem duo perfectly in sync.

Rattled by her family's utter disinterest in carrying on a conversation, Desi scooped her coffee from the table and went back inside. She needed to go for a run and clear her head.

She refilled her coffee and stood at the entrance to the living room, leaning against the mantel. When they'd first visited the land that would become their summer escape, they'd all been overcome by the beauty of the Blue Ridge Mountains. She and Jules had studied their origin on a map, snaking their fingers from Carlisle, Pennsylvania, to Maryland, Virginia, and here, to this tiny town at the tip of North Carolina.

She turned her attention back to the living room. It was large but cozy with two oversized leather couches, a glass coffee table, twin Ansley armchairs, and the updated fireplace, which was the focal point of the entire room. The back was nothing but sweeping glass. The twenty-foot ceiling was capped by ornate wooden beams she'd salvaged from the original farmhouse.

The living room bled into the dining room, then the separate

kitchen behind her with its Sub-Zero fridge, her professional
gas range, the island, and the covered patio. Down the hallway,
three guest bedrooms, along with the master, branched off the
back, away from the heart of the home.

God, I'm lonely.

She ignored the gloomy thought and took her coffee down the
hall to the master suite. She peeked into Jules's room, which
was simple and open, the oversized windows capturing the ro-
bust acreage just beyond the glass. The silence hummed in her
ears. Here, there were no Chicago buses, ambulances, or fire
trucks to muddy her thoughts.

She kept walking to their bedroom at the rear of the house. The
understated king took up the center of the room with built-in
nightstands and lamps. Her spa bathroom with the immense
soaking tub and dressing area sat behind a set of antique French
doors.

She opened the drapes and stepped onto the balcony that overlooked a spray of reedy trees and the glittering infinity pool
off the back patio. The sun pricked the water and turned the
surface to diamonds. A few leaves bobbed at the deep end, and
she eyed them distractedly. Jules and Peter were still splashing
and talking.

Peter made a joke then dunked Jules, who took his back
and sunk in a rear naked choke she'd learned in jiujitsu. Peter
tapped, and they went at it again, always turning quality time
into some sort of tactical training.

Desi missed the days when Jules was small and life was less
complicated. She could so easily conjure the little girl who used
to sprint around their kitchen with panties on her head. The
child who always refused to wear dresses, who made her stuffed
animals cardboard beds, and adored reptiles. The daughter

who'd fold into her side and beg to be tickled, carried upside down, or to snuggle any available second of the day.

Her heart ached just thinking about it, because so often, Desi *hadn't* snuggled or tickled Jules. She'd been so busy, she'd distractedly say, "Sure, honey, in just a sec," and then after so many minutes of hopeful waiting, Jules would retreat from the room, dejected. Now, it was too late to snuggle. It was too late to carry her in the very arms that had created her. She'd missed the only precious thing a mother was supposed to witness.

She was out of time.

She changed into running clothes, slipped on her shoes by the front door, and clipped a bell to her shorts to keep bears away. She contemplated grabbing her AirPods but decided against music today. She stepped outside to check her phone before her run, as the reception inside was practically nonexistent. The wind had stalled, and the sun rose higher overhead. She saw that she had one unread text.

She swiped it open and paused. It was from Carter.

Where are you? We need to talk. Please.

Her stomach clenched and she searched the trees, feeling as if there were eyes somewhere beyond them.

After a few uncertain moments, she deleted the text and replaced her phone inside.

She stretched her quadriceps and calves. Her feet scurried through freshly laid gravel, dusting her shoes white. Taking a momentary detour, she walked the perimeter of the property and pushed through thickets of trees to find the mountain's edge. She moved east until the trees abruptly ended and opened to a clear, cobalt sky. She wrapped her hand around a sappy trunk and stared into the vast wilderness. Her brown hair whipped across her face and her eyes roamed the land. Hillside cottages dotted various peaks. Downtown was a small rectangle at the mountain's base—a few blocks at best.

Desi stood like that for minutes, taking in the stillness she never got in Chicago. Finally, she eased back through the branches, a few scraping her cheeks. The earthy scent of pine mixed with the pungent aroma of dirt. The magic of this place had already seeped into her bones and settled.

Desi took off toward the back of the house, where they'd carved a three-mile trail through their land. Back home, she ran on the lakefront, dodging cyclists and other runners every few steps. Here, she had her own personal path.

She started off at a slower pace until her body loosened. The bell's jingle faded to the background as her mind wandered. Once again, her nightmare floated to the surface. She imagined Jules running ahead of her, panting, Peter calling after her in a low, playful growl.

Pursuit.

She sucked a breath and picked up the pace. Carter's text hammered her conscience and her mind lingered over his last word—*please.* That word gutted her for so many reasons. She could imagine that one simple word rolling off his lips, and everything in her had to keep from turning around and racing back to the house to call him.

Right before they'd come here for the summer, she'd thought about sitting Peter down and finally telling him the truth. If they were going to make their marriage better, then all the cards had to be on the table. But if she told him, would it only be to assuage her guilt? She hopped over a branch, her feet sturdy on the path.

Out of the corner of her eye, something darted through the trees, the quick spray of leaves evident beneath some creature's feet. She kept going and glanced behind her to make sure it wasn't a bear.

She rose up an incline, her thighs burning, and looped to the right. She quickened into a sprint, the soles of her Nikes slapping fresh wood chips, which provided a spongy floor beneath her feet. She watched for spare rocks or branches, so she didn't accidentally roll an ankle.

She concentrated on her breath, lost herself to the rhythm of the bell. When she felt her lungs would burst, she slowed, suddenly parched. She rested her hands on her thighs and sucked air. Birds flapped from tree to tree, and she kept her eyes peeled for predators. She stood upright, her left hip sore. She kneaded the palm of her hand into it when a blast of hot breath tickled the back of her neck.

She whipped around. "Hello?" She looked left and right, the shaggy trees casting her in shadow. Sweat beaded down her temple. Her fingers traced the back of her neck. Thoughts clashed for space in her brain. She stood there, breathing and thinking.

She turned and began running again, faster, as if she were being chased. Wasn't she though? Her past was chasing her, the truth was chasing her . . . *He* was chasing her. She blocked out the worry and completed the three-mile loop in just twenty minutes and emerged from the mouth of the trail, gasping. Her muscles throbbed. She raised her hands over her head and paced the gravel drive.

She hadn't pushed herself like that in so long. She closed her eyes until her heart rate slowed, but she could still feel the breath on her neck, a firm hand around her wrist, his voice in her ear.

She opened her eyes and walked back inside. She removed her shoes and found Jules and Peter at the dining room table.

"Did you guys eat yet?" Desi cleared her throat and waited for Jules to look up from her book long enough to acknowledge the question. Peter busied himself packing some sort of kit.

"We did." He zipped the bag. "Sorry." He offered her a smile. *He wasn't sorry.*

Desi ignored him and gripped the back of the dining room chair. "I was thinking we could go into town today."

Peter tightened a strap on his pack. "We're going exploring."

"Right now?"

"Yep."

"Can I come?" The words wobbled unsteadily from her lips. Desi watched the disappointment cloud Peter's face, then just as quickly disappear.

Jules rested her paperback on the table and gauged her mother. "You seriously want to come? Like, to build with us?"

Desi bit her tongue, then forced a laugh. "Is that so hard to believe?" She wanted to remind them that *she* built this house they were sitting so comfortably in—and it was much more complex than a shelter in the woods.

Jules and Peter looked at each other. "Yes."

Peter shoved his black hair back with a rough palm. His crow's feet deepened around a set of stormy eyes. "You sure?"

She hiked a shoulder, dropped it, heard something crack. All this recent tension had coiled the muscles she tried so hard to stretch. "Just let me change."

Jules and Peter exchanged another look—always ganging up on her, even with their silence. She jutted her jaw, turned on her heel, and strode to her phone instead. "You know what? Never mind. Have fun."

"Des."

"Mom, come on."

Desi lifted a hand, swiped her phone from the entryway table, and walked back outside in the same futile attempt to get reception. It's the one damn thing she couldn't seem to pay for here. Many people would say that was the point, but not when her livelihood depended on it. *Their* livelihood.

Peter made a good living since he'd retired from the military, but she could tell he was tired of training urbanites in tactical self-defense. He came alive in River Falls the same way Jules did. She'd heard their whispered plans about creating an outdoor survivalist course for locals. The only problem was their plan had nothing to do with her.

Whenever she pressed him on it, Peter would say it was just a way to expand his business someday. But she knew better. He had that look in his eye, and she didn't want to be the one to talk him out of it. However, her career was wrapped up in the city. As much as she loved having a second home, she was tethered to Chicago, and that would always be the dividing line between them.

She finally connected to her assistant, James, and asked for an update. She didn't need to call him, but she was antsy and needed something to do. They'd already survived six weeks of her three-month absence. But she was growing restless without work.

After a few minutes of updates, she hung up and gazed at her masterpiece, remembering the old one in its place. The gleaming compound welcomed her with its silver solar panels and painted black brick. No one would ever know how much work it had taken to construct this house in the middle of nowhere, tucked up here in the clouds.

The original 1964 farmhouse had been in irreparable condition. When she'd first stepped inside the property that would become their summer home, she'd wondered if she could salvage it. But after crunching over dead june bugs and fisting thick clumps of cobwebs, she knew it would be a teardown. Inside was nothing more than one open, dusty room with sturdy beams and weed-choked windows that overlooked acres of burnt grass and towering trees.

However, as she'd walked from left to right, she could feel the history and love in those walls, could sense it from the tiny scoop of a kitchen, with its well-seasoned cast-iron pots and pans hanging from a fishhook, the grease-laden stove, the retro beaded curtains, plaid furniture, and wrinkled, dog-eared paperbacks stuffed in a woven basket among skeins of vibrant yarn and knitting needles. Who had lived here, and why had they left? She'd spun in a circle, her toes scattering bug shells, and imagined what she could create. After endless renovations that spanned exactly fifteen months, The Black House was finally ready.

Desi checked the time. She wanted to go to town to get a few things. She walked around the side of the house to the garden. Peter and Jules had helped till soil and plant all their summer favorites: squash, lettuce, kale, corn, tomatoes. She squatted down, grabbed the shears in a nearby pot, and snipped some lavender. She'd toss it in her bath later.

She circled back to the front, still rattled by what had happened on her run. The dark black of her hidden truth gnawed at her conscience, but she knocked it away and let herself back inside.

"What's the verdict?" Peter asked.

Desi lifted the lavender to her nose. "You guys go. It's fine."

"Are you sure?" Peter looked relieved.

"I'm going into town," she said instead. "Okay if I take the car?"

"Do what you want," he offered and motioned for Jules to join him. She closed her book and grabbed her own pack.

"Have fun." Desi forced her lips into a smile.

She walked the long hall back to her master bedroom, showered, dressed, and adjusted her blouse in the mirror. She slicked a finger under her bottom lip and blotted her Chanel lipstick, Merry Rose. She tried not to locate the insecurity behind her eyes, all of the untold truths and buried secrets that threatened to erupt.

In the dining room, the remnants of her family's mess remained: paper, sketches, charcoal pencils, breakfast plates, crumbs, books, a carabiner. She sighed, swept the random objects into a heap, and hurriedly did the dishes. She checked the time, pulled on a sweater, and circled the grounds, keys in hand. To her surprise, her phone dinged again. She jumped to life, charged by the possibility that there might be one modicum of land she hadn't discovered that got cell reception.

She froze when she saw Carter's name again.

Please, Des. I need you.

Her heart hammered wickedly. She glanced behind her to make sure she was alone and before thinking too much about it, she responded.

We're away for the summer. Maybe we can speak when I get back?

She sent it, knowing what an empty promise that was. They hadn't spoken in years—not until they'd bumped into each other recently at the farmer's market, and she'd startled as though she'd seen a ghost. They'd shared pleasantries, and he'd asked for her card. She could have lied and said she didn't have one, but deep down, she wanted him to have her number. He'd rubbed his thumb over the embossed gold lettering and smiled.

"I always knew you'd do big things." He'd kissed her cheek and disappeared as suddenly as he'd arrived. It's all she'd been thinking about since.

She stared dumbly at her phone, practically willing a response. The text bubbles began, then disappeared. She held her breath until his text came through:

Can I come to you?

She laughed out loud. She could just imagine Carter showing up on her doorstep. What that would mean for her family. What that would mean for her.

She shoved the phone in her pocket, unsure of how to respond. She started toward the car, but suddenly, she didn't want to be alone. Peter and Jules would already be on the trail. She called their names anyway, the syllables echoing through the forest.

She walked closer to the edge of the trees and clenched her sweater from the sudden chill. The wind cried. Should she go into town as planned or should she join her family?

Carter's text bounced through her mind again. *Can I come to you?*

She closed her eyes and willed away the panic. Though she'd kept her secret safe for all these years, she'd opened the door of communication when she shouldn't have. Sooner or later, she was going to have to find a way to deal with all of this. They all were. She calmed her mind, told herself to stay calm.

Carefully, she pushed her way inside the trees.

2

Jules

THEY'D been looking forward to the Fourth of July festival all summer.

While most of the locals lived for winters, slogging through the heat of summer just to get to ski season, Jules couldn't wait to see what River Falls had in store. She texted Will a quick *I can't wait to see you* and waited for his reply.

I miss you madly. See you soon, gorgeous.

Her stomach flipped. Before Will, she'd never even had a serious boyfriend—instead always losing herself in schoolwork, sports, or focusing on bettering her outdoor skills. But the moment they'd met, she couldn't think of anything else.

"Jules? You ready?" her dad called from the foyer.

"Coming!" She assessed herself once more in the mirror. She was wearing blue jean shorts, a white midriff top, and red sandals. Her skin had darkened from all the time outside, and her face was bare, the way Will liked it. He loved that she didn't buy into the beauty standards set by society. She tied her hair up in a red-checked handkerchief.

Her parents were waiting for her, both of them standing feet apart. A few years ago, they'd each jokingly dressed like two halves of the American flag. Now, they were barely speaking.

Desi grabbed her purse but absently left the keys in the foyer. "You ready?"

Jules grabbed the keys, locked the door, and tossed them to her dad.

He caught them with ease, cupped his hands around his mouth, and shouted, "And the crowd goes wild." Jules rolled her eyes good-naturedly as they crunched through the gravel.

On the way into town, Jules drank in the lush mountains and jagged rock faces that marked the sky. When they'd first driven here from Chicago, Jules had watched flat farmland feed into rolling hills and murky brown fields blossom into vibrant green mountains, burly with life. Steep inclines had replaced congested roads. Livestock roamed freely. Homes studded the horizon, spread far apart rather than stacked together like Legos on every block.

Now, she emptied her mind as the SUV chugged down the craggy mountain face, rich with trees and glistening rocks. She fixed her eyes on the jade landscape that whipped by in a flurry. She jabbed the window down to suck in the fresh air. She smelled dew, dirt, and the fragrant sweep of pines.

"Is Will excited?" her mom asked.

"Yeah, I think so." Will had graduated early from Western North Carolina Aviation with his pilot's license. Today, he was in charge of flying a fifty-foot American flag above the festival.

Will loved to fly, but he also dealt with the guilt of leaving his terminally ill mother at home with the nurse. Lenore had stage 4 lung cancer and had been given just months to live.

"I miss flying," Peter said, peering at the cloudless sky. "Especially on a day like this." Her dad also had his pilot's license and used to fly Jules around when she was younger. However, a few years ago, she'd had an especially horrible flight into Chicago with her mother.

She closed her eyes, remembering. The plane plunging from the sky. Her mother's tiny yelps as she shoved an arm in front of Jules's chest, as if to restrain her. Jules's own obliviousness until she'd glimpsed the fear in her mother's eyes. The collective panic that spread like a virus across the plane, resulting in chaotic screams and hushed prayers. The uncertainty about whether they would live or die as they braced for landing.

She hadn't been on a plane since.

She shivered from the recollection and focused on what she could physically see outside her window: *Trees. Pavement. Horses. Cows. Fences. Men and women in rocking chairs.*

At the base of the mountain, people clogged the streets. American flags rippled in the wind, hoisted high by skinny white poles. Patriotic men wobbled on stilts, and a drumline vibrated their car. They turned onto Coventry Street toward the main drag and searched for a parking spot.

After endless circling, her father finally found parking behind Pal's Grocery. The drumline twirled their sticks and beat a punchy staccato on their snares. Tall hats with feathers jiggled as the boys—and two girls—bobbed their heads and walked sideways, their shoulders stiff and elbows set. Her mother shook her hips in time to the music. Her dad smiled. While her parents rarely fought, they'd spent the majority of the summer being cold to each other. She was happy to see them lightening up.

She walked a few paces behind them and checked her phone. Jules was meeting up with Will's sister, Ava, who worked in their mom's clothing boutique.

They were meeting at Ted's Soda Shop, which was situated between a used bookstore and the lone dry cleaner at the end of the block. She loved downtown—the chalet-style shops that hugged both sides of the street and then abruptly ended at the bowl of the mountain. She'd made a point to become a patron at almost every one.

"What should we do first?" her mother yelled. Her face was flushed, her body loose. Jules shrugged, not wanting to distance herself so soon, but at the same time, she wanted to explore. Her dad pointed to a booth selling funnel cakes. As they crossed the street, a little boy rammed into Jules's hip.

"Be careful." She patted his head as the little boy dashed ahead of her, his arms wild, something chocolate smeared across his sugar-crazed lips. A few other kids followed, their parents nowhere in sight. Here, kids were free. In Chicago, she'd literally seen parents walk their kids on leashes.

She rested her elbows on the snack cart as her father paid for their greasy treat. Her eyes panned the throngs of people. It seemed the whole town had shown up.

Because they were on the curb, she got a clear view of the shops and the mountain looming behind them. Her eyes continued to work over the crowd. She searched for Will but didn't see him yet.

"Earth to Jules?" Her mother handed her the funnel cake. She licked the powdered sugar from her fingers.

They walked up and down the block, stopping at random shops and making small talk when the opportunity presented itself.

They finally reached Ted's Soda Shop. A line spilled out the door. Jules checked her watch. She wadded up the rest of her funnel cake and tossed it in the green metal trash can. "This is where I'm meeting Ava and her friends."

"Do you want us to wait with you?" her mom asked.

"Des, let her be." Her dad jerked his head back down the block. "Let's meet at the funnel cake stand at five. Sound good?"

She nodded. "You guys have fun."

"You too."

She watched her parents walk away. The space widened between them. Jules longed for the days when her dad would sling an arm around her mother's shoulder and make her laugh because of something he said.

Jules searched the line again, but didn't see Ava, so she worked her way to the rear. She got lost in thought as she inched forward. Inside, the place smelled like a milkshake. Red, shiny barstools, wooden booths, and a real ice cream bar screamed 1950s. Employees wore candy-striped aprons and crisp paper hats. An antique jukebox sat in the corner with a cluster of kids around it. Jules saw the back of someone that looked a lot like Ava. The girl turned. No luck.

Jules sighed and wondered if she'd somehow missed them. At the register, she swiped a box of matches for her collection, checked the menu, and ordered an ice cream sundae.

"Hey, Jules!"

Jules turned and saw a bunch of kids crammed in a U-shaped booth in the very back. She spotted Ava. She waved, collected her oversized sundae, and joined them.

"You made it." Ava patted the seat next to her, and Jules squeezed in. The red leather stuck to her thighs. The dome of her ice cream sundae oozed with caramel and chocolate. She wasn't even hungry after the funnel cake.

"This place is great," Jules said by way of introduction.

"Ted's is the best," Ava said. She tugged on a strand of her hair, which was dyed purple and shaved on one side. "Let me introduce you. This is Bricks. Not his real name obviously, but he'll tell you the story someday." A chubby guy, probably her age, made a fist and shook it playfully at Ava. Ava slapped it away and continued. "Then we have Lindsay. We've known each other since what? Kindergarten?"

A model-worthy blonde with dark eyebrows and full, pouty lips rolled her ice-blue eyes. "We're practically sisters." She smiled at Jules. "Nice to meet you."

"The twins, Gwynn and Lynn," Ava continued. Two redheads with curly, shoulder-length hair and a face full of freckles waved at the same time.

"And last but not least, Trevor. My boyfriend." A gorgeous African-American boy with a shaved head and an eyebrow piercing nodded.

"And this is Jules. Is that short for Julia?" Ava asked. "Will never said."

"Juliette, actually. My mom read the French version of Romeo and Juliet, and the rest is history," she explained. To her relief, the kids laughed. They eased into conversation, and luckily, Jules didn't have to ask questions, as they wanted to know all about living in a big city like Chicago.

"I love cities." Lindsay sighed. "I mean, food delivery? Walking everywhere? Ice removal? Culture?"

"We've got culture." Bricks snorted.

"You know what I mean," Lindsay said. "It just must be nice to live somewhere with modern conveniences."

Before she could respond, Ava turned in the booth. "Well, look who decided to grace us with his presence."

Will pushed in beside Jules, smelling of sunshine-warmed skin. She looked up as a familiar punch of heat spread wildly in her chest. Will tucked a strand of dirty-blond hair behind his ear. Every time she looked at him, it was like the first time. His skin, darkened from the sun. His chiseled cheekbones.

The bend of his smile. His grass-green eyes that probed hers when she spoke. His beauty mark, the size of a pencil tip, that grazed his top lip.

"Hey you." He leaned down and kissed her softly on the lips, as all the kids made a gagging sound. Jules pulled back and blushed, never much for public displays of affection.

"So, the gang's all here," Ava said. "What's next?"

"We could go to Old Willard's barn and ride horses before Will flies?" one of the twins suggested.

They tossed around ideas, and Jules was disappointed they didn't want to stay and watch the parade. To them, it was probably old and boring, but to her, it was all so new.

The table broke off into several simultaneous conversations and the twins squealed when Bricks spit a thin stream of water at them through his straw.

Distracted, Jules leaned closer to Will. "How's your mom?"

He sighed. "Hanging in. The nurse is a godsend." His eyes were pained, and she knew it was a struggle for all of them. His father, William Sr., was a commercial pilot, and had to constantly fly to handle the medical bills. While they all wanted to be there for her, Lenore insisted they not wait around watching her die.

He checked the time. "I don't have to fly for another three hours." He leaned in, his lips sending chills down her arm as they grazed her ear. "Up for an adventure?"

Jules hesitated and glanced around the table. Ava had specifically invited her here today to hang with her friends, but any time with Will was time well spent. She stood up to join him. The backs of her thighs were clammy from the sticky booth. Her sundae dripped onto the table, uneaten.

"Where do you two think you're going?" Ava wiggled her eyebrows suggestively.

"I'm just going to borrow her for a quick second and will bring her right back," Will said. "Meet back here in a bit?"

Ava rolled her eyes. "Yeah, yeah. Go be in love."

Jules and Will hadn't yet said those words to each other, but she was—madly. She told everyone goodbye before they slipped out onto the street.

"So, where's this adventure taking place?"

"You'll just have to wait and find out," he said.

She loved how he always found new ways to surprise her. They walked for about a quarter of a mile until the crowd thinned and they stopped in front of a motorcycle. Will unclipped his helmet. He reached into the pillion and offered her a matching one.

"Ever ride?" He fastened his chin strap.

She had ridden in Wisconsin with her uncle Dan. "Once." She took the helmet and put it on. "Is this the surprise?"

"Not even close." He straddled the bike and motioned behind him. "Hop on."

She sat behind him, her jean shorts inching to the tops of her thighs. Her fingers glided around his middle, which was hard and lean. He started the bike, and they were off. The cool mountain air studded her skin. She gripped him tighter when he shifted gears. They raced toward the base of the mountain. He took the first turn so fast, she slid sideways on her seat. She focused on the scenery. They rose up the mountain, mingling with the trees. Below, the town reduced to nothing but colorful specks. A few early fireworks exploded into the sky, fizzing with color and then vanishing into the blue.

They rode for five minutes, winding up and up. The sun disappeared as they approached the mouth of a cave. He sped up until they were inside a tunnel. Will howled and she joined him, tossing her head back to scream.

The tunnel was black and cool, and she shivered from the unexpected temperature drop. He said something over his shoulder, but she couldn't hear. With the throttle of the engine, they burst out of the tunnel. Fractured light glinted through the heavy spruce and pines. He revved through a small dirt path, which opened into a private parking lot. He slid into a space before killing the engine and stomping down the kickstand. He dismounted, removed his helmet, and shook out his hair. "You okay?"

Her ears rang from the speed and vicious wind. She dismounted too, swinging a shaky leg to the ground. Her entire body felt boneless, her skin chilled. She nodded and handed him her helmet. "That was thrilling."

"You're thrilling." His smile blinded her. "Now for the surprise." He extended his hand and led her down a narrow path. Fresh wood chips scattered the trail, just like at The Black House. Pathway mulch lodged into her sandals and Jules tapped her toes against the earth to kick them free.

While most people would get nervous traipsing through the woods, she felt instantly at home. The trees bowed inward along the path, their tangle of branches arching toward them at various angles. She stared at Will's back. Had he brought other girls here before? She killed the thought in its tracks. So what if he had? She knew he'd had plenty of girlfriends before her. They passed signs to stay out of the woods to preserve the natural wildlife. Will lightly touched her arm, pointed. "Look. Deer."

They stopped to stare at a group of deer, their long brown necks bent in search of food. She'd hunted deer most summers, and her dad had showed her how to break down the entire animal so nothing went to waste.

They padded silently past, and after a few more minutes of

walking, Will pointed to a small trail that veered uphill. He glanced at her gladiator sandals. "It's steep. You okay to climb?"

"Why don't you find out?" Jules heard herself say. She rocketed ahead of him and broke into a run. He yelled in surprise and chased after her, but years of cross country meant she could keep a five-and-a-half-minute-mile pace, easy. Her lungs burned until the lactic acid flushed from her system. She found her rhythm, but Will was right. It was a challenging climb full of switchbacks and turns, but she followed it effortlessly and beat him with two minutes to spare. When he got to the top, gasping, he bent over, hands splayed on his knees.

"How did I not know my girlfriend was an Olympic sprinter?"

She was barely out of breath. "Cross country, not sprinting," she reminded him.

He moved closer and placed his hands on her shoulders, kissed her softly, then turned her around. "Walk."

She approached a set of stairs, formed by large, wide rocks, and descended. The temperature fell again, and she marveled at the glossy boulders perched in space above them. The rush of water roared as they approached. At the very bottom stair, she rounded the corner and almost screamed in delight.

Rich green water gushed over a massive inky rock. The waterfall seemed endless and powerful, and Jules took a moment to admire its majesty.

The cool spray drenched her cheeks and clothes, and she opened her arms wide. Behind her, Will kicked off his boots and peeled away his T-shirt. Jules stared at his stomach carved with muscles. Desire rattled her insides. He unbuckled his jeans slowly, and her eyes tracked him like prey.

"What are you doing?"

"Living," he joked. "Come in." He motioned to the water then dove straight in. He emerged and slapped the top.

"Get in!"

She stared at the froth of the waterfall churning anything below it. Surprisingly, he swam right toward it, unafraid. She removed her top and shimmied out of her shorts. She was wearing her only nice lingerie, ironically bought at Will's mother's shop at the start of summer.

After a huge breath, she rocked back on her heels and jumped off the side, propelling her body outward to avoid the rocks. A thousand icy needles pricked her skin as she plunged deep into the black before clawing her way back to the top. Finally, she broke the surface, steadied her breath, and freestyled toward him.

"This way." Will turned and dove underwater again. She followed him until they bobbed near the edge of the waterfall. He swam to the right and pulled himself up onto a rock. "Careful. It's slick," he said.

She eased out of the water and instantly found her footing. Once she was stable, they walked over moss-speckled rocks, which were furry beneath her slick soles. At the right side of the waterfall, he wedged himself into a sliver of space just wide enough for two bodies to slip through. Suddenly, they were behind the water, being sprayed by its clean, pure mist. She huddled beside Will to get warmer. "This is incredible," she said. Her teeth chattered involuntarily.

"Cold?"

"I'm good." In the dark, she could only make out the whites of his eyes.

"I used to come here as a kid. Sneak away from the house and swim for hours." He hesitated. "I've never brought anyone here before."

Pleasure rippled through her body at the admission. "Why not?" she asked.

"I've never wanted to share it with anyone. Until now."

She leaned into his wet shoulder, their bare bodies so attuned to each other. Time stretched under the hypnotic rush of water. She wondered what it must have been like to grow up with nature all around. The waterfall drowned out her thoughts.

A few minutes later, he led her up to a trail so they didn't have to swim back. They walked silently through the woods, the branches lashing her bare skin. Dead leaves clung to her wet feet. He looped them around to a clearing on top of the rocks, with the crush of the waterfall below.

He pushed past a few trees. Inside the cover of leaves, a rectangle of earth was covered with a red blanket. Twinkle lights hung between the pines, and a wicker picnic basket dangled from a leaning branch so critters didn't devour its contents.

"Will." She said his name softly. "When did you do all this?" She shivered once again in her bra and panties, but her body was primed and alert. He reached down and unfolded another blanket from a stack and wrapped her in it, warming her arms.

"I wanted to do something special for you," he said. His voice quivered from the cold.

The water shimmered and rippled below, and a gust of wind rustled the leaves, pricking her skin with a fresh layer of goose bumps. She opened the blanket and invited him in.

"Every day with you is special," she said.

There was so much they hadn't talked about: their four-year age difference, the fact that she was going to college in a couple of months, the preposterous conclusion that they would have to say goodbye in just four weeks' time. The unspoken truth existed between them, but for now, she didn't want to think about living on borrowed time.

He kissed her hungrily, and she kissed him back. Their slippery bodies molded into one, until they lowered themselves to the earth. She could feel how aroused he was, and she pressed her weight on top of him, kissing him deeply. He moaned and pulled her closer. They were never alone, always at his house, where his mother was just a room away, or out in public, where all eyes were on them. Here, she felt free. She was in her favorite place with her favorite person, and she wanted to give herself to him completely.

She straddled his body and unhooked her bra.

He inhaled sharply. When his hands cupped her breasts, her body throbbed in anticipation. How had she ever lived without his touch? His fingers wandered down her hips, squeezing and rubbing every inch of her. She leaned in and kissed him again. Gently, he rolled her onto her back and stared down at her. His skin on her skin. His breath on hers.

"You are so beautiful." He trailed his fingers from her jawline to her breasts and stomach and gently parted her thighs. "Is this okay?" His fingers moved over her panties, tracing slow, agonizing circles.

Jules moaned yes. If she thought her body had been alive before, she was mistaken. Now, every nerve ending sizzled as he pulled her panties to the side and slipped a finger inside. She succumbed to the feeling of him, wanting more. She fumbled with his underwear, pulling them lower. He stood up, fully naked, and her eyes trailed down to the most vulnerable part of him. She crawled to her knees and took him in her mouth. He moaned and gripped her hair. Finally, he pulled away and she lay on her back. He climbed on top of her again. She opened her legs, an invitation.

"Are you sure?" he whispered.

"Yes." She'd never been surer of anything in her life.

As he entered her, she relaxed into him. The first sharp moments melted into liquid pleasure. He kissed her as he rocked in and out of her body. She cried out and bit into his shoulder as she climaxed, but he slowed, wanting it to last. He pulled back, his eyes locked on hers.

"I love you, Juliette," he whispered.

She looked at him, the bright sun bathing him in golden light. "I love you too, Will."

He kissed her again and in that kiss, she knew: she wanted to spend her life here, with this man, doing this exact thing, for as long as they both lived.

After, they both lay on their backs, sweating and sucking fresh air. She rolled onto his chest and smiled.

She'd just had sex for the first time, with a man she loved. She knew other girls weren't so lucky. She'd heard horror stories of girls losing their virginity. She'd never made decisions about her virginity either way, but now, she was glad Will had been her first. And she hoped he'd be her last.

"What are you thinking?" he asked. He rubbed light circles on her shoulder.

"I'm just so happy," she said. "I love it here. I love being with you."

"Me too."

She sighed and rotated her watch to check the time. "Oh shit." She sat up. "I was supposed to meet my parents at five."

They'd completely lost track of time, and Will still had a plane to fly. Will packed up the picnic they didn't get to eat and said he'd clean the blankets and lights up later. They stalked back to where their clothes were and hurriedly dressed. She hated to rush them, to rush this moment.

At his bike, she pulled on her shoes and refastened her helmet. She hopped on behind him, kissing his neck, before they sped back down the mountain. As they neared town, a little of the magic faded. She wanted to hold on to it just a little bit longer, hoard the memory all for herself.

Will parked the bike and they both dismounted.

She shook out her hair, still damp. "Do you want to walk with me to meet my parents before you have to go? Or do you need to find your sister?"

"I'll walk with you." He gripped both sides of her face and kissed her deeply. Even their kisses felt different. *She* felt different.

He slid his hand in hers. Together, they walked back to the mouth of the parade.

3

Desi

DESI tapped her foot in time to the music and sipped her second glass of white wine.

Her cheeks hurt from smiling so much. She glanced up at Peter, whose neck was beet red from the heat and alcohol. When's the last time they'd enjoyed themselves like this?

Just the other day, she'd been agonizing over their distance, and today, there was a sliver of life pulsing between them. She took a shaky breath. The sun was fierce, even this late in the afternoon. She adjusted her wide-brimmed hat and checked the time. She was shocked to see it was already fifteen minutes past five. Jules should have been back.

She shook Peter's arm, who was chatting with Stan, the guy who ran the cheese shop. He laughed and turned to her, completely unencumbered. She choked on her own worry; why worry him too? Peter looked so at ease, so happy. She didn't want to ruin his mood when he was having such a good time. Jules was responsible. If she was late, there was probably a good reason. *Like Will*. She laughed to herself.

She remembered how all-consuming it was to fall in love. It was like everything else paled in comparison, but Desi didn't want Jules to lose sight of what was really important. She turned her attention back to Peter. Instead of saying anything, she surprised herself by leaning in and kissing his cheek. It smelled of aftershave and the sun.

To her relief, he didn't pull away. He turned to stare at her. His eyes trailed down to her lips, and then he went back to talking.

She longed for the way they used to be. She chugged the last of her wine. Like so many other people she knew, they'd become just another disgruntled married couple who'd grown apart and succumbed to a sea of parental and financial obligations.

She crumpled the plastic cup in her fist, tossed it in the trash, and continued to search the crowd for Jules.

She checked her phone out of obsessive habit, even though she had zero reception. A man in the crowd bumped into her from behind. He murmured his apologies and kept moving. She couldn't tear her eyes away from his back. Broad shoulders under a plaid shirt. The same dark hair. He even walked with a bit of the same swagger.

Carter?

She fanned her blouse and attempted to gulp air. Suddenly, she wanted to get out of here, to climb back up the mountain and hide from all these people. She searched for the man again, but he'd vanished. She tugged on Peter's arm, this time more insistent.

He shot her an annoyed look, and the momentary alliance between them dissolved. He didn't like being interrupted. She pointed to her watch. "Jules is late." His annoyance evaporated, but his eyes turned razor sharp. He stood straight, cutting off his conversation with Stan midsentence. He stepped into the street and tented his hand above his eyes, searching. She knew Jules's name was on his lips. He wouldn't dare shout his teenage daughter's name in front of all these people, but she understood the urge. The urge was always there if you lived in the city. But even here, with Jules on the precipice of adulthood, Peter was still so protective.

Desi hunted for water from one of the vendors. A bead of sweat trickled between her breasts, and she blotted it with her shirt.

Peter stepped closer. "She's never late."

She laid a hand on his arm. "She probably just lost track of time."

He bolted into the crowd anyway, the back of her strong, capable husband slicing through red, white, and blue bodies like a switchblade.

Desi walked to Pal's and bought a bottle of water. On the way back, she spotted Will and Jules making their way to the snack stand. She laughed as they approached.

"Go for a swim?"

Jules glanced at Will, and something flashed between them. "Will took me to the waterfall." She stared at her sandals. "It's beautiful, Mom. You should see it."

She assessed the two of them, their wet hair and rumpled clothes. Before she could come to any obvious conclusions, Peter approached and clapped a hand on Will's shoulder.

"You ready to fly?" Peter asked.

She didn't know how he did that—how he went from strict and concerned to calm and casual. It made it so that she could rarely figure out what he was actually thinking.

"I am. Anyone want to join?" Will squeezed Jules's waist, and Desi glimpsed the panic behind her daughter's eyes. Will knew her fear of planes, of course, but maybe not how deep.

"I'd love to go," Peter interjected. "You don't mind, do you, Jules?"

Jules appeared relieved. "Is that okay with you?" She glanced at Will.

"I'd be honored, sir." He shook Peter's hand. "Let's do it."

They said goodbye. Desi cocked her head and watched Will and Peter walk away, chatting like they were old friends.

"That was awfully nice of your father," Desi said.

"I guess I'm going to have to get over the whole hating to fly thing, huh?" Jules gnawed at one of her cuticles, a leftover habit from childhood.

Desi wrapped an arm around her. "Probably."

Jules adjusted her shorts and Desi glanced down. A small trickle of blood ran down her leg.

"Oh, honey. Did you start your period? You're bleeding." Desi rustled in her purse for a tampon. She was always prepared. She also pulled out a cardigan, which Jules promptly tied around her waist. "I know I have one in here somewhere."

"Mom, I didn't start my period."

Desi blinked at her. "So why are you bleeding?"

Her hair had dried loose and wavy around her shoulders and Desi resisted the urge to brush a few errant strands off her face. Jules opened her mouth to speak, but the crowd pushed in and they bustled forward until they found an edge of curb to claim.

"Answer me, please."

She shrugged. "Will and I had sex." Jules lifted her chin and stared her mother squarely in the eye.

"Like, today? Just now?" She was instantly shuttled back to her first time, which had been fast and nothing to write home about.

Jules adjusted the cardigan and lowered her voice. "Yes."

Desi nodded. She didn't want to overreact and cause Jules to clam up, but she didn't want to underact or seem like she didn't care either. She racked her brain for when they'd had the sex talk. Jules was such a studious person, she'd never really asked a lot of questions. If she ever wanted to figure something out, she did.

"Were you safe at least?" Desi watched Will and Peter disappear. If Peter knew what Will had just done with their daughter . . .

Jules opened her mouth, then closed it and nodded. She was a terrible liar, always had been. "Juliette, you didn't use protection? Why?"

She shrugged, her cheeks reddening from the admission. "We were just in the moment."

Desi took a deep breath. "That's the same excuse uttered by every woman who's ever gotten unexpectedly pregnant. Or an STD," she added. "We'll get you the morning after pill."

"Mom, no. I'm not putting that crap into my body. I'm not ovulating. It's fine."

She couldn't believe she was having this conversation during the Fourth of July. *Happy birthday, America! Did you know my daughter just had unprotected sex?*

"Juliette, stranger things have happened. You're taking it."

Jules rolled her eyes, then began chewing on her cuticle again.

Desi lowered Jules's arm. "Stop that." Jules had the hands of a worker: calluses; short, uneven nails lined with caked dirt; bloody cuticles. Whenever she took Jules to get a manicure, her nails were ruined the next day.

"Please don't tell Dad."

Desi scoffed. She'd gotten so used to not telling him things, she could just add this one to the list.

Sensing the tough part of the conversation was over, Jules released a breath and started clapping as the parade began.

"Weren't you supposed to meet Ava and her friends?"

"I did." Jules covered her eyes with one hand and searched the crowd. She bit on her bottom lip in lieu of her cuticles, tearing at the tender flesh until a prick of blood dotted her lower lip. "I'm going to meet back up with them."

"Not dressed like that you're not. Let's go get you an outfit from Lenore's shop."

Jules rolled her eyes again, but then nodded. They were in and out in five minutes flat, and Desi stuffed the bloodied jean shorts and underwear into her purse. They claimed a fresh patch of curb and waited for Will's plane.

"Are Will's parents here today?" She hadn't yet met Lenore or William Sr., but she understood the gist of the situation from snippets of Will and Jules's conversation. She didn't understand how any woman in her forties could face the surrender of her own body, how she had to say goodbye to her children while still alive.

"William Sr. is flying. Lenore didn't feel up to it." Jules glanced up at the bright blue sky again. "You think they'll be okay?"

Sometimes, Desi could still see the kid in Jules, that innocence bubbling up when she was uncertain, which was rare.

"I know they will."

She nodded, her eyes serious, before she broke into a smile and waved. Ava and her friends knotted together on the next street corner.

Jules turned back to her mother and before she could even ask, Desi shooed her away. "Go be with your friends."

"You sure?"

"Positive." She checked her watch. "We can meet up once Dad and Will are back on the ground?"

Jules nodded and jogged over to her friends, who swallowed her in a gaggle of teen gossip and excitement.

To be so young again, Desi thought wistfully. Watching Jules fall in love reminded her so much of her past. She'd been older than Jules, but those feelings were fierce.

She tried to put herself in Jules's shoes now. It probably felt like her whole world was just cracking open, and she'd have to leave this place and the people in it. She'd been there too, but she also had the hindsight now to realize that young love was sometimes just that, and that you couldn't bet your whole future on it working out.

Desi walked a few paces and bought herself a lemonade. She sipped the sickly sweet drink and then found a vacant spot on the same curb. Bored, she fished her phone from her back pocket and checked for service. To her surprise, her phone began to ring in her palm, the volume cranked high. She smiled apologetically at the woman next to her, who gave her a stern look, and quickly lowered the volume.

Blocked number.

Probably just a telemarketer. She declined the number, but it rang again. Desi sighed dramatically. Rather than turn it off, she set her lemonade on the ground and answered.

She waited. The parade ballooned around her, and she pressed a finger to her ear to hear better.

"I didn't know you still drank lemonade."

Desi whipped around as she searched the pink cheeks, wide smiles, and festive community for her brother, Tommy. Every tall, lean guy in a baseball cap. Every lanky male in his early forties. She turned in a complete circle. "Why are you calling me from a blocked number?"

"You know I've always loved the element of surprise," he joked.

"Where are you?"

He ignored her question. "Jules has grown a foot."

"Well, if you were ever *around*, you'd know that," she snapped.

Her brother, also a Marine, still occasionally suffered from PTSD and mood swings, had had a brief but nearly fatal stint with drugs, and usually only showed up when he needed money. Desi began to work her way toward Jules, except she wasn't on the corner. "When did you get back?"

"Last week," he said.

"Where were you this time?"

"Morocco."

Desi didn't ask him what he was doing there. He came and went as he pleased, borrowing money, crashing with her or other friends when things got really bad, then disappearing just as quickly. Desi struggled to listen for sounds in the background, to figure out exactly where he was.

He said something else but cut out and then the line went dead. Desi stared at the phone in her hand, annoyed, then gathered her thoughts and searched for Jules and her friends.

Suddenly, the band started and the crowd erupted into clapping, yelling, singing, and marching. Someone bumped her from behind and she spun around, but it was just a teenager. She thought of the man in the plaid shirt again. She wasn't sure if she secretly wanted Carter to show up, or if that would literally be the worst thing that could happen.

The band marched down the wide street, their brass instruments noisy and slightly off-key. Desi moved farther onto the curb, feigning excitement as her eyes scanned the crowd.

A few minutes later, Will's plane shot into the sky, the giant American flag surging behind it. The crowd whooped. The sun pierced the edge of the plane and made it sparkle.

Suddenly, Will took a nosedive, and the crowd gasped. A small jolt of terror stiffened her body, until he righted and hooked left. She relaxed. He was just showing off. She looked down at her cell again, practically willing Tommy to call her back. Now, a red stream of smoke inked the sky, and everyone cheered.

She continued to watch the plane and simultaneously search for Jules. A little girl on her father's shoulders clapped, her chubby thighs squeezing both sides of his red neck.

"Plane!" she cheered. "Plane, plane!" Her blond, curly hair bounced under her yellow sun hat.

Desi steadied her thoughts and continued to watch the plane carve tracks in the sky. What was supposed to be a relaxing summer had instantly turned complex. Her brother was here, she was receiving texts from Carter, Jules was having sex, and Peter seemed to grow less and less emotionally available.

But more than that, her past was catching up to her, whether she was ready or not.

4

Desi

AFTER Will's performance, she walked briskly to the airport hangar, where they'd arranged to meet.

She kept checking behind her, expecting to see Tommy. As she neared the hangar, Jules adjusted her red dress, already talking to Peter and Will, who seemed to be buzzing from their air time. Before she reached them, a figure appeared from behind the hangar. She stopped in her tracks as Tommy extended his arms and shouted Peter's name.

Peter shielded his eyes from the unrelenting sun to see who it was. Jules turned too, and then she yelped and ran toward Tommy.

"Uncle Tommy!" Jules practically threw herself at him.

Peter broke into a grin. Though Peter also got frustrated with Tommy's immature behavior, they'd served together, which bonded them in ways she couldn't comprehend. Yet she was always the one who shelled out money or dealt with his debilitating mood swings. She'd suggested therapy a million times, but he always refused.

"Mom!" Jules looked at her incredulously, holding Tommy by the shoulders. "Did you know about this?"

Desi wiped the concern from her face and joined them. "Nope! I'm as surprised as you are." She turned to Tommy, hands on her hips. "How *did* you find us, Tom?" She hadn't seen or talked to her brother in months.

"Your assistant. He just adores your big brother." He batted his long, thick eyelashes, and she wanted to punch him. He'd always been part protector, part bully. He was trying to bully her now, playing a twisted game of hide-and-seek. But, if she knew Tommy, he just wanted somewhere free to crash for a while.

Jules wrapped her arms around his waist and squeezed. Though she wasn't an affectionate girl, she always made an exception for Tommy. When Tommy playfully tapped a dramatic submission to Jules's strong grip, she pulled away and assessed her uncle. She flicked a finger toward his face. "What's with the creepy porn 'stache?"

"What? You don't like it?" Tommy stroked his blond mustache.

"It's totally creepy," Desi confirmed. "You look like a pedophile."

"Mom," Jules said. "Gross."

"I like it," Peter said. "Very 1980s."

"Exactly," Tommy said. He snapped at him and erected a cheesy pose. "Plus, the ladies love it."

Jules rolled her eyes. "You wish."

Tommy turned toward Will. "And who's this asshole?"

Jules slapped Tommy on the arm. "This is Will. My boyfriend."

"Boyfriend?" He slung an easy arm around Jules's shoulders. "Does Dad approve?"

Peter crossed his arms, widened his stance as if he were about to give some sort of lecture, and stared intently at Will. Finally, he nodded. "I do approve."

Will mimed wiping sweat from his brow.

"Mom, can he stay?"

Beside her, Tommy steepled his hands in a mock prayer.

"Is that why you're here?"

"I mean, I could stay a few days, sure." Tommy nodded like he'd just thought of it.

Rather than argue, she tried to diffuse the situation. "We'll talk about it, okay?"

They weaved back toward the parade. Desi wanted to go home, soak in a long, hot bath, and begin again tomorrow. Instead, once they were back on the main strip, Tommy grabbed her elbow. "We'll go get everyone drinks. Any takers?"

They rattled off their requests and Tommy steered her toward a food truck that offered nonalcoholic drinks and local craft beers. Desi jerked her arm free and moved ahead of him to stand in line.

"Don't be mad," he said.

She turned and really studied his face. "How could I not be? You only show up when you need something." She lowered her voice. "What kind of example does that set for Jules?"

"Jules is grown," he said. "Plus, my landlord rented out my place while I was gone."

"Let me guess: because you didn't pay rent?"

"This isn't on me," he said, stabbing his chest. "Do you know how hard it is for veterans to get work?"

"I do know," she snapped. "But some manage just fine."

He sighed. "We can't *all* be like Mr. Perfect Peter."

She wasn't just thinking of Peter. She massaged her temples. She didn't have the energy to argue. If she gave in, he would milk her dry. First, it would be a few days, then a month, then he'd find a way to live in The Black House permanently for free.

She dropped her hands, inched forward in line. She started to speak, then stopped.

"What?"

"Are you in some kind of trouble, Tom?" She searched his face and arms, to make sure he wasn't using.

"Hey. Look at me." His grip was strong and reminded her of when he'd taught her a few core wrestling moves as a kid. Somewhere under this righteous facade was the brother she adored, but right now, she was pissed. "I really did just want to see you. I want to spend time with Jules before she leaves. Is that so wrong?"

She took a step back. "No, it's not wrong. But a phone call would have been nice."

"It'll be fun." He spread his arms wide again, revealing a few new tattoos on both forearms: a scrawled quote on his left, a woman's curvy body covered by a thick green snake on his right. "I've got the rest of the summer."

Desi shook her head. "You're not staying with us until the end of summer. No." She sliced her hand in a firm line in the air.

He ignored her declaration as they stepped up to the window. "Plus, I'm just dying to see this black house everyone's going on and on about," he tossed over his shoulder. "I want to see my little sister's masterpiece for myself." He rattled off their drink orders, not a care in the world. *Was he actually enjoying this?*

She slapped her credit card on the counter and walked back to the group with two cold beers in hand.

The man in the plaid shirt darted through the crowd again, and she stopped, ramming into Tommy's back. Beer sloshed from the plastic cup. She murmured an apology and whipped around, but the guy was gone.

"You good?" he asked, pinching his eyebrows together in concern.

She stared into the empty void where the man had just been. Was her mind playing tricks on her, or could that possibly be Carter?

She nodded, her body primed for fight or flight. "Yeah, I'm good."

5

Desi

SHE couldn't sleep.

She bypassed the guest room, where Tommy had made himself immediately at home. She kicked his shoes from the middle of the hallway and laced up her own. She slipped out the door and sucked the frigid air into her lungs. *Medicine.* She stretched her quads, limbered her hamstrings, and took off toward the trail.

Her head pounded from all the drinks coupled with Tommy's sudden appearance. She crunched over leaves as the temperature dropped even more in the shadow of trees.

Desi's foot snagged on a root and she stumbled, then righted herself before slamming into a low-hanging tree branch. *Jesus, I can't even clear my head on a run.*

A sudden rustling made her stop, but it was just a squirrel launching itself between two trees. She picked up the pace and completed the loop, drenched and gasping. No matter how far or fast she ran, she couldn't escape herself. She couldn't escape what she'd done or what she really wanted, and she was starting to feel desperate.

She entered through the back of the house, removed her shoes, and flipped on a few lights in the kitchen. Inside, she grabbed her phone from her purse and asked Siri to call Beth. She stepped outside and walked to the golden spot with so-so reception.

Beth had twin girls and was always up, so she knew it wouldn't be too early to call. Roommates in college, she and Beth had remained friends through exams, drugs, binges, boyfriends, engagements, marriage, babies, depression, emergency room visits, and losing relatives. Though their lives were different now, Beth still remembered the pre-wife, pre-mother version of Desi, which she struggled to remember herself. And while Beth didn't know everything, she knew enough about Desi's past, and the possible consequences.

After two tries, it was clear the call wouldn't connect. Desi walked back into the kitchen and realized her phone was still on Do Not Disturb. She had a few unread texts. Before she could thumb through them, Peter shuffled into the kitchen, dragging a hand through his hair.

"Morning," she said. She pocketed her phone. His hair was rumpled, and he looked more rested than he had in quite some time.

He studied her outfit. "Did you already go for a run?" He almost sounded impressed as he filled the carafe for coffee and shook some grounds into the filter.

"I did. Couldn't sleep." She kept her voice neutral; she didn't want to give away how much Tommy's appearance had rattled her.

"How long is Tom staying?"

That was a loaded question. "Not sure," she said. She sat on an island stool, her heart still pounding from her run and the possibility of another unread text from Carter.

"Kind of crazy that he just showed up out of the blue like that, huh?" Peter scratched his two-day stubble as the coffee hissed into the pot.

"You know Tommy."

"That I do."

She searched his face. "I have a question."

"Shoot." He leaned against the counter, arms crossed.

"What's happening with us?" What she really meant was what was going to happen after the summer?

Peter looked out at the pool and sighed. "What do you mean?"

"Peter, we came here as a last-ditch effort, and you can barely stand to be in the same room."

"That's not true."

It was true, but she didn't bother arguing. "I thought we were going to try what my therapist suggested." Her therapist thought a new environment might loosen some of their old patterns, but here they were, avoiding each other, sprinkled with moments of normalcy.

"Aren't we?"

Desi didn't know what to say. "We've just drifted so much."

"People drift."

She nodded. "They do, but . . ."

"But what?"

She thought back to the first part of the parade. "Yesterday felt different. Lighter."

He nodded. "It did."

She wanted to know why the tenor of their relationship hung on his every mood. She constantly walked on eggshells, and she was tired of it. "With Jules going off to college, I just want to make sure we know what we're doing."

He studied her, his face impenetrable. "What do you want to do?"

What a loaded question. "I was hoping this summer would bring some answers, but I feel like we're running out of time."

Peter again ran a hand through his hair. "It's not just on you, Des."

"I know, but I feel like you always just adapt to the situation, even if it's not a favorable one. I want you to *want* to make our marriage better too. Because if you don't . . ." The thought faded. She didn't want to finish that sentence.

Peter turned back to stare at the pool and the land beyond it. "I'm ready to have my life back."

At first, she thought he said *wife* but then realized he said *life*. "What does that mean?"

Before he could answer, Tommy sauntered into the kitchen, stretching his long arms above his head. "Morning, fam." He smiled and came behind Desi to massage her shoulders. She resisted the urge to tell him to go away and instead decided to play nice.

"How'd you sleep?"

"Like a baby. It's quiet as shit up here."

"You should go for a walk on the trail," Peter said. "Freshest air you'll ever breathe." He turned back to the coffee and poured them each a cup.

"Thanks, dude." He took his coffee and slurped it loudly.

Desi rolled her eyes and took a tentative sip. What was Peter going to say? Did he want to fix their marriage or did he just want to get Jules out of the house and then go their separate ways? She knew too many couples who played nice until their kids went off to college, and then they got divorced. Desi rolled that scenario around in her head. In some ways, isn't that what she deserved? She slipped off her stool, coffee still in hand. "I'm going to take a shower."

Peter and Tommy barely registered her response. They were

deep in conversation about Peter's business in Chicago. Tommy helped out on occasion, but he was such a floater, hopping from job to job, place to place, that Peter could never count on him as regular help.

In her bedroom, she started the shower and waited for it to warm. She eagerly read through her texts. A few were from work and one was from Beth, but no more messages from Carter. A pang of disappointment was instantly replaced when she read Beth's last text.

Carter posted this on Facebook and then immediately took it down, but I'm pretty sure this is your house? WTF?! Call me. XOXO

Her heart jumped as she viewed the selfie. In it, Carter had a full-blown beard, a backward baseball cap, and was giving the peace sign. His blue-jean eyes were bright and mischievous. The caption read *Home Sweet Home*, and behind him, a bit blurred, was a black house.

Her black house.

Desi clamped a hand over her mouth. She zoomed in to see the house behind him, and sure enough, there was her silver roof. She zoomed out and saw the edge of Carter's shirt— plaid, like the man she'd seen yesterday. She read Beth's text below it.

Hurriedly, Desi pulled up a browser to search Facebook, but the rainbow wheel spun and spun until she threw her phone on the bed and sat, thinking. So she *had* seen Carter yesterday? How had he found her?

She heard Tommy and Peter laughing down the hall. They'd both served with Carter before he lost a leg to an IED. If Tommy had found out where the house was so easily, perhaps he'd told Carter. She grabbed her phone and looked at the photo again, studying Carter's face. It was familiar and strange all at once.

She moved to the balcony and tried to pull up Facebook. After an eternity, it connected. She perused Carter's page— something she never allowed herself to do—and her stomach kicked as she saw random pictures of him fishing, hiking, at a bar with friends. He'd put on a little weight over the years and seemed weathered, but he'd mostly stayed the same.

Still, Beth was right. The photo wasn't there. She thumbed through old images, her heart contracting with every one. Next, she navigated to Tommy's page, which housed all his worldwide adventures. And there, at the top, was a photo of The Black House with the caption, *My new summer home. Thanks, sis.*

"You're kidding." She gripped the phone and stormed back down the hall, wagging her phone in the air. She hoped Jules was out and not in the kitchen, because she was about to give her brother an earful. Tommy and Peter were still in the same spot, absorbed in conversation.

"Did you really post a photo of our house on Facebook?"

Tommy glanced at Peter. "Um, yeah. Have you seen this place? It should have its own account."

"This house isn't for posting. It's private. I don't want this all over social media."

"I didn't share the location."

"Tommy, come on." Peter knew, as well as Tommy did, how easy it was to find someone's location. Had Carter somehow seen Tommy's post and just hightailed it here? That made zero sense. There had to be another reason.

"Take it down," she barked.

"Sis, come on."

"Now."

She waited, arms crossed, as he pulled up his phone, grumbling in the process. "No service."

She marched him to her balcony and had him try from

there. After waiting for the Internet to kick in, he deleted it and stared out over the railing and then down at her. "What's this all about?"

She showed him the photo of Carter.

He shook his head in confusion. "Why would Carter be here?"

"You tell me."

"I have no idea."

It would make so much more sense if Tommy and Carter had just gone on a road trip together and ended up here. But for both of them to be here at the exact same time, separately, didn't register. "So you had no idea he was here?"

He shook his head. "Maybe it's not this house." He peered at the photo again. "Then again . . ." His voice trailed off. "If he is here, maybe we can have a little reunion. It's been forever." He was talking about him, Peter, and Carter of course, but it would also be a reunion for her.

"I need to shower."

He took the hint and left her bedroom. She dropped the phone, undressed, and tossed her clothes in the hamper. The water enveloped her in a steamy cloud, the hot spray pricking her sun-soaked skin. She tried to block thoughts of Carter from her mind as she lathered her body, but he crept in.

Before they'd seen each other at the market, she'd avoided him at all costs. They didn't run in the same circles, and the last she'd heard, he'd been drinking pretty heavily and had a new girlfriend. She never ran into him. Most days, it was easy to convince herself he didn't even exist.

Thoughts continued to tumble. Should she see him? Should they finally just talk about what they'd been avoiding all these years?

She tipped her head back and rinsed away the shampoo. Still, she didn't like games. She'd never snap a photo in front of someone else's house and post it for the world to see. Not when it came with such a deeper meaning. When she opened her eyes, Peter hulked on the other side of the foggy glass, watching her.

"Jesus!" She slapped a hand to her chest and slid the door back. "You scared me."

He was looking at her strangely, not saying a word.

"You okay?"

"Don't talk." He disrobed and entered the shower.

For a moment, fear rioted through her. *He knows.* She glanced down and swiftly realized he wanted to have sex. How long had it been? Before she could overthink it and ruin the moment, he turned her around and fastened her arms above her head. She gave into it, into him.

Her worries evaporated with the steam.

6

Desi

"ARE you nervous?" Desi asked. She flipped down her visor and checked for lipstick on her teeth.

Peter glanced at her. "Should I be?"

"I don't know," she confessed. "We've just never done this before." They were meeting Will's parents for dinner. Even though tonight was about Jules, all she could think about was Carter and that photo. She hadn't told Peter, but she knew she was going to have to figure it out, especially if Carter was in River Falls.

"It'll be fine."

Every time she looked at Peter, she replayed what happened in the shower. Her hands above her head. His lips on her neck. His fingers in her mouth. The way he'd felt inside her.

He hadn't even kissed her after—just rinsed off and returned to his side of the house, almost as if disgusted by what they'd done. Since then, he'd spent most of his time with Tommy, in the woods, completing the shelter he and Jules had started at the beginning of summer.

"So, I got a text from Beth the other day," she said now. "It was strange."

"Well, Beth *is* strange," Peter joked. He flicked on his blinker and changed lanes.

She hesitated. "Carter posted a selfie on Facebook."

"So?"

"He was standing in front of our house."

"What?" Peter glanced at her, concerned. "In Chicago?"

She swallowed. "No, here."

He said nothing. Though Beth loved to gossip, this felt bigger than that. She picked at the fabric of her skirt. "Why would he do that?"

Peter punched the horn as someone pulled out in front of him. "Are you sure it was our house?"

She hesitated. She wasn't positive, but it seemed too ironic: a black house, the silver roof, the *Home Sweet Home* caption.

"How long has it been since you've seen him?"

Peter scratched his jaw. The sandpaper scrape filled the car, irritating her. "At least a year." While Carter, Tommy, and Peter served together years ago, they occasionally saw each other at veteran meetups. She knew Tommy kept up with Carter more, as he'd always felt a great responsibility to check up on his brothers.

"What about you?" he asked.

The farmer's market flooded her memory. She'd been picking out a ripe pair of watermelons when he'd approached from behind and made a joke about her melons. She'd turned and almost dropped them when she'd seen his face. He hadn't hugged her; hadn't dared touch her, but she recognized all the pain and emotion on his face because she felt it too. "Me? Why would I see Carter?" She kept her voice light, but inside, her heart began to race.

Peter shrugged, his face impassive. "Just curious."

Desi fumbled for something to say. She and Carter had kept

the conversation neutral. He'd asked about Peter and Jules. She'd asked about his life and where he lived. They talked to each other like strangers, but the unspoken truth crackled between them. When he'd left, she'd literally had to fight the urge to run after him.

She adjusted in her seat, suddenly eager to change the subject. "I can't believe Jules turns eighteen in a couple of days."

Peter clenched his hands on the wheel. "Don't remind me."

Desi knew this was especially hard on Peter. His daughter was not only in love, but she was about to head off to live an independent life without them.

Desi stared out the window, admiring the simplicity of the land. The backdrop of the mountains lent itself as a spectacular view from every house. They ambled past downtown and then farther away from the main strip, deep into the forest on the other side of the mountain. The houses shrank. Some crested hilltops, jabbed into the side of the rock face like an afterthought. She marveled how the land dwarfed their modest nature. A few trailers splattered with junk—old refrigerators, tires, torn couches, cars without wheels—filled the spaces between quaint ranches, barns, and occasional brick buildings.

She was so used to her city friends, with their million-dollar homes and insane renovations. It sometimes didn't dawn on her that there was another way to live—a life where making your home beautiful wasn't a top priority. Where surviving was the only thing that mattered.

Peter turned right down a dusty dirt road. They rumbled past open fields, parched from the dry summer. After a quarter of a mile, Peter slowed and squinted at the numbers on the mailboxes, some of them stripped bare and worn from weather.

"Aha." Finally, he spotted one with cursive script: THE SAGERS.

He flicked on his blinker and crunched onto a gravel drive.

The house, a white brick ranch, sat far back from the road. Their front yard sprawled toward a massive flower and vegetable garden. A white picket fence lined the perimeter. Behind the house, the mountain surged, blotting out the rosy pink sky.

Already, she could imagine small touches that would make this house pop: a gazebo over the rose garden, a new roof, a fresh coat of paint. "This is adorable."

"It is." Peter parked, unbuckled his seat belt, and squeezed the steering wheel. "Look, before we go in . . ." His voice faded and he cleared his throat. "I know how important this is for Jules. So let's keep an open mind, okay?"

Desi laughed. "Me keep an open mind? Don't you mean *you* should keep an open mind?"

Peter scratched his forehead then pointed to their house. "Des, you're judgmental when it comes to how other people live."

"I am not!" Desi exclaimed.

Peter shot her a look. "You are. It's your job. I get it. But Will's mom is terminal. I'm sure her home isn't on the top of her priority list, so just, you know . . ." He gestured toward the house. "Don't think about giving them a reno or something."

Hadn't she just been thinking some version of the same thing? She tried to be offended but realized she didn't have it in her. Tonight wasn't about her or her profession. He was right. "I won't," she conceded.

"Good." He opened his door, but she reached forward and touched his elbow. "But the same goes for you."

He hesitated before climbing out of the car. "What do you mean?"

"Don't get all weird with Will's dad or protective over Jules. This is about her. We both agree, right?"

"I know that."

His curt response hurt her feelings. Wasn't she allowed to

offer advice too? She unbuckled her seat belt, smoothed her skirt and blouse, shouldered her purse, and balanced her tray of homemade brownies, which were Lenore's favorite, in the crooks of her arms. The pan was still warm. They padded down the brightly lit path to the blue front door. Oak shutters highlighted multiple sets of windows across the front. Peter stabbed the doorbell. She glanced at her feet to find gravel dust coating her shoes. Inside, a dog barked.

Peter looked at her. "Did you know they have a dog?"

Desi shook her head. Before she could say anything, the door opened and a tall, thin man with a gray mustache and close-cropped hair answered. She searched for an older version of Will somewhere in there, but didn't see the resemblance. The man smiled and extended a hand. "You must be Peter and Desi. Welcome." His voice was tender and had a slight southern twang. They shook hands and William Sr. took the tray of brownies from her. He lifted it to his nose and sniffed. "Lenore will be over the moon."

They shuffled into the foyer as a beautiful black Doberman trotted up to Desi and Peter. Desi loved dogs and had wanted one forever, but they never could because of Peter's allergies. She dropped to her knees. "What a gorgeous dog," she said. "I used to have a Doberman when I was small. Memphis. He was the best."

"This is Mabel. She's a good girl, isn't she?" William Sr. scratched behind her pointed ears.

Peter backed away slightly while Desi ran a hand over Mabel's sleek fur. She stood up and assessed the foyer. The floors were refinished white oak. The bedrooms lined the right side of the hall and the rectangular living room opened to the left. The furniture was warm and traditional, though there were a few modern touches in the fixtures and art. "You have a lovely home."

"Thank you. Please, come on in. I'll just pop these in the kitchen."

They followed William Sr. down a long, narrow hallway into an open-concept kitchen that dumped into a family room. A woman sat in a recliner, knitting, listening to Billie Holiday. Desi's heart lurched at the sight of her. Lenore looked up when they entered, the movement slow and full of effort. Her green eyes were piercing, even from across the room. They matched the emerald scarf knotted around her head. She smiled, her lips colorless. She placed the knitting needles in a woven basket and braced each hand on the edge of the chair to stand.

"Leni, now don't get too excited," William Sr. said. He hurriedly deposited the tray on the kitchen counter and rushed around to help her. He kissed her paper-thin cheek. She wrapped her bony hand around his arm.

Desi and Peter stood awkwardly in the kitchen, embarrassed by the intimate glimpse into this family's pain, but something about it made her long for a love like that. A love she thought she'd have with Peter, no matter what. In sickness or in health.

In lies or deceit.

Lenore inched slowly toward them, her breath audible. She stopped at the edge of the counter, those stunning eyes still teeming with life. "I'm so happy to meet you," she said. Desi didn't know what to do. Hug her? Shake her hand? She was afraid any point of contact might break this woman in half.

Peter moved in first and extended a hand, but Lenore waved it away. "Germs." She rolled her eyes. "Not a woman's best friend when her immunity is shot. I'll take a hug?"

Peter retracted his hand, embarrassed, and stepped into a stiff hug. Desi commented on Lenore's scarf.

Lenore patted it self-consciously, then looked down at her plain shift dress. "I feel like I'm underdressed in my own home," she joked.

"You look lovely," Desi said. "Why don't you sit and I can help with the food while we chat?"

William Sr. pulled over a bar-height chair and Lenore slipped into it as Desi acclimated to their kitchen. She understood she was succumbing to her usual overfunctioning mode, but she wanted to stay busy.

Peter thrust his hands in his pockets and rocked back on his heels. "So, where are the lovebirds?"

William Sr. smiled. "Good question." He checked his watch. "Will texted a little while ago and said they'd be here soon." He rolled his eyes. "Young love. Am I right?"

"How did you two meet?" Desi asked. She opened a drawer and located some tongs to toss the salad. This was her element. She loved getting to know people, hearing their stories, making them feel comfortable. Some would say her superpower was around gatherings. She always felt she came to life among groups.

Lenore laughed, and it was a beautiful sound, throaty and rich. It transformed her entire face, and Desi took a moment to mourn for this family, how empty this house would be without her laughter to fill it someday soon.

"Well, believe it or not, I was actually a flight attendant for William." They launched into a back-and-forth tale of how they'd met and fallen in love somewhere over Philadelphia. Their very first dates in Tokyo and Paris. How he proposed under the Eiffel Tower, like a movie. They traded details beautifully; it was evident they'd told their love story many times throughout the years. When they finished, she'd put together the salad and set the table. Peter slipped outside to help William Sr. fire up the grill.

"Where's Ava?" Desi asked as she washed her hands.

Lenore waved. "She's probably at the shop still, closing up."

Desi wondered what it must be like to have such a full life—your own business, a wonderful marriage, two amazing kids—and then to have it ripped away before you could witness how it would all turn out. Lenore couldn't have been any older than she was. How did one face their own mortality when they were just entering midlife?

Desi dried her hands on a bright yellow dish towel covered in hand-sewn baby chicks. "Your shop is amazing, by the way. We've been many times."

Peter rejoined them, beer in hand. Desi smiled at him and slid a glass of ice water over to Lenore, who graciously took a sip with a straw.

"Thank you. It's been so long since I've even been in . . ." Her voice faded, and some of the light drained from her eyes. Desi struggled to change the subject while Lenore fixed her attention on Peter. "So what do you think of all this?" Lenore asked him.

Peter pushed off the wall. Desi noticed his eyes were a little red from the dog. "All of what?"

"Our children," she said.

Outside the patio door, Desi watched William Sr. flip burgers and stare at the mountain.

"Will's an exceptional young man," Peter said.

Lenore motioned for Peter to come closer and Desi felt like she should leave the room. There was such a *knowing* about this woman. Being in her presence felt intimate in a way she wasn't used to. All of the people she surrounded herself with were obsessed with appearances and their place in the world. It was boasting about vacation spots, a pretentious knowledge of wine, or their investment portfolios. Desi poured herself a glass of water and stared into the cup. Was her entire life really about covering up who she really was?

Peter walked over and Lenore slid her hand across the counter and grabbed his forearm. He cleared his throat, never one for obvious outward affection—especially with strangers. But Lenore didn't care. Once she had his attention, she looked him square in the eye.

"I just want to say thank you. You've been here for my boy. Everything in Will's world is spinning right now, and he needs guidance. He needs another strong male in his life." Her eyes glistened with unshed tears and she squeezed Peter's arm. "Will respects the hell out of you and never stops talking about you and your family. Both of you." She stared between them, and Desi could sense all the things Lenore wanted to say—how she wouldn't be around to see how this all played out, how much she adored Jules, how appreciative she was of the time she had left, to take care of her boy when she was gone.

Desi stared intently at Lenore. "You did good," she said softly.

Lenore's stoicism wobbled, but then she nodded once, firmly, and retracted her hand. "Now that *that's* out of the way." She smacked the counter. "How about one of those brownies?"

Desi and Peter laughed. "Before dinner?"

Lenore glanced behind her. Steam hissed from the grill as William Sr. pressed a spatula into the sizzling meat. "I won't tell if you won't." She lifted her eyebrows, and Desi peeled back a corner of the aluminum foil and cut off a big hunk of the gooey dark chocolate–walnut brownies. She slid the piece onto a paper towel and watched as Lenore devoured it. She closed her eyes and moaned. "This is the best brownie I've ever had in my entire life." She smiled, her teeth sticky with chocolate. "Oh my God. Give me another."

For some reason, Desi wanted to cry. "Will told me that dark chocolate and walnuts are your favorite, so . . ." She proudly cut her another piece. She cut herself a piece too. Peter took a drink and looked at her, surprised.

"What? A woman should never eat alone, am I right?" Desi tapped her brownie against Lenore's in a mock toast.

"I'm going to go check on William," Peter said.

He left the two women, and Lenore waited until Peter was outside before continuing. "I just want you to know that your daughter is a revelation. Bright, beautiful, strong. She's got Will . . ." She lifted her arm. Blue veins snaked just beneath thin, ivory skin as she wagged her index finger.

Desi laughed. "I could say the same. Jules has never been so smitten. I'm so glad they met."

William Sr. and Peter entered the kitchen and set the steaming platter of food on the center of the dining room table. William Sr. removed his grilling apron, just as the front door opened and Will called out, "We're here!"

He glanced at his watch. "Right on time."

Desi, Peter, and Lenore hung back as William Sr. walked down the hall to greet them.

7

Jules

JULES paused on Will's doorstep.

"Wait." She took a breath, grabbed his arm. "I'm nervous."

"Don't be. My parents love you."

That's not why she was nervous. She was nervous *her* parents would somehow embarrass her. Before she could think too much more about it, the door opened and William Sr. stood there with a goofy grin and a pair of grilling tongs in his free hand.

"Juliette, my dear!" William Sr. crushed her in a hug that smelled of hamburgers. She waved at her parents who stood in the kitchen. "Hey, son." William Sr. closed the door behind them. Jules loved their home. The photos on the walls. The eclectic art, stacks of blankets, and homely personalization her mother would never tolerate. Lenore stood in the kitchen, always so striking, even at this stage of cancer. Jules leaned in for a hug. She smelled like Dial soap and something floral. Before Lenore released her, she gripped Jules's face. "How's my girl?"

Jules felt her mom bristle from a few feet away, but Jules smiled. "I'm good. How are you?"

"Fucking fantastic."

Everyone laughed, and Lenore looped her arm through Jules's and leaned her head on her shoulder. She caught her mother's expression, which she couldn't quite read. Every time she was with Lenore, an entire world of mother-daughter closeness rioted through her, and she envied Ava for having a mom this comfortable with invading personal space to create authentic moments.

"Hi. Remember me?" Will laughed, slinging an arm around Lenore's shoulders. He was a foot taller than his mother and tenderly kissed her head scarf. "You look good today, Mom."

"I *feel* good today." She rubbed his lower back. As always, Jules was enthralled with the physical closeness of this family. She couldn't ever remember a time of snuggling with her mother, of her mother holding her face or holding her. Her father would give her light hugs or high fives, but not this. This was another level of familial intimacy.

"Shall we eat?" William Sr. clapped his hands and ushered them to the table. Jules sat by Will, who gripped her hand underneath the table. His parents were at opposite ends, and hers sat across from her and Will. This was the part she'd been dreading the most—if their parents would have anything in common, if there would be awkward lulls or complete silence. Suddenly, behind them, the door burst open and Ava exploded in, dropping her bag by the door.

"Sorry I'm late," she said. She walked into the kitchen, smacking gum, in jean shorts and a matching jacket studded with purple rhinestones.

"I thought you weren't coming?" her mother said.

"Will wanted me here." She karate-chopped his shoulders playfully. "So you guys didn't totally embarrass him and scare Jules away."

Jules laughed and waved. "You remember my parents?"

"Of course. Hi." She slid into the empty chair next to Will, and everyone glided into easy conversation.

Lenore scooted closer toward Jules and rested her chin in her hand. "So, tell me more about Columbia," she said. "It's approaching fast."

Her parents were deep in conversation with Will and William Sr., while Ava joked about something and covered her mouth with a napkin. Jules leaned in, ready to give the prerequisite, "I can't wait" speech. Instead, she offered up radical honesty, because she knew Lenore would cut right through the bullshit anyway. "Too fast."

Lenore waited for her to say more.

"I don't want to go." Though she'd been thinking this for weeks, it wasn't until she confided in Tommy and he told her she should follow her own path, that she'd really considered another option.

Still, she catalogued all the reasons why she should go. She'd already accepted. She'd made plans. She had a dorm and a roommate. The first semester had been paid for. Of course she was going! That's what you did after high school. But being here, in this place, after just two months, she knew that going to a city like New York wasn't what she wanted next. She wanted The Black House. She wanted River Falls. She wanted a year to just work, build, and *be*. She wanted Will and his family. She wanted conversations like this. She waited for the obligatory "Oh, everyone feels that way, but you'll come around," or some other adult pearls of wisdom.

Instead, Lenore shrugged and said, "So don't go."

Jules almost burst out laughing. Was it really so easy? She glanced around the table, at all these accomplished people who had all gone to college or were planning to. She couldn't disappoint her parents like that, all of *their* hopes and dreams so tangled up in what she would someday achieve. There seemed such little room for her own happiness when she thought about her future.

"Don't do that." Lenore shook one bony finger her way.

"Don't do what?" Jules asked. Had she said something out loud?

"Don't sit here and think about who you owe or why, or shove your feelings down until you can't feel them anymore. Listen, honey." She inched closer. "This is your *life*. As Mary Oliver says, your one wild and precious life. You need to do what you have to do to feel the way you want to feel. If I could go back, I would stop time and never spend one second agonizing over something I knew in my heart to be true." She lifted a hand to emphasize her point, and a group of razor-thin silver bangles slid toward her forearm. "Good decisions are the hardest. But hard is where the good stuff is."

Jules practically memorized Lenore's words. *Hard is where the good stuff is.* She glanced at Will, who caught her eye and smiled. Her parents were still talking, but she lowered her voice. "It's like when I got here . . ."

Understanding filled Lenore's entire face so that Jules could imagine just how vivacious she'd once been. "This place takes hold, I know." She sighed. "The moment we moved to River Falls, I knew I wanted to spend the rest of my days looking at those mountains. Breathing in this air. Walking the main strip. Believe me, I get it. It's a special place." She took a sip of water and narrowed her eyes. "Just promise me you'll do what's right for *you*."

"What's right for Jules?" Her mother had turned her attention their way, and Jules felt her stomach drop.

She figured Lenore would change the subject. "That Jules will make the right decision regarding her future," she said simply.

Her mother straightened in her chair and dabbed her mouth with a napkin. "Her future? She's got a bright one. Columbia will be lucky to have her."

Jules stopped breathing. This was the very thing she'd feared. Her mother, with her massive pride and even bigger ego, would somehow ruin everything.

"I think River Falls is lucky to have her too." Lenore also straightened, the unrolling of her spine audible as it cracked into place.

Jules searched for something to say, but instead, a collective hush roared across the table.

"What are you talking about?" Peter asked.

"College," Desi said brightly. "When Jules goes to New York in the fall."

Lenore looked at Jules expectantly, but she remained silent. The table was eerily still. Jules thought her lungs might explode because she refused to take a breath. She clenched her napkin in her lap until her knuckles turned white.

Ava tried to lighten the mood. "I've always wanted to go to New York."

"Jules is going to love it," Desi said matter-of-factly. "Right, Jules?"

Jules felt the words bubbling in her chest. "I don't want to go."

Desi studied her incredulously, her nostrils flaring. "Since when? It's already been *decided*, sweetheart."

"No, *you* decided."

Desi balked. "No, *you* decided to go to Columbia. Everything is already set."

"Well, now I want to stay."

Lenore dropped her fork and Jules bent down to retrieve it as it bounced off her plate and clattered onto the floor. She wished time would stop, that she could rewind and start tonight over.

Finally, Peter spoke. "Well, I for one love it here. We've already talked about building a survivalist course here someday, haven't we, Jules? William, what's the entrepreneurship market like in River Falls? Would the town support something like that?"

The tension diffused a bit as William Sr. and Peter talked about specifics. Will grabbed her hand under the table again, but Jules stared at her lap, ashamed of her mother, ashamed that she'd made a scene in Lenore's home. Will leaned in and whispered in her ear. "You okay?"

She nodded and scooped up another bite of food, chewing and staring at the table.

"Don't do that either," Lenore suddenly said.

Desi and Jules looked at Lenore, unsure of what she meant.

"Do what?" Jules asked.

"Silence how you feel to make other people comfortable. This is your life, honey. You are a human being who has her own desires, wishes, and dreams. It doesn't matter if you're seventeen or seventy-five. You want what you want for a reason. So don't apologize for wanting what you want, Juliette. Ever."

"So now you're giving my daughter advice on how to live her life?" Desi's voice lifted another octave.

"Mom, stop." She started to say more, then reconsidered. She could say nothing and life would carry on as usual, or she could speak up for herself and put an end to this now. She weighed her options, knowing that the repercussions would last long after tonight, but she'd been raised to be honest, and what was the point of all those life lessons if she couldn't be honest with her own family?

"The truth is . . ." she started. She licked her lips, losing a bit of her nerve when she looked at her mom, but then she glanced at Lenore, who gave her a small nod. *Permission*. She took a breath and tried again. The truth was she'd never wanted to go to Columbia, or any college for that matter. She'd spent her entire life overachieving, working hard, and was expected to have the same life many other people had the privilege to live: college, degree, work, marriage, babies, death. She wanted something more.

She pointed to the mountain outside the window. "I feel alive here. I don't want a fancy degree or a bustling career like yours that keeps me so busy I miss everything else. I want to build a *real* life that means something to me." She shrugged and looked around the table. "I want to stay."

Jules could already feel the effect of her words as they performed a silent echo around the room. She'd never spoken to her mother this way. She glanced at her father. He sat in stony silence, but he didn't look angry. Her mother, on the other hand, looked like she'd been slapped. Lenore crossed her arms, staring at her with respect. Never one for a public scene, her mother forced a smile.

"We'll talk about this at home, Juliette." She turned to Peter and scooted back from the table, tossing her napkin on her half-eaten plate. "I've suddenly got a splitting headache. Peter, drive me home?"

Jules expected her father to oblige, to rush out of there and leave her to clean up the mess.

"No." He said it once, softly. "We are here for Jules and Will, and we're going to stay until the evening is over. And if I recall, there's a plate of brownies that needs to be eaten, am I right? Will, help me clear the table?"

Bodies sprung to life around them as Desi excused herself to the bathroom. Jules had never seen her mother so embarrassed, and she looked at Lenore, opening her mouth to apologize on her behalf.

"Honey, don't. What you did just changed your life and hers. Trust me." She winked, and Jules almost threw herself into Lenore's arms. Something about this woman and this place made her want to stand up for herself. She wasn't just a robot being told what to do, how to dress, what to eat, or how to feel. In the span of one night, she'd become more than just the topic of adult conversation and how they dangled their offspring's accomplishments like shiny trophies. She was her own person. Even though she was young, she knew exactly who she was and what she wanted. It had just taken a new environment to really drive it all home.

Will kissed the top of her head and her dad nodded as if to tell her everything would be alright. Jules helped Lenore out of her chair. "Come outside with me for a second?"

"Of course."

Jules helped her outside, while Ava washed dishes with the men. Her mother still hadn't reappeared, and she wondered if she should check on her. A wave of guilt crashed over her for what she'd said. All of the damage control she would have to do. But all of it had been true. She wasn't trying to hurt her mother; she was trying to be honest with herself. When had her own self-worth gotten so tangled up in her mother's?

Outside, the stars popped and the mountain's backbone rose in dark, undulating waves. Lenore sank into a patio chair and patted the one next to her.

"I'm going to tell you something, and I want you to listen."

Jules nodded. She was learning pretty quickly that she'd listen to anything Lenore had to say.

"Will isn't as strong as he appears."

The change in topic threw her, but she clung to every word.

"A year ago, everything was different. We were all going about our lives, staying busy, and then the cancer hit." She tipped her head back and sucked in the clean, crisp air. "You think you're prepared for anything. That nothing can really change your life, or that everything you obsess about matters. When I first got diagnosed, it was terrible. I've never smoked a cigarette a day in my life, can you believe it? And with all this mountain air, I didn't understand how I could get lung cancer, of all things." She sighed. "But I worked in a factory with my father when I was a child, so I possibly ingested toxic chemicals for years. Anyway, that's not the point. The point is, after the shock of the diagnosis wore off, we developed a new routine, one where we learned to *co*-exist, not just merely go through the motions. My family basically quit their lives to be here for me at first, take me to appointments, research, and help me fight this thing." She shook her head. "I realized that they wanted to stop their lives to take care of mine. William Sr. wanted to quit flying, Will wanted to drop out of school, and Ava wanted to homeschool to be here for me. But I said no." She laughed. "While selfishly, I might have wanted them around, I knew that their lives were theirs, and they weren't going to stop to watch me die. So I made them keep living. But as a result, Will has taken on the brunt of helping around the house. He loves his father dearly, but William Sr. flies most weeks, all week." She rolled her eyes. "But since he's met your father . . ." Her voice faded, and Jules's heart gave a kick. "I'm just glad he's got all of you."

Jules knew there was an end to that sentence, an unspoken truth about when Lenore would no longer be here. She wanted to point out that maybe some miracle drug would surface, but Lenore was terminal. They all knew it, so there was no use pretending the inevitable wasn't going to happen.

"Promise me you'll love each other the way you both deserve to be loved."

Love. Such a powerful word, especially since they'd only been dating such a short time, but Jules heard herself speak from the very truest part of herself. "I promise."

"Good. That's all I need to hear."

Jules reached over and grabbed Lenore's hand. The two of them sat together, staring at the star-studded sky, holding hands. The clouds drifted across the mountaintops, turning wispy. In the span of a single night, they'd gone from friends to understanding each other in a way she never even knew was possible.

Almost like family.

8

Desi

DESI replayed the scene at the dinner table.

Her anger intensified as she washed and dried her hands with a baby-blue towel. Lenore had known her daughter for all of five minutes and assumed she knew what was best. As she stared into the mirror, a bit of the anger slipped. What really bothered her was that Jules had more in common with Lenore—starting with the fact that they both felt they belonged in River Falls. She wasn't sure what was worse: that her daughter wanted a simple life or that she wasn't the kind of mother who could celebrate their differences, instead constantly wanting Jules to conform to a life that didn't fit.

She knew she had to apologize, but she'd never been good at saying she was sorry. Hers was a family that ignored issues until they just went away. She flipped off the light and thought of Peter, who had put yet another wedge between them by not standing up for her.

She opened the door. Peter stood on the other side, leaning against the wall, arms crossed, waiting. "You good?" he asked.

"What do you think?" she snapped. She looked around to

make sure they were alone. "You embarrassed me out there. Why didn't you have my back?"

"Because I didn't agree." He took a step toward her. "You didn't listen to anything Jules said or how she feels."

That admission stung. She wanted a daughter who could tell her anything, and yet hadn't she gotten angry when Jules expressed herself?

"You need to go back in there and apologize. To everyone." He stabbed a finger toward the kitchen.

She recoiled. "I most certainly will not." She had no problem pulling Lenore aside, but she wasn't going to give a goddamned speech.

He leaned in, squinted at her. "Yes, you will. You will do it for our daughter and for that poor boy in there with his dying mother. You will make peace because Will—*and* his family—are going to be in our lives, Desiree. You will do this because you love your daughter and you will put her wishes above your own selfish ego. Do you understand me?"

Desi opened her mouth to retort, but then closed it. She knew he was right, but she also hated to be told what to do. Finally, she stalked past him and into the family room, where they were all sitting in various positions of relaxation listening to music and talking. It was such an idyllic family picture: her daughter on the floor with Will, flipping through a photo album, Ava curled up with her mom and William Sr., talking about their days.

What did she really know about family?

She took a tentative step into the room, and Lenore was the first to look up. There was no trace of anger or disdain; rather, she looked curious about what was going to happen next.

"I just wanted to apologize," she began. She looked at Jules.

"You're right in that this is your life and you should be able to make your own choices. When we get home, let's sit down and talk about everything, okay? I promise to listen. Your feelings are important."

Jules nodded, looking relieved.

Desi turned to Lenore. "And Lenore, I'm so sorry for the way I behaved in your home."

Lenore cut her off. "Please. You showed me I still have a bit of fire left. Took my mind completely off my cancer for once, so I should be thanking you." She patted the couch cushion next to her. "Come and sit. I must get this brownie recipe from you."

Desi eased into the room, feeling the tension dissolve with every step. Is this what an unconditional family looked like? Where they didn't walk around for weeks in silence until the storm had passed? Peter moved into the room behind her. As Desi sat beside Lenore, sadness wrapped its arms around her. Maybe she'd gotten it wrong all these years. The things she valued, all that she'd worked so hard for. What was the use of having such an outwardly pretty life if, inwardly, her own family didn't want the same things?

She joined the conversation, but her heart wasn't in it. Instead of pretending, she sat quietly, observing the scene around her. She watched Jules with Will, the way they touched and looked at each other, and she knew that it would be impossible to tear her daughter away from this place. Hadn't she once been in a similar position?

Lenore coughed beside her, which tugged her back to the present. It was harsh and wet. She pressed a balled-up handkerchief to her lips, and when she lowered it, Desi could see it was stained with blood. Jules looked at Will, alarmed, and William Sr. helped Lenore stand.

"I think this lovely lady has had enough action for one night. You guys are welcome to stay, but I'm going to put her to bed."

Lenore had instantly transformed with one cough. One moment, she was vivacious and laughing, the next she appeared used and limp. Desi and Peter told her good night, and all the joy drained from the room as William Sr. escorted Lenore down the hall.

Desi locked eyes with Peter. "We should get going. Jules?"

Jules looked prepared to argue, but seemed to reconsider.

"Dad and I will just be outside," Desi interjected. "Come out whenever you're ready." She said good night to Will and Ava, collected her purse, and couldn't get to the front door fast enough.

When she reached the hallway, the bedroom door was open. Lenore's back was turned, her spine visible through her silk nightgown. She was curved over like a C, trying to reach for a fallen sock. Her scarf had been removed to reveal tufts of downy brown hair sprouting from her smooth scalp.

Before she knew what she was doing, she rushed into the room.

"Desi," Peter hissed. William Sr. was in the bathroom, the door closed, water running, and Lenore turned, startled.

Before she could protest, Desi scooped up the sock, then wrapped her arms around Lenore and held her there until Lenore melted into her arms.

They stood there, mother to mother. While they were wildly different, they both loved their families. They were both trying to do what they thought was best. They both had to be strong. There *were* no right answers or perfect mothers, but there was this: a unitedness that could only happen in moments like these, when a strong mother needed another mother to lift her up when she was so weary, she couldn't even pick up a damn sock.

Desi stood with Lenore until William Sr. walked in with a humidifier and set it gingerly on the nightstand. Desi extricated herself and cradled Lenore's face in her hands, just as Lenore had held Jules's face hours before.

"You have a lovely family," she said, tears slipping down her own cheeks. "You did good." She repeated her words from earlier, but the meaning felt deeper.

Lenore nodded and closed her eyes. Desi said goodbye and pushed past Peter. Outside, she gazed at the star-flecked sky and took a long, shaky breath. Peter approached and slowly slid his arms around her waist. He said nothing but held her there, his chin resting on the crown of her head, for minutes or hours, she wasn't sure.

Finally, Jules announced she was ready. Desi broke away from Peter, walked to the passenger side of their SUV, and climbed inside.

They made the long journey home, silently ascending the mountain toward The Black House.

9

Desi

THE next day, Desi had the house to herself.

Jules, Tommy, and Peter were in the woods, working on the shelter for Jules's upcoming birthday party. Desi enjoyed a lazy morning of coffee, a hot bubble bath, and reading a book. She tried to luxuriate in the self-care, but her mind filled with the college discussion at Lenore's.

She hadn't yet talked to Jules about it, partly because she didn't know what to say. She vividly remembered being that age, feeling like the whole world was condensed to what was in front of her. Boyfriends. A happy life. Not a care in the world.

She too hadn't necessarily wanted to go straight to college, desperately asking her parents for a gap year. In hindsight, she was relieved she hadn't thrown her future away to go travel the world, but she did know a thing or two about having regrets.

She understood that Jules was madly in love for the first time, but that feeling would fade. It *always* faded. And when it did, she needed something concrete to fall back on, like a legitimate, thriving career, not just wounds from a failed relationship.

After her bath, Desi got dressed and went outside to tend the garden. She filled her basket with dandelion greens, arugula, spinach, fresh basil, thyme, and a few vine-ripened tomatoes. They'd already stocked up on seafood. Perhaps she'd make pesto and some homemade pasta with scallops.

She lost herself in the work, her fingers digging deeply into the earth. Back in Chicago, she'd had a small urban garden, but here she could explore her green thumb. She put on some music and worked until her shoulders were pink and sore from the solid effort. She brought her bounty inside, rinsed the greens, and poured a fresh glass of lemonade when the doorbell rang.

She jumped from the sound, partly because they never used it. She wondered if it was Tommy, because no one could get through their gate without the code. Had Jules given it to Will?

She walked slowly to the front and glimpsed a pair of work boots at the bottom of the door. She worked her gaze up and froze.

Carter.

He lifted his hand in a sheepish wave and then put both of them up, as if to surrender. Desi's breath caught in her chest, and she stood there, unable to move, her lemonade glass sweating in her dirt-caked palm. She was too stunned to worry about how he'd gotten through the gate or how she must look, sweaty and crisped from the sun. She didn't see a vehicle in her driveway and hadn't heard any tires disturb the gravel.

Setting the drink down on the entry table, she tentatively opened the door.

"Hey, Des." He stared at her until a warm blush crept from her neck to her scalp.

A flood of memories—equally beautiful and agonizing—hit her in a rush. It was like looking at a ghost.

"What are you doing here?"

He peered behind him and shoved both hands into the back pockets of his jeans. He tipped back on his heels, stared at his boots, then at her. He lifted an eyebrow and cocked a shoulder. His gaze jolted her entire body, tiny spasms that shocked her into silence. "I wanted to see you," he said simply.

She'd wanted to see him too over the years, but this was insane. You didn't go almost twenty years without talking, run into each other randomly, and then suddenly show up out of the blue. "How did you find me?"

He opened his mouth to answer right as Tommy, Peter, and Jules rounded the corner, smeared in dirt and sweat. She froze again, this time from guilt.

"Carter?" Tommy was the first to spot him and rushed over to clap him on the back. "So the rumor's true. You are in town."

Jules said hello and excused herself, avoiding eye contact with Desi, which sent another spasm through her heart. They really needed to talk. Peter was the last to approach and eyed Carter warily. "You lost, brother?"

Carter laughed and gave him a hug. "I saw my boy Tommy took a road trip and I thought, why not? Haven't been to the mountains in ages." He dropped his arms, but Desi noticed his hand tremored. When he saw her looking, he stuffed it back in his pocket.

"Beer?" Tommy asked.

Desi shot him a look, but he ignored her and ushered Carter inside. Peter assessed her as he wiped his face with his red bandanna. "You good?"

"Not really," she said. "This was supposed to be our family vacation, and now we have *two* uninvited guests." She pushed past him before she said more. Peter had no idea what it really meant for Carter to be here, and she was intent on keeping it that way.

She rushed to her room, cleaned up, and headed to join them in the kitchen. On the way, she hesitated outside of Jules's door and lightly knocked.

"What?" her daughter called.

Desi peered inside. Jules was spread out on her stomach, work clothes still on, sketching in her journal. She closed it and sat up.

"Can we talk for a sec?"

Jules scratched her head and nodded. "Who's that guy?"

Desi eased herself into a chair across the bed. "A friend of your father's and Tommy's. They served together."

"Does he live here or something?"

"No, he lives in Chicago."

Desi saw the confusion pass across her daughter's face, but she wiped it away and focused on her. "What do you want to talk about?"

"Listen, I wanted to talk to you about dinner last night." She swallowed. "I'm sorry if I came across as harsh. I'm just surprised."

"I am too," Jules confessed. "But this place is amazing, Mom. I can see myself here."

"And I'm happy about that, sweetie, I am, but I just want you to really think about it. You have all the time in the world to set up a life here, to visit. We own this place." She gestured around. "It's yours whenever you want it. I just don't want you to give up what you've worked so hard for."

"I'm not."

Desi braced herself for an argument.

"Plus," she added, "Tommy thinks it's a good idea."

Desi attempted to keep her face impassive. "What do you mean?"

Jules fiddled with the journal ribbon, sliding it between her fingers. "He said I should take some EMT classes or something. Remember how I wanted to do that? And I can help Dad with his survivalist courses too."

She ignored that last statement and backpedaled to the first. "I didn't know you were still interested in becoming an EMT."

Jules's face hardened. "I never stopped thinking about it." She shrugged. "I think it's cool to be a medic. Uncle Tommy loved it."

She wanted to remind Jules that while being a medic was noble, she shouldn't use Tommy as a poster child for any future endeavors.

"Being a medic is a wonderful path," Desi said. "But with a biomedical science degree, you could do so much more. Help change the world even." Desi could hear the desperation in her own voice and knew by pushing, Jules would just want to do the opposite. That was parenting 101. Sensing her daughter's discomfort, all the fight drained from her body. She stood. "You know what? Why don't we talk about this later?" At the door, she turned. "Again, I'm sorry if I upset you."

Jules deflated and offered a tight-lipped smile. "It's fine. Is it okay if I go to Will's?"

Desi almost protested, but she didn't want Jules around Carter. It was time they had a serious talk, and the less distractions, the better. "Sure, see if Dad can drive you." She paused at her door, turned. "I love you, Juliette."

"I love you too," she said, distractedly rolling back to her stomach to sketch.

Desi closed her door and inched down the hall, straining to hear what the boys were talking about. Instead, she found an empty kitchen. She sighed, retrieved her lemonade glass, and dumped the remnants into the sink. Antsy, she went outside and searched the grounds, hearing the men by the pool. Sure enough, they were all nursing beers around her patio table. Carter's feet were propped up on the empty chair—her chair. As she approached, they fell quiet. Carter's eyes traveled slowly up to her face as he lowered both boots to the ground.

"Can I get you anything?" she found herself asking. Here he was, encroaching on her space, and she still didn't have the courage to rock the boat.

He lifted his beer and took a swig. "All good." He wiped his mouth with the back of his hand.

"I'll leave you boys to it then."

"Aw, why don't you stay? We can all catch up," Tommy said. He patted the empty chair.

"I think I'm going to take a walk actually." She turned to Peter. "Jules needs a ride." She offered a short wave. "You guys enjoy."

She wanted to scream. Carter was on her back patio, drinking a beer with her husband and brother, when he'd really come here to see her. She didn't trust herself to be near him, especially not while around Tommy and Peter.

She pushed through the gate and crunched over the earth. She'd not yet walked this path, instead always running, the land a blur around her. She attempted to clear her mind and slow her thoughts, taking in the birds, the trees, the slivers of sunlight that pricked through the leaves. But she kept seeing Carter: his probing eyes, the beard that covered a silver scar along her jaw, those hands at once so familiar yet completely foreign wrapped around a bottle's neck.

She couldn't breathe. She felt trapped, claustrophobic, lost in this vast land with nowhere to escape. Despite her intentions to walk, she began to run and veered sharply off course, pushing through rough terrain and overgrown trees and brush. Thorns nicked her skin, but she kept going, wanting to feel anything other than this agonizing uncertainty.

Finally, when she reached an open meadow, she walked in small circles, clearing her head. She'd never wandered this far off the path and was floored by its beauty—the open, expansive mountains, the rich green of summer, the trees that gave everything a padded hush. She lay on the ground and closed her eyes, gathering her thoughts, when she heard a branch crack behind her.

She sat up too fast and her back tightened, sending a twinge of pain to her thoracic spine. She turned. Carter marched toward her, with an imperceptible limp from his prosthetic, an intent look on his face.

She let out a small yelp and scrambled to her feet, searching for Peter or Tommy. "What are you doing out here?" She took a few steps back, afraid to get too close.

"Calm down," he joked. "I'm not going to jump you."

Desi visibly relaxed.

"Peter left to drive Jules to town, and I wanted to talk."

A small thrill rippled through her body at the thought of being alone with him. It had been so long.

"Where does Tommy think you are?"

"Exploring." He moved closer.

Her body hummed with expectation.

"Can I give you a hug at least?"

She hovered in space, caught between wanting to fling herself into his arms and run away. Instead, when his hands clasped around her waist, she melted against him and buried her face in his neck. He smelled like wood smoke and soap. He cradled her gingerly, as if she might break, and despite herself, she took a giant inhale and squeezed him as tightly as possible.

As if reading her thoughts, he spoke first. "God, I've missed the way you smell." She used to wake up with his nose pressed gently into her spine, high off her scent.

She finally broke away. She grazed his beard and let her hands fall. They were mere inches from each other, and his eyes were glued to her mouth. She put some distance between them, but still felt unsteady. "Why are you really here?"

He sighed. "Des, I've wanted to see you for years. You have to know that. I've never stopped thinking about us."

The term *us* made her skin flush, but she stayed silent. He reached for her hand, and when she threaded her fingers through his, she was at home. Their time together shuttled back into focus, so that she could glimpse that younger version of herself, happy and madly in love. But she had too many questions: How had he found her? Why now? It seemed a dangerous game to be playing.

She tugged him to a small patch of wildflowers bursting in a rainbow of blue, purple, and yellow under their feet. "Talk to me," she said, as she sat.

He eased himself onto the flowers, drew his good knee to his chest, and looped his arms around it. "Where do I begin? It's been so long."

The distance cried between them. She hated that she'd missed so much of his life. He filled her in on the last several years—going to veterans meetings, keeping odd jobs, trying to stay afloat as city crime drove people out and prices continued to escalate. He turned to her. "But it seems like you've done really well for yourself, Desi. I'm proud of you."

She soaked in his words, but tugged herself back to the present. "All these years, we've lived in the same city. You could have reached out any time."

He sighed, bowed his head, and closed his eyes. "I've thought about reaching out so many times, but that didn't seem fair to you." He looked off in the distance. "I've had a lot of time to reflect recently. About my life, about my mistakes. I know you can't live in the past, but it's all I'm drawn to." He dragged his gaze back to her. "Every time I dwell on the past, there you are. The happiest times of my life were with you."

The same admission lodged in her chest, but she didn't dare utter a word. She was the one who had everything to lose: a husband, a daughter, a reputation. There was so much less on the line for him.

"Are you happy?" he finally asked.

She shook her head. "Don't ask me that." Her eyes filled with tears, but she cleared her throat and looked away.

"Des, look at me." He tugged her arm free, slid her hand into his, and caressed her palm with his thumb. A few tears slipped down her cheeks. "Are you happy?"

She could easily say that she was; that she and Peter were still in love, that everything was as good as it appeared. Instead of saying anything, she just stared into his eyes. Finally, she spoke. "Peter and I came here this summer as a last-ditch effort to fix our marriage. We've been slipping for a long time."

At the mention of Peter, he put a bit of physical space between them. "Peter's always been hard to figure out," he said, scratching his beard. "A fantastic soldier. Not so sure about a fantastic partner."

The jab hurt; mostly because it was true. So much sat unsaid between them. All the hurt she must have caused when she chose Peter over him. Though she'd met Carter before Peter, she'd always assumed the illusion of their flame would fade with time. Carter had nothing to offer but his love. In fairy tales, that was enough. But not in real life.

Once they paid bills together and did the hard work of

sustaining a relationship, they'd tire of each other. They'd sink into the same comfort zone that plagued most long-term couples. She didn't want to remember Carter like that. She didn't want to become a bitter wife to the man who'd shown her a different way of being.

While Peter offered stability and protection, she'd always felt too unbridled with Carter, too emotional. She couldn't sustain a life like that. She needed certain and familiar, not wild and unpredictable. In so many ways, Carter had become her mental escape, her ultimate what-if. She needed it to stay that way.

"What are you thinking?"

She sighed. "We were so young back then. What makes you think it wouldn't have faded with time?"

"Do you think it would have faded with time?"

No. She shrugged.

"Has it faded with Peter?"

She brushed a small lavender petal from her lap. "Marriage is complicated. When I met Peter, he seemed so . . . grown up. So responsible. I thought he was the safer choice."

Carter smiled painfully. "Never pegged you for a woman who wanted to be safe."

She narrowed her eyes. "Well, I wasn't *that* safe."

When Peter deployed, she'd been a lonely newlywed who'd felt betrayed that her brand-new husband wanted to serve his country rather than build a life with her. She'd been selfish and weak. She'd run into Carter at a bar one night, and they'd picked up right where they'd left off. Because they'd been so in love, it didn't even feel like cheating. It was easy not to face the consequences when Peter was away, but when he returned, she'd broken it off with Carter and promised to commit herself to Peter and give their marriage a chance.

As the years went by and her business grew, she and Peter

spent less and less time together. They were parents, room-mates, partners. There was so little time for romance.

"I want you to know that I understand why you chose him." He motioned around. "I mean, look at this. What you've built. You've always been so capable, Desiree. You don't need a man. You've never needed a man." He smiled. "I just had this foolish idea that after we ran into each other at the farmer's market, that maybe we were supposed to reconnect." He scratched his head, embarrassed. "Maybe I was reading too much into it. I shouldn't have come."

She placed a hand on his arm. Heat pulsed between them. "I'm glad you came." She meant it. All of this mental obsessing, the few random texts . . . She wanted to ask him about the Facebook photo, but it could wait. It was all so much less threatening to have him here. She'd forgotten how easily they got along, how she could just be herself around him.

Her hand slipped into her lap. "But I have to figure out what I'm doing first." She glanced over her shoulder, as though Peter might be waiting there, watching. She lowered her voice any-way. "If he ever found out what we did when he was away . . ." She shook her head. She plucked a handful of wildflowers and let them flutter around her. "Perhaps that's why I've stayed with him all these years. To try and prove that I can honor my com-mitments."

"But it's your life," Carter said. "Some relationships aren't meant to last forever. That doesn't make it a failure. It just means it's time to move on."

Desi laughed. "Listen to you, giving relationship advice. From what I know, you aren't someone who *has* long-term relation-ships."

"See?" He bumped her shoulder playfully. "Exactly my point."

She studied him. "Do you want to stay for dinner?"

Carter studied her. "Yes."

Desi stood and picked the petals from her pants. "We're all adults, right?" Perhaps it was a selfish move, but she wasn't ready to see him go yet. And she was sure Peter and Tommy would like more time with him. Now that he was here and they'd talked, she assumed she could handle it.

Carter stood and gestured for her to lead the way. The two of them walked side by side, a familiar desire aching between them.

Desi didn't know if she was playing a dangerous game, but tonight, for some unexplainable reason, she was willing to find out.

10

Desi

THAT night, Desi did her best to play hostess.

Tommy seemed thrilled to have Carter stay for dinner, while Peter was aloof. Jules was staying at Will's for the night, so it was just the adults for the evening.

Desi kept the wine flowing as the men complimented her seafood pasta dish.

"I can't get over the vegetables here," Desi heard herself saying. "So much fresher than anything in Chicago."

"It seems like an amazing place," Carter affirmed. "I can see why you built here." He turned to Peter. "And I hear you're going to do survivalist courses too?"

Tommy slapped Peter on the arm. "We should all go into business together. Teach locals survival and tactical skills. Get out of the city. Think about it: mountains, fresh air, using our skills for good."

Desi laughed. Her brother would get restless after a month and want to move on. And Peter and Carter working together? It would never happen.

Peter swirled his wine and pretended to consider it. "I'm not sure Carter would be willing to leave Chicago. Born and raised, right?"

Carter nodded. "Actually, I've been wanting a change. There's nothing there for me anymore." He glanced at Desi then averted his eyes.

"Well, change can be good," Desi offered. "Maybe it's time."

"Maybe."

"How long you staying?" Tommy asked.

"I'll probably head back tomorrow," Carter said. "Maybe keep driving to one of the Carolina beaches. It's been a while since I've taken a road trip."

"Nonsense," Peter said. "You can stay here. You should see the town, try it on."

"Oh no, I wouldn't want to impose."

"We insist. Right, Des? The more, the merrier."

He knew damn well it was never the more, the merrier, but she found herself nodding, unable to speak. Carter showing up randomly was one thing. But Carter sleeping down the hall from her was quite another.

Peter refilled Carter's wineglass and assessed him. "I am curious though . . . how did you find this house? We haven't shared the address with anyone."

A chilly silence passed around the table as Desi hunted for something to say.

"I texted Tommy to ask where he was," Carter said smoothly. "He sent me a photo and told me the address." He shrugged. "It's been so long since I've seen all of you . . ."

"You didn't think to ask first?" There was an edge to Peter's voice that only she could detect. She needed to defuse the situation, but she didn't want to make anything worse.

Carter nodded. "I probably should have. Just got a wild hair and jumped in the car."

Peter's cold eyes softened as he smiled. "I'm just giving you shit, man. It's great to see you. Too rare for all of us to be together. What's mine is yours." He looked directly at Desi, and she pushed back from the table and began clearing dishes.

"Why don't you boys go show Carter the shelter? I'm sure he'd love to see it. I'll just clean up." She'd had too much wine and focused on enunciating every syllable. This wasn't good. This wasn't good at all. The more Carter stayed, the more paranoid she'd become. Reading into every word, every look . . .

As she scraped the first dish into the trash, that sick sense of foreboding worked over her body. What in the world made her think Peter didn't know already? He was one of the smartest men she'd ever met. Though he'd never outright asked her, and she'd never shared that she and Carter had dated, he had ways of finding anything out. She took a shuddering breath and stacked the plates in the dishwasher before pouring herself a glass of water.

She needed to have a clear head if she was going to make it out of this intact. Her earlier confidence that this was a good idea evaporated into an obvious truth: She was still drawn to Carter and Peter could sense it. This was a disaster.

"Need a hand?" Tommy entered the kitchen. She heard the sliding glass door open as Carter and Peter stepped onto the patio, bathed in moonlight by the pool.

She turned to Tommy as he handed her a dish. "You okay?"

She rearranged her face to neutral. "Of course. Why?"

He placed his hands on her shoulders so that she had to stop what she was doing to look at him. "Is something going on between you and Carter?"

The words knifed the open room. Was it so obvious? "Don't be ridiculous." She laughed and bit her tongue from saying more.

"You can tell me, you know. I know that you and Peter aren't doing well."

"And how do you know that?" she asked.

"Because he told me," he said. "He does talk, you know."

Desi couldn't imagine Peter confiding in anyone, much less her brother. "What did he say?"

Tommy lifted his hands. "Nope. Not getting involved."

"Oh, really? Is that why you're being a total shit stirrer right now?"

"Fine, fine. I'm just saying, if you need to talk, I'm here." Tommy glanced at his phone, smirked, and texted a reply.

Desi swatted him with a kitchen towel. "Who is that?"

He jumped out of the way. "Just a new lady friend. We're going to meet for a drink."

She had no idea how her brother had found time to meet anyone, much less find any sort of reception in their kitchen. He kissed her on the temple and told her to be good before saying goodbye to the guys.

She rolled her eyes as she pushed start on the dishwasher and wiped down the dining room table. Her mind spun on a relentless loop. She needed to think. What if Peter came right out and asked her about Carter? Would she lie directly to his face? Or would she finally tell him the truth?

She glanced at the two of them outside, standing by the pool, chatting. Sometimes, she forgot that they shared secrets she'd never understand. Secrets of war, murder, sacrifice, loss. She dropped her dish towel on the counter and despite her better judgment, joined the boys out by the fire pit.

"Are you going to head to the shelter?" she asked.

"Nah," Peter said. "We'll take him in the morning." Peter yawned. "Des, do you need help setting up the guest room?"

"No, I've got it." Ironically, Peter had been staying in the guest room, which meant he'd have to share her bed tonight.

He clapped Carter on the shoulder. "Good to have you here, man."

Suddenly, the landline rang from inside, which startled all three of them. "I'll get it." Desi rushed to the phone. "Hello?"

"Mom, can you come get me please?" Jules's voice wavered and she could tell she was trying not to cry.

Desi flagged Peter from outside. "Honey, what's happened? Are you okay?"

"It's Lenore . . . she's having a horrible night. Will says it would be better if I came home."

"Of course, sweetheart."

Peter motioned to give him the phone. Poor Lenore. It seemed she was having more bad days than good. She wished there was more that she could do.

Peter hung up the phone and snatched his keys from the table. "I'll be right back."

"Do you need me to come with you?" she asked.

"No, I've got it." He hesitated before pulling open the door and turned to her. He opened his mouth to speak and a spasm of fear jolted her chest. She waited for the inevitable question, but he closed his mouth. "Tell Carter I said good night."

He shut the door behind him. She felt as if she was wading through water. They were all alone, at night, in her house. She locked the door and leaned against it, gathering herself. She'd have at least an hour before Peter made it back. The roads could be treacherous at night, which is why she wasn't comfortable driving here beyond daytime errands yet.

She smoothed her hands over her hair and joined Carter outside. "Everything okay?" he asked.

She filled him in and took a seat by the fire. The earlier heat had drained from the sky and she pulled a blanket from the basket and draped it over her legs. "Join me?" she asked.

He sat across from her. The flames licked the black fire pot and cast playful shadows over his face. He watched her intently. Neither of them spoke. Finally, after a few minutes of trancelike staring, he started. "You have such a great family, Des." He sighed when he said it, as if he was conceding to something.

"It's not as great as it appears." The words poured from her lips and she quickly backtracked. "I'm grateful—of course I am. But I don't know. Sometimes I can't tell between how my life looks and what it really is." She shook her head. "You know I envy you, C. You have no ties, no obligations, nobody to disappoint. You could get in your car tomorrow and start over wherever you want, become whoever you want. You're free in a way I won't ever be."

He seemed to digest what she said before speaking. "You could be though. Jules is almost out of the house. You can change your life at any time."

Could she though? Could she walk away from her marriage, from her secrets and lies, from her business, from her penthouse and possessions? Where would she even go? She closed her eyes and imagined hitting the road with Carter. They'd done it so many times before, on weekends when the city got so achingly cold, they could barely stand outside. He would warm up his old beat-up truck and surprise her by taking her someplace completely unexpected—a random cabin in Wisconsin, a bed-and-breakfast in Michigan, a hotel in Indy. He never let her pay, even back then, though she knew he struggled to make ends meet. But he never complained and always wanted to make her happy.

"I'm sorry I didn't choose you." The admission tumbled free and seemed to suck all the energy from the starry black night. She held her breath, unsure of how those words would land, or what they would even mean.

"I'm sorry I didn't fight harder," he whispered. "I shouldn't have let you go . . . I just thought Peter could give you a better life, and it was what you wanted. You seemed so sure."

He didn't know what really happened, but she couldn't tell him now. It would hurt too much.

"Is it too late?" He sat perfectly still, his hands clasped in his lap, leaning forward over his knees in anticipatory silence.

She didn't know how to answer. On one hand, she wanted to scream that it wasn't, that these past couple of months, he was all she'd obsessed about, but that in order to move on, she had to be honest with Peter. But when she thought about divorce—about getting lawyers involved, dividing properties and money, and especially telling Jules—she wasn't sure if she could sacrifice all that she'd built for her own selfish agenda. "I'm honestly not sure," she said. All the alcohol had muddled her thoughts. She suddenly felt wiped and wanted to go to bed. But she also wanted to stay and talk to Carter.

"I should get your room ready," she said. He said he'd snuff out the fire.

Inside, she steadied her nerves and prepared the room, which sat at the front of the house, across from Jules's room. Tommy's was next door. She flipped on the bedside lamp and was hurriedly changing the sheets when Carter entered behind her and leaned in the doorway.

"This is nicer than my entire place back home," he joked.

"I doubt that," she said. She folded her arms across her chest as she faced him. She didn't trust herself, didn't trust her body not to override the logical side of her brain. It was one thing to think about Carter, it was quite another to cross a line in her own home, when her husband would be back shortly.

His eyes landed on some of Peter's clothes on top of the dresser, as well as the sheets.

"Peter's been crashing in here." She sighed. There was no use pretending. Why did it take saying it out loud to make her realize how far gone her marriage actually was?

"I'm sorry to hear that, Des. That must be hard."

She shrugged. It should be hard, but the truth was they'd been living such separate lives for so long, she didn't really remember what true intimacy felt like. Not until looking into Carter's eyes and feeling everything she'd been denying herself for the better part of twenty years. "Let me know if you need anything," she said. She checked her watch. It was already close to midnight. She never stayed up this late.

He stopped her in the doorway and tugged one of her arms free and tenderly pulled her forward into a hug. She clung to him, threading her fingers through his hair and sighing against his neck. Before she could think, she pulled back and gripped his face in her hands.

"Desi . . ." He could barely breathe. He would never cross that line unless she gave him permission, and she did now, nodding.

"Please," she said.

He dipped his head, pausing one agonizing second before giving in. Her entire body pulsed. His lips pressed against hers and their world together spilled back through her body, back before she was a mother or wife. She remembered everything in that kiss—from the first moment she fell for him until their last torturous goodbye. This was just another secret, another level of deceit she couldn't take back.

He pushed her farther into the room, then kicked the door closed behind him. They fell on the bed, entangled and kissing. Her body woke from its frigid dormancy. God, she'd forgotten. She'd forgotten the way he made her feel.

He pulled back and looked at her, brushing a few hairs from her face. "You're still so fucking beautiful," he said. "I've missed you so much."

A tear slipped from her cheek as she tugged him back on top of her. Her body felt wild and dangerous; she wanted to rip all his clothes off and feel him inside her, but they would never do that to Peter. Even this was too much.

Finally, he sat back and ran his fingers through his hair and then over his beard, calming himself. "Holy shit," he said.

Her lips were swollen. Her skin smelled like his. She wanted more. She searched eyes she used to know so well. Their life together consumed the inky black of the bedroom. He used to tell her everything under the veil of night, and she would listen without judgment, rubbing a hand along his chest, memorizing the heavy thud of his heart beneath her ear. She'd trace his scars or massage the ragged flesh of his knee. When she looked at him now, his eyes were timid, uncertain even. He didn't know where he stood.

"I don't want to put any pressure on you," he said. "But Des, if there's a chance that this could happen, that we could really give this a shot somehow . . ." He motioned between them. "Then I need to know. Otherwise . . ." He roughly raked a hand through his hair. "I can't go through this again. I can't lose you three times." The first had been when she started dating Peter. The second had been after their affair and she'd chosen Peter again. It hadn't been fair to him then and it wasn't fair to him now. She couldn't go through it either.

There was an indefinite moment of silence where Desi's choices fired through her heart: Breaking up with Carter in the first place. Lying to Peter. Lying to herself. Then, Jules's face flashed through her mind before the sharp crack of her conscience followed suit. She didn't know what to do.

She gripped his hand across the bed. Headlights flicked across the windowpane. She moved forward and kissed him again, deeply. "Don't give up on me" was all she said. She wanted to tell him she still loved him, that she wanted what he wanted, but she was afraid. He nodded and breathed her in before she walked toward the door.

"Des . . ."

She turned in the doorway, anguished.

He shook his head and smiled, burying whatever it was he was going to say. "Sleep well."

She nodded and shut his door before bursting into tears.

11

Jules

SHE'D never been a huge fan of her own birthday.

Jules threw on jean shorts and a crop top over her ruby-red bathing suit. She stared at herself in the mirror, reciting her new age: eighteen. Today, she turned eighteen. This birthday felt special, and not just because she could finally make her own decisions. This year, she had someone she wanted to share it with.

A few days ago, her mother had been so excited about her birthday, making plans, buying supplies for the pool party, and now she moped around, barely offering a word since Carter had shown up and then taken off the next morning without another word.

Wordlessly, she helped her mom set out the appetizers and her dad gather wood for a bonfire. A few s'mores kits sat stacked in the shade. It was a perfect day for a pool party.

"Hey, kiddo. Can we chat for a sec?"

She dropped the last of the wood near the fire pit and turned to find Uncle Tommy with his hands clasped behind his back.

"Sure."

He motioned to one of the patio chairs. She took a seat. The hot iron seared the backs of her thighs. She grabbed one of the folded pool towels and sat on that instead. "What's up?"

"Just wanted to check in on you. See how you're feeling."

Jules scratched her leg. She had a raised mosquito bite, and she thumbed the small itchy mound. "About?"

"Turning eighteen. Leaving for college. Will. You know . . ." He lightly punched her arm. "Life."

"I'm okay." She didn't elaborate.

Tommy studied her and then broke into a grin. "Okay, I get it. No serious talk for the birthday girl." He slapped his hands on his shorts and then fished something from his pocket. "I was going to give this to you later, but . . ."

He handed her a small wrapped package. She shook it like she used to when she was a kid. She tore into the paper. A Leatherman box. She ran her fingers over the letters. "I thought Marines used Gerber?"

"You know me." He waved his hand dismissively. "I've always been a rebel."

She lifted the top of the box to find a Skeletool nestled inside. "No way." She unfolded it. It had a knife, screwdriver, bottle opener, carabiner, and pair of pliers with wire cutters attached.

"I thought you could use this in the city." He shrugged. "Or here. Pretty versatile."

She gave him a hug and clipped it to her shorts. "This is perfect. Thank you." She touched the cool steel at her side, already itching to use it.

"And one more." He brandished another wrapped package.

"Uncle Tommy, you shouldn't have."

"Shut it. You only turn eighteen once."

She unwrapped the second present to find an even smaller

box. Inside was a gorgeous pair of stainless-steel shears with an oxygen tank wrench, ring cutters, and a carbide glass breaker. It folded up to the size of a bottle opener. "These are beautiful."

"I would have killed for these when I was a medic. All my tools were super old-school."

Jules fit the shears into a holster and fastened them to the other side of her shorts. "These are the best. Thank you." She gave him a hug and then checked the time. She wanted to go for a walk before the party to clear her head.

Back inside, she threw a few items into her pack, told her parents and Tommy she was going to get some fresh air, and charged through the cleared path she and her dad had carved out back. She bypassed her mother's running trail and walked the parallel trail that forked off to their shelter.

After three-quarters of a mile, she veered left, paying close attention to the breadcrumbs she'd left. A green ribbon, tied artfully around exposed branches, guided her the right way. After pushing through some brush and respraying her legs with DEET, she came to a glittering black pond surrounded by mossy trees. The water stretched in front of her, a few birds swerving down to nab fish. She dropped her pack and sat by the water. She'd found this pond a few weeks ago, and it had swiftly become one of her favorite places.

She gripped a handful of pebbles and skipped them across the glassy water. They sped over the surface and sank. She emptied her mind, focusing on the rocks in her hand and the sounds around her. Birds. Bugs. Wildlife so few people paid attention to. She craned her neck to gaze at the flawless sky. Sometimes, she came here at night to watch the stars, as if the entire solar system was just mere feet away. She'd never experienced darkness like this back in the city, and she'd stay out for hours until she could count the number of shooting stars on both hands.

Already, she couldn't wait until the pond froze in winter, so she'd have her own private ice rink.

She checked the time again and realized she was officially eighteen. Somehow, this was supposed to signal she was an adult, but she still felt like she needed her parents' permission. When would that go away? She'd rehearsed her speech a thousand times over the last few weeks: she was going to stay in River Falls instead of going to Columbia in the fall. She'd find a way to pay them back for any fees they'd already incurred. She would prove that this was the right decision.

She lay back on the dirt and stared at the swaying leaves above her. Pines rippled in the sunlight, casting needles of light around her. Why couldn't this just be easier? She suddenly had everything she'd ever wanted, but there was this great big obstacle ahead of her: college. She wished her parents could understand that she wasn't going to sit around and take advantage of their good fortune. She would take EMT classes and work on getting the survivalist courses up and running. She sat up and fiddled with both presents Uncle Tommy had given her. Even though he wasn't around much, he seemed to understand her.

She started back, gearing herself up for the day ahead. As long as she could remember, she'd celebrated her birthday the same way: a camping trip with her dad followed by a dinner or movie with her mom and sometimes a few friends. Today would be different.

At the back of the house, she could hear her dad laughing. She was now covered in a thin film of sweat and reeked of bug spray. She wouldn't have time to freshen up. She let go of her pack inside the back gate as her mother waved to her.

Ava and the gang were all there, fanned out in lounge chairs. Ava lifted her iced tea. "Happy birthday, J!" she exclaimed. The others joined in a chorus of happy wishes.

"Thanks, A," she called back.

Ava laughed. "I love it. J and A. JA. AJ." She laughed. "We'll work on it."

Bricks removed his T-shirt unselfconsciously and waded into the pool. His stomach was pasty white and large, and he shivered as he entered the shallow end.

"Just do it, you baby," Lindsay called. She threw in a foam noodle after him.

"Don't rush me, woman," he joked. He clasped his hands in front of his chest and dipped lower, inch by inch.

"Jules, this place is sick." Lindsay wore a two-piece green string bikini, while the twins wore matching pink one-pieces that clashed with their bright red hair.

"Yeah, *sick* sick," Gwynn said.

Jules searched for Will, but she knew he was coming directly from work and would be running late.

When her mother went inside to get some snacks, Jules stretched out next to Ava, who adjusted her two-piece lavender bikini. Black tattoos inked her left hip up to her ribs. "Dude, how do you have all of this?"

Jules shrugged. "My mom has a really successful design company."

"And your dad?" Lynn asked.

"He was a sniper. Now he runs survivalist courses."

The twins looked at each other. "That's so cool."

She guessed it was pretty cool. She didn't really think about how other kids saw her or her family. At her private school, everyone's parents were millionaires, investors, or had their own company. It was like a giant pissing contest to see who had the most money or privilege, and somewhere along the way, she'd grown bored of it.

But it was a nice reminder of how lucky she really was, how

she shouldn't take any of it for granted. Jules was antsy and kept glancing over her shoulder every few minutes.

"Expecting someone?" Ava asked, pursing her lips around her metal straw. Her 1950s white polka-dotted sunglasses made her look slightly less edgy.

Jules laughed. "Just your brother."

Ava flapped her wrist, and a slew of bangles—just like Lenore's—slid up to her elbow. "He'll be here. He'd never miss spending time with you."

Pleasure trampled her insides. "Really?"

Ava laughed, revealing a row of slightly crooked teeth. "J, you know he worships the ground you walk on. He's smitten. You two are totally getting married."

Jules's face warmed. "We are so not getting married."

"Uh-huh. Mark my words. *Mar-ried*."

Secretly, Jules was thrilled. Though marriage was the furthest thing from her mind, she knew she wanted to spend her life with him.

Bricks sprayed Ava from the pool. "Get in here, you two!"

Ava tossed aside her towel and jumped in the pool. Jules peeled off her sweaty shorts and tank and dove off the deep end. She swam all the way to the bottom and hovered. Her friends' milky legs thrashed above her. A great gaping hole of longing forced her to the top. She sucked in air and swam toward her friends. She couldn't believe how much she missed Will when they weren't together.

After swimming, her mother brought out the food, and they wrapped themselves in towels and ate.

"Dude, what is it about swimming that makes you so hungry?" Bricks bit into his third hot dog and a giant glob of ketchup stuck to his cheek.

Ava rolled her eyes and handed him a napkin. "You swam for like a minute."

Jules laughed. When she'd been on the swim team, her parents couldn't keep enough food in the house.

"It *is* weird," Lindsay said, pushing her salad around on her plate. "It's, like, scientific or something, right?"

Her parents disappeared inside to give them some privacy. Jules tried not to worry that Will hadn't yet shown up, but if he didn't hurry, he was going to miss the entire party.

Bricks slapped his belly and sighed. "Now what?" he asked. "Nap time?"

Jules wiped her mouth and took a swig of water. "Actually, we've been building a shelter on our land. Want to see it?" She, Tommy, and her dad had been furiously finishing the shelter the last few days. She couldn't wait to show her friends, but she was most excited to show Will.

"I could use a walk to burn off all this food," Ava said.

The twins yawned. "Mind if we stay here?"

Jules shrugged. "Whatever you want. My house is your house."

Ava laughed. "I'd be careful saying that. The twins might literally never leave. Come on, you two. Don't be babies. Let's go."

To her surprise, Gwynn and Lynn did as they were told, and Lindsay jumped up too. Jules tossed everyone the DEET, grabbed her pack, and led them all to the path. She pointed out the species of trees along the way and gave them some history about the plants and their medicinal purposes.

"What are you, a nature guide?" Bricks huffed. His cheeks were bright red and his hairline was damp with sweat.

Jules automatically slowed her pace. "I just like learning about the land."

"I've never really liked the woods," Ava offered.

Jules looked back at her. "Really? Why not?"

She shrugged and jumped when she stepped on a stick. "I had a lot of allergies as a kid, so I spent most of my time inside."

Jules could relate. She'd grown up in a concrete jungle and practically begged to go outside any chance she could, hunting for patches of green in the city. She'd often remove her shoes and walk barefoot to ground herself at parks, even when she was young. That's when her dad started taking her to different campsites.

Lindsay and the twins took turns throwing things at Bricks's back. Each time, he'd jump and yell for them to stop. The girls giggled and shushed each other and then started up again.

"Seriously, guys." Bricks huffed out an irritated response as the girls snickered behind his back.

Ava jogged to catch up with Jules. "Sorry Will isn't here yet."

"Me too." She hadn't talked to him all day, and because she didn't get good reception, she didn't even know if he'd tried to call her or wish her a happy birthday.

"How's your mom doing?"

Ava shrugged. "More bad days than good, lately."

She wondered if they'd already made arrangements for Lenore's funeral. She never felt like it was her place to ask.

They drifted back into single file, falling into silence, until they came to the shelter. A small clearing, once full of trees and overgrown brush, now opened up to a small A-frame cabin with a thatched roof, using only parts from the land.

"Holy shit. You built this?" Ava exclaimed.

"Like, by hand?" Lindsay asked.

"With the help of my dad and uncle, but yeah." As Jules surveyed the shelter, she realized it was pretty amazing. She'd painted the door bright green, and they'd even insulated the roof with greenery to keep the cold out. They'd also built a custom fire pit, a drying rack, and a retractable worktable.

The twins approached the table. "You could totally sell this!" Lynn exclaimed. "This is legit, like one of those tiny homes!"

Bricks opened the door to the cabin and stepped inside. "Yo, check it!" he yelled. "Twins, come here."

Ava surveyed the shelter and crossed her arms. "I'm impressed."

"Beyond impressed," Lindsay agreed. She bent over to inspect the fire pit, her stick-straight golden hair brushing her cheeks. "I don't know anyone that's built something like this."

"Really?" Jules asked, surprised.

Ava shrugged. "Most locals spend their time skiing or snowboarding."

Suddenly, behind them, a snort sent every hair on Jules's body to full attention. She turned slowly. "Don't move," she whispered to Ava.

About ten feet away, a black bear was braced to either retreat or attack. Jules quickly searched for cubs and grabbed the bear spray hanging from her pack. Behind her, Ava sucked in a shaky breath. The twins and Lindsay gasped, and Jules shot them all a look to be quiet. The bear's long black fur swayed as it moved a few steps forward, its snout stuffed into the earth.

Jules pressed her finger on the trigger when Bricks burst out of the shelter and exclaimed, "I'm moving in!" He dropped his arms and went pale when he saw the bear. Suddenly, it let out a guttural roar and charged forward. Behind Jules, the kids screamed and scattered, startling the bear even more.

Jules took a few defiant steps forward, looked the bear in the eye, and shouted "Get away, bear!" like she'd been taught. At the same time, she pressed the trigger. The bear stiffened and growled, rising up on its hind legs so that it towered over her. Jules continued to unleash a steady stream of aerosol and screamed even louder until the bear dropped off its hind legs and loped off in the opposite direction.

Jules's heart thudded violently in her chest. She held the spray in front of her, searching for other bears beyond the trees. Her breath rattled her entire body, and she turned, but her friends had all bolted to different places.

Rather than yell their names, she took a few steps toward the shelter and found Bricks huddled inside, near the back. "Is it gone?" he whispered.

She nodded. Together, they found the twins behind the shelter and Lindsay halfway up a tree. She'd skinned her shins and was bleeding from one knee.

Jules began to breathe a sigh of relief, both amazed that she'd finally come that close to a bear and freaking out that it could have killed her. She assessed the group.

"Where's Ava?"

The twins clung to each other, while Bricks and Lindsay stood, shell-shocked, both of their faces contorted with worry. Before she could narrate what to do next, a gut-wrenching scream shattered the silence of the woods. A few birds took flight overhead, their wings slapping furiously against agitated air.

"Oh my God," Lindsay said. "Is that . . . ?" She clamped a hand over her mouth and whimpered behind it.

"Stay here," Jules ordered. "Get into the shelter and do not come out. Do you hear me? Lindsay, you're in charge." She tossed her a utility knife from her pack and sprinted toward the sound, keeping her eye out for other predators. She stopped on the path, searching the leaves for bear scat or tracks. Off to the left, it looked like there'd been some sort of tussle, as the path was dented and muddy. As she got closer, she saw a thick stream of blood leading to a copse of trees.

Ava.

Jules slowed her pace and braced herself for what she might see. She didn't dare let herself think about the worst-case scenario. She'd watched documentaries about bear attacks, had trained with her father and Tommy on scenarios just like this. She listened for the bear and then heard audible moans coming fifty yards out. Jules shot between the trees and found Ava behind a large stump. She held a giant branch in one hand, which Jules guessed she'd used as a weapon, and there was a pool of blood beneath her. Her left arm was gone, only mangled tissue and bone flapping like shredded fabric below her elbow.

"Oh my God, Ava."

Ava's eyes were glassy, blood and dirt smudged across her face. "I hit it with the stick. I played dead. I . . ." Her teeth chattered, and Jules was afraid she might go into shock.

"It's okay. It's okay. You're going to be okay."

Jules took off her pack and found hand sanitizer. She doused her hands in the gel and situated Ava to lift the bloody stump onto the tree in order to elevate it. Ava screamed and began shaking uncontrollably, and Jules reminded her to stay calm. She took off her shirt and used the new scissors Uncle Tommy had given her to cut it into a tourniquet. "Ava, look at me, okay? This is going to hurt, but I have to do it." She gingerly lifted her arm, wrapped the shirt around the wound, right above the amputation, and tied it as tightly as she could. Ava howled in pain and threw up into a pile of leaves.

"We have to keep you warm." She searched for anything to be used as a blanket, but they were both barely wearing anything. She racked her brain to think about what was at the shelter. Maybe a blanket near the fire pit? "Listen, we've got to get you to the shelter, okay? That way, I can go get help. But I need you to come with me. Can you do that?" Ava was going in and out of consciousness. "Shit." Jules debated what to do. She needed to find Ava's arm if there was any chance of reattachment. The sooner she got it on ice, the better.

"Stay here." She gave Ava the bear spray, which she loosely grasped in her limp palm. Jules followed the trail of blood farther into the woods and gave herself approximately two minutes to search. She felt desperate as her eyes tracked every inch. She counted down in her head, knowing how precious every second was. She was preparing to turn back when she saw something fleshy sticking out by a clump of leaves.

She dropped to her knees and there was the remainder of Ava's hand and forearm, the bangles still there, slathered with blood. Jules took off her jean shorts and carefully wrapped it up, knowing she had to get it on ice immediately. She darted back to Ava, who had slipped off the stump and lay in a patch of bloody leaves, eyes unblinking. For a horrifying moment, Jules worried she was dead.

"Ava?" She twitched, while Jules struggled to think. "We've got to get you to the shelter. I'm just going to help you stand." She gently laid the arm in her pack, zipped it, and got Ava to her feet. She half-dragged, half-held her, noticing the shirt she'd used as a tourniquet had already been soaked through with blood. She calculated the time it would take to get back to her house and down the mountain to the hospital.

Too much time.

The very stark realization that Ava might die kicked her in the chest. She couldn't let that happen.

"We're almost there," she said. She guided Ava, encouraging her with every step. At the shelter, she screamed for Bricks to open the door. When he did, his face grew even paler as he glimpsed Ava, mangled and bloody.

"Holy shit," he said.

The girls immediately started crying, and Jules gave a sharp command to stay calm. Everyone quieted, though the twins continued to whimper.

Jules grabbed the blanket from the corner, propped Ava into a sitting position, and draped it over her legs. "We need to elevate her arm." She calculated how fast she could run a mile, and knew she could get back to the house in five minutes flat. "Keep the door shut. Whoever has the cleanest shirt needs to rewrap her arm just like I did." She tossed the hand sanitizer to the floor, as well as the bear spray. She registered the shocked look on all of their faces. "I'll be right back."

She strapped her pack as tightly as she could to her back and sprinted out of the shelter. She took off through the woods, running faster than she ever had. Her bag bounced with Ava's severed limb, and she tried not to think of it—of how Ava might die—right here on her birthday. Lenore would never forgive her. *Will* would never forgive her.

She picked up her pace until she had no breath left. Sweat mixed with Ava's blood and made her skin slick. Her heart continued to pound in her chest until, after what felt like an eternity, The Black House emerged through the trees. She began screaming for help as she neared the back gate. Her dad, Will, Uncle Tommy, and her mother all stood from their chairs at the pool, drinks in hand. When they glimpsed Jules, bloody in her bathing suit, her mother dropped her drink, the glass shattering around her bare feet.

"Ava's been attacked by a bear!" She flung off her pack and handed it off to her dad. "Her arm is in there. Get it on ice and call an ambulance. Now!"

Uncle Tommy was already gathering supplies. In two minutes flat, bag in hand, he ran toward the shelter before anyone else could utter a word. Jules collapsed against the black brick wall as Will walked over, speechless. "What happened?" he finally choked. "Is she . . . ?"

She looked up at him, tears in her eyes. "I did everything I could. I . . ."

He cradled her head against his chest. His hands and voice shook, and she realized she was the one who was trembling, not him.

Her mother called an ambulance from the landline and her father emerged with another pack. "Stay here."

"No way." Will released her. "I'm coming."

Her father didn't have time to argue, but he cast a look her way in an invisible question. Jules was completely physically depleted, her throat screaming for water, but she gave him a nod. The men took off at a sprint. She cast one look at her mother, who stood at the entrance to the black gate, a hushed terror between them.

"Jules." Her mother said her name only once, an alarmed whisper. Her eyes were large and uncertain. Her right shin was bleeding where the glass had exploded.

"Mom, your shin." Jules's voice was hoarse from screaming at the bear.

When her mother looked down to assess the damage, Jules mustered every ounce of strength she had left, and began to run back to help.

12

Jules

SUMMIT Memorial was an hour outside of town.

As River Falls didn't have the proper resources to reattach a severed limb, Ava had been medevacked to the nearest major hospital. Jules didn't have time to take a shower or do anything other than throw on a pair of shorts. Her red bathing suit top was stained darker from Ava's blood. She'd been in surgery for over three hours, and Jules was utterly drained. The waiting room was nearly empty. She glanced around the room with its stiff maroon chairs and shiny linoleum floors. Nurses walked to and from the front desk in scrubs with clipboards, pushing carts up and down the hall.

William Sr. and Lenore had arrived over an hour ago. Lenore wore a surgical mask due to her compromised immune system and had nodded off in the chair beside her. William Sr. had an arm looped around Lenore, and she'd slumped against his chest and was snoring lightly. Will had been pacing the halls for hours. Jules had told her own parents to go home, but they'd insisted on staying until Ava was out of surgery.

Thanks to Uncle Tommy's medical supplies and quick thinking, he'd been able to clean the wound and get it properly packed and ready for transport.

Jules kept replaying the incident. She should never have dragged those kids into the woods when she knew there could be bears. Not everyone was trained, even if they'd grown up here. Jules was terrified William Sr. and Lenore blamed her, though they'd insisted that it was just a freak accident.

Jules finally approached Will, who stopped pacing and gave her a hug. He'd barely spoken three words to her. She shivered under the harsh hospital lights and crisp, dry air. It was a stark contrast to the muggy night outside. Jules tipped her head back to look at him, searching for words, but she didn't have any. Nothing she said could make the situation better.

Finally, Ava's surgeon—Dr. Wang—walked through the double doors. Everyone snapped to attention, even Lenore, who shook herself awake and slowly made her way over to hear the news. Jules's parents hung back, within earshot.

Dr. Wang smiled and waited for Lenore. "Ava did very well," she began. Her voice was calm but serious. "We were able to re-attach the arm, though we won't know until she's out of surgery how successful it was. She's lost a lot of blood and has received a transfusion." She paused. "We've got a long way to go, but we're optimistic. We'll let you know when she's awake and is able to have visitors." She turned to walk away, but then stopped. "By the way, whoever handled the wound right after the attack literally saved Ava's life." Dr. Wang prepared to push back through the doors, but William Sr., Lenore, and Will pulled her aside to ask more questions.

Tommy slung an arm around her shoulder. "Did you hear that, kid? You're a natural. Maybe medicine runs in your blood after all."

"Not now, Tommy," Desi snapped. She assessed Jules. "Honey, why don't you let us take you home and get some rest? I'm sure they're only going to allow family visitors for tonight." She lightly rubbed her arm, which was studded with goose bumps. Jules was too tired to argue.

"Let me just say goodbye."

She approached the family and gently pulled Will aside. "I'm going to head home. Let me know how she is, okay?"

"Okay." He scratched his neck distractedly and turned back to the doctor, obviously not wanting to miss what she had to say. "I'll call you tomorrow?" He absently kissed her cheek, and Jules turned, tears in her eyes.

She met up with her family, who were waiting by the automatic doors. They slipped open and shut, ushering hot air in, pushing cold air out. Outside, the enormity of what had happened washed through her system in its own version of shock. Her dad's SUV alarm chirped as he unlocked the car.

"Jules!"

Will ran from the automatic doors into the bare parking lot. His shoes slapped the pavement. Her heart leaped at the sight of him.

"Give me a minute," she told her family.

Tommy winked, before they all climbed into the car to give her privacy.

"I'm such an idiot. I never even told you happy birthday." He pulled her into a real hug, his heart thudding against her ear.

Relief washed over Jules, and she held him tighter. "That's okay. We can celebrate later." She finally pulled back. "Go be with your family."

He reached into his pocket and pulled out a tiny blue jewelry box. "Open it when you're alone, okay? I love you."

He gave her a kiss, and her lips trembled under his, but she willed herself not to cry. She palmed the box as she climbed into the car, itching to discover what was inside.

They were mostly silent on the climb back up the mountain, all of them processing the day.

"Well, this is a birthday you'll never forget, huh?" Tommy finally offered.

"Really, Tommy?" Desi glared at him from the front seat.

Jules turned the box over and over in her hands, running her fingers along the velvet. Tommy tried to keep the conversation going, but she wasn't in the mood. She stared out the window, watching the roads grow black and treacherous as the milky moon guided them deliberately up the mountain.

At the house, she was the first through the door. She locked herself in her room and started the shower, peeling off her bathing suit and shorts and throwing them in the trash. She didn't want any physical reminders of this day. She climbed into the shower and watched the water turn pink as she scrubbed herself clean. Ava's blood rinsed into the drain, and Jules let herself come undone, sliding down to the tile floor. She rested her head on her knees and cried.

After an eternity, she stood, her limbs heavy, and turned off the shower. She changed into pajamas and climbed into her bed with Will's present. She opened it slowly and found a small steel heart on a thin silver chain. There was a little card that read:

I had this made from scraps of my first plane. You are my entire heart, Juliette. This is a little piece of it to carry with you, always. Happy birthday.

The tears continued to flow as she studied the delicate heart. She traced her fingers over the steel and then fastened the chain around her neck and stood to study herself in the mirror. She adjusted the heart until it landed right in the center of her clavicle. She stared into her own eyes, wanting Ava to be okay, wanting to just go back and redo that one part of the afternoon.

There was a soft knock on her door.

She sighed and turned away from the mirror, preparing herself for a pep talk. "Come in."

"May I?" Uncle Tommy stood at the threshold, and she nodded. She climbed onto the bed and he joined her, crossing his long legs at the ankle.

"Have you ever worn matching socks a day in your life?" Jules joked.

Tommy pointed and flexed his toes, showing off the drastically different pair of socks. "Nope." He turned to her. "So, how you really doing, kid?"

She shrugged. "I'm okay."

"Listen, what you saw out there." He cleared this throat. "That's pretty big stuff. It's important to talk about it, so you can process everything."

"What, so I don't get PTSD?" She knew all about PTSD. Her dad had suffered from flashbacks, waking with night terrors, jumping at loud noises. For years, she and her mom had walked on eggshells, until he got professional help.

"Yes, exactly."

She leaned back against her headboard. "It was so gnarly. I've never seen an arm like that. It made me realize how fragile we all are."

"Or resilient, right?" Tommy added. "I mean, because you found Ava's arm, they were able to reattach it and she might not have to go through life as an amputee. And that's all thanks to you."

"You mean the fact that she even had an arm ripped off to reattach is all thanks to me." Jules pressed her palms into her eyes. "God, I've cried more today than I have in years."

"Hey." He rubbed her shoulder. "Don't do that. It wasn't your fault. That could have happened anywhere, anytime. Ava knows the risks when going into the woods. We all do. Plus, you saved her life."

"No, you saved her life."

"I'll fight you." Tommy put up his fists, and she slapped them away.

No matter how serious things were, he always found a way to defuse the situation. It was an endearing but quirky trait and reminded her of so many good memories with her uncle. She turned to him. "Why haven't you been around lately? I miss seeing you."

He offered a sad smile and something passed behind his eyes. "I'd love to see you every day if I could, kid." He scratched his nose. "I'm just trying to figure out my life."

Jules looked at him, confused. "What do you mean?"

"Personal stuff. Adult stuff."

She bumped his shoulder. "In case you haven't noticed, I'm an adult now, so I can totally handle it."

"Oh, that's right, that's right." Tommy tapped his chin. "Well, see if you can handle this." In one fluid motion, he grabbed the pillow from behind her back and whacked her on the head.

Jules screamed in protest and grabbed another pillow, smacking him square in the chest. They both hopped off the bed and faced off.

"You don't stand a chance, Grandma," he said. He lurched right and left, trying to fake her out.

"Oh really?" Jules feinted, then went high, catching him right in the temple. Tommy gripped his head dramatically and collapsed onto her bed.

"Victorious!" she screamed, pumping her fists in the air.

Her door opened, and her parents stood there, concerned, until they saw Tommy on the bed, the pillows by their feet.

"She started it." Tommy pointed to Jules.

"Lies." She scooped up her pillow and looked at her parents. "Want to join?"

Desi opened her mouth, but then she sprinted off. Jules looked at Tommy and her dad before they all crept down the hallway. Her father put his finger to his lips outside the bedroom door.

He threw it open and her mother balanced on the bed, with every pillow piled in her arms. "Don't come any closer." One slipped from her arms, and she kicked it away.

"Attack!" Jules screamed.

Desi squealed as Tommy and Peter ripped most of her pillows away, and they all went at it, smacking and batting each other, laughing until Jules couldn't breathe.

After endless pounding and a lot of laughter, the pillow fight died, and Tommy and her parents led her to the kitchen, where her pine tree cake was ready to be lit. Eighteen candles strategically placed in the pine's leaves were also green.

"Feel like a slice?" her mom asked. She was still winded, her hair free and loose around her shoulders, her cheeks flushed.

Jules wanted to hold on to this moment just a little bit longer—all of them together, as a family. "Sure."

Her mother got to work pulling down plates while her father lit all the candles. It looked like a Christmas tree. When they were ready, they launched into an out-of-tune version of "Happy Birthday." When it was time to make a wish, she prayed for Ava.

She closed her eyes and blew.

13

Desi

DESI adjusted her wide-brimmed hat and gazed at the water.

Lake Medley sat at the edge of town, surrounded by a pebbly coast. The parched, sunbaked earth cracked beneath their shoes. Despite the lack of rain, the lake seemed full and endless.

She hadn't slept in weeks. The night Carter had stayed over, she'd been so excited to see him the next morning, she hadn't even bothered to get dressed in proper clothes. But when he wasn't at breakfast, or in his room, or on the grounds, a sinking feeling pushed in. She tried calling, but his phone was turned off. She'd scoured the guest room for a note or some other hidden clue of where he'd gone. But there was nothing. No trace. She'd had too much time to think. Perhaps it wasn't fair to ask him to wait, when really, hadn't he been waiting for decades?

Desi gazed at the water, trying to forget the image of their kiss that slithered through her brain like a snake. She'd been checking her phone religiously, practically willing him to call or text. Something that would allude to why he'd suddenly left when she'd just asked him not to give up on her.

Restless, she stood on the edge of the dock and snapped a photo of Lenore. Her reflection gleamed off the mirror-smooth water: her green scarf knotted at her crown, the flowing flower-printed tunic, ruffled from the breeze, and a handful of healing crystals clutched in her upturned palm. Her chin lifted toward the sky. Desi clicked the shutter, perfectly capturing her long, elegant neck and look of contentment.

Lenore turned to her and smiled. "Let me see."

Desi brought her camera over.

"Oh my goodness." Lenore smoothed a hand against her chest, settling the fabric into place as it fluttered from a sudden, gusty wind. "You're talented."

"It's all about the subject," she insisted. "So where's William Sr. flying to today?"

She waved a hand. "I forget. After so many years, you stop asking." She smiled, her teeth almost translucent from her constant bouts of nausea, heavy antibiotic usage, and lack of nutrients.

Will was helping Jules with her fishing pole, baiting it with slippery worms. Lake Medley was well known for its black bass and redbreast sunfish. Jules yelped as one slipped from her fingers and splashed into the lake. Ava sat cross-legged on a towel, her healing arm bound in a sling. It had been less than a month since her accident. Her scar was red and puckered and formed a jagged zipper around her entire bicep. She patted it self-consciously and obeyed Lenore's commands to keep it out of the sun.

Peter and Tommy were sitting on the edge of the dock, drinking beers and chatting. Their feet dangled over the edge. Tommy's long limbs skirted the surface, then disappeared beneath the black.

She set her camera down. Between Carter and Ava, her nerves were fried. This summer, with all of its quiet moments, had become a rampage of tragedies, interruptions, and lies.

Her phone buzzed and she jumped in anticipation. But it was just a text from Beth. They'd only spoken a few times the entire summer. She scanned the text. *Have you heard? Carter is missing! What in the world is going on?*

Desi almost dropped the phone. She reread the text, her breath rattling around in her chest. She glanced over at Tommy, who laughed at something Peter said. She pulled up a browser, thankful for service, and punched in the phrase *Carter Abbott missing* and waited. Sure enough, there was a short article in the local paper.

Carter Abbott, celebrated Marine veteran, was reported missing by his girlfriend, Haley Shanks, on Thursday, July 25th. Authorities are looking into Mr. Abbott's whereabouts. He was last seen in late July. Haley reported Mr. Abbott had been going on a road trip. If you have information, please contact . . .

Desi searched for more information, but it was mostly vague. She reread the article, unsure of what was more shocking: the fact that he had a girlfriend or was presumed missing. Her hand landed against her chest in a futile attempt to slow her heartbeat. Lenore glanced over.

"You okay?"

"Excuse me for a second."

Desi approached Tommy and tapped him on the shoulder. "We need to talk."

He peered at her, his cheeks ruddy from the alcohol and sun. "Now? We're having bro time."

Peter laughed as Tommy bumped his shoulder.

"Yes, now." She gestured to the end of the tidy dock that jutted several feet over the lake. Tommy made a production of standing up and followed her until they were out of earshot.

"What's shaking?"

"This." She handed him her phone. His eyes skimmed the report, then darkened.

"Is this for real?"

"Have you talked to him?" she asked. "Did he tell you where he was going?"

He didn't answer and instead took her phone. She waited, chewing on her cuticle, just like Jules. Though Desi had peppered Tommy with questions those first few days after Carter left, she'd stopped so as not to make him suspicious.

Finally, he shrugged and gave it back. "Maybe he just went off the grid for a while. His girlfriend can be a little nuts. I'm sure it's fine."

So he did have a girlfriend. She ignored the pinprick of jealousy and glanced at Peter. "You're not worried about him then?"

He shrugged. "Have you checked his social?"

"No." She had, but there was nothing new. "Has Peter said anything?"

"Nope." He didn't look at her when he said it, his eyes skimming the water instead.

"Tommy." Her brother was a terrible liar. He forgot that she'd been trained to spot his lies: when he sneaked out of the house and would bribe her not to tell, when he lied to their parents' faces about a grade, and especially when he was trying to impress a girl.

He looked her square in the eye. "There's nothing to worry about, Desi. Drop it."

How could she possibly drop it? One second, she and Carter were finally discussing being together, and the next, he was officially missing? Something didn't add up.

He crossed his arms over his bare chest. "Why are you so interested in Carter? I thought you'd be glad to have one less visitor." He scoured the lake again and his jaw twitched. "Unless there's more to that story?"

She turned to go and he latched onto her wrist. "What aren't you telling me?"

She opened her mouth, then snapped it shut. He waited, but she said nothing and yanked her wrist free.

She once again saw Carter knocking on her door. His mouth on hers. Their entangled limbs in bed. She'd worked for years to keep Carter away, but now she wanted to know where he'd disappeared to. "Nothing."

He hiked a shoulder and carelessly dropped it. "I'm just saying . . . you seem really bent out of shape over a *friend*."

She pushed past him, irate. Her sandal snagged on a wooden plank and sent her flying forward, but she righted herself before her knees smashed onto the dock. A searing pain shot through her back, but she massaged it and kept moving forward.

Back at the other end, Jules whooped and jumped to her feet. A fish tugged on her line, bending the pole in her capable hands. Will coached her through it, and after a bit of a struggle, Jules cranked up a gorgeous striped bass. Its heavy body sprayed droplets of water as she hoisted it up like a prize. The fish flopped and bucked, silvery scales glinting in the sunlight. Never one for cruelty, Jules unhooked the fish and tossed it back in. It sliced through the water and disappeared from sight.

"What'd you do that for?" Tommy goaded, walking toward them. His flip-flops slapped the dock, and he extended his arms dramatically. "That was dinner!"

Jules rolled her eyes and baited her line again, hooking the worm and casting it back in.

Desi occupied the empty chair beside Lenore. A stew of emotions warred through her brain. She knew panicking wouldn't help, but what else was she supposed to do? She had to find Carter.

"This is heaven," Lenore said. She rolled her head toward Desi, the skin of her forehead suddenly pinching in concern. "What's wrong?"

Desi forced herself to appear relaxed and offered a smile. "Oh nothing." She laughed. "Just my brother."

"I loved being an only child," she said.

"I can imagine," Desi joked.

"Don't stress," Lenore offered. "Whatever your worries are, they'll go away."

If only it were that easy. Her worries had started as simple omissions. Little gaps that had turned into years of secrecy, and now they seemed irreparable. They fell into a comfortable silence, and then Lenore coughed and sat up.

Desi placed a hand on her back. "Are you okay?"

"Fine, fine." She waited until it passed, her knuckles taut as she gripped her chair, her body seizing and racking in angry, relentless spasms. Lenore rode the wave, her eyes bulging and watering, her face cranking from red to purple. Desi watched helplessly, knowing by this point that Lenore couldn't resist what was happening to her. She had to allow it, in all its brutality. Sensing her distress, Will and Ava jumped up to help, but Lenore waved them away.

Finally, she settled back, a thick blue vein bisected her forehead.

Desi rummaged in the cooler and offered her a bottle of water.

Lenore unscrewed the cap and took a healthy sip. "Thank you."

She sipped again and patted her mouth. Desi searched for blood and spotted a few drops.

"You know, I always heard when you were on your deathbed, life would become clear," Lenore continued. "We hear it all the time—what's important, what we should focus on, what really matters, blah, blah, blah—and then we live our lives with all these trivial concerns and worries anyway." She sighed, took a raspy breath, and sifted her crystals from one hand to the other.

"Now, I see how silly I've been in my life, how much time I've wasted. Every stressful day. Every time I complained about William or the kids. My false sense of urgency." She paused. "When the kids were young"—she cast a woeful look at Ava and Will—"I was desperate for them to just go to sleep so I could be alone with my thoughts. When they went to school, I could breathe a sigh of relief. And now . . ." Her voice died and she steadied her shallow breath. "Now, I would give anything to have that time back, to snuggle them close, to tell them everything, to spend every second that is going to be robbed from me." She placed a hand on her chest. "I'm not angry. I'm really not, but I am heartbroken." Her voice cracked and she took a moment to compose herself. "How can I miss all this?" She knocked a bony hand toward the lake and then around to the group.

Lenore seemed like she wanted to say more, but Desi stayed quiet, the unsaid truth passing sorrowfully between them. *Why me? It's not fair. Life is devastating.*

"I know I have to be brave now," Lenore said.

"You're one of the bravest people I've ever met," Desi said. And she meant it. She reached for Lenore, and they sat, hand in hand, watching the water. Desi's mind spun on an infinite loop. Life was so fragile. She closed her eyes, wishing she could make her own worries disappear, but instead, they scraped and taunted. Suddenly, Tommy and Peter jumped in the lake.

"You'll scare away all the fish!" Jules exclaimed in outrage.

Tommy broke the surface of the water and tugged on Jules's ankle. She slid into the water, fully dressed, and screamed. Will ripped off his shirt and did a cannonball, while Ava laughed from her place on the dock. She couldn't get her arm wet—not yet.

"I'm going to the bathroom," Ava announced.

"Okay, sweetie." Lenore watched her walk away. "I'm worried about her," she said after a minute.

Desi waited for her to explain.

"She's taking too many pain pills. She hasn't seen her friends."

"She'll be okay. She just has to heal," Desi said. "It takes time."

Lenore smiled woefully, knowing she probably wouldn't be around to witness it. She turned her attention back to Desi. "Why don't you go on in and swim?"

Desi removed her hand. "I'm just fine right here."

Lenore's eyes searched Desi's. "Be with your family, Desiree. Every moment you can."

Desi opened her mouth to protest and then shut it. Isn't that what Lenore had just been preaching? Desi nodded, removed her cover-up, and gingerly stood at the edge of the dock. Her reflection wobbled in the water. She lowered herself in, adjusted to the shock of cold, then swam over to Peter, Jules, Tommy, and Will. Her back was tight where she'd almost fallen on the dock, but she ignored the pain. She rolled to her back and floated. Her ears dipped below the surface. The water fizzed through her ears. Someone pinched her leg underwater, and she righted herself, her heel jamming into a sharp rock. She slipped on slimy moss.

"Who did that?" she teased.

Peter surfaced a few feet away, shaking the water from his hair. "No idea."

She hesitated. They'd had such little contact since Carter had disappeared, but she swam toward him anyway and wrapped her wet limbs around his back. Her heels hooked onto his hips, and she sunk in a rear naked choke.

"Holy shit! Go, sis!" Tommy exclaimed.

Desi ignored Tommy and squeezed tighter, half playing and

half intentionally. Peter tapped, but she didn't immediately release him. He'd been so smug ever since Carter left; so much
so, she'd started to wonder if he'd talked to Carter that night
and threatened him. Peter wrenched her arm free and grabbed
his throat.

"Jesus, Desi. Tap means *let go*." He splashed in her direction.

She rearranged her face. "I was just playing." The tension
was obvious between them, yet no one uttered a word. Tommy
made a joke and everyone swam around her, splashing and
playing. She glanced back at the dock. They'd drifted at least
a hundred feet out.

"Let's play chicken!" Jules climbed onto Will's shoulders and
challenged Peter, who awkwardly balanced on Tommy's shoulders and goaded her with a mock boxer's stance. Jules did the
same, then Will charged forward and Jules and Peter locked
arms, attempting to knock the other down. Jules held her own
against her father, before she finally tipped back and slapped
the water with a loud splash.

Desi began to swim a few laps, dipping underwater, then
emerging in a freestyle. She couldn't shake what she'd read
about Carter. He'd never stage his own disappearance, would
he? When she was out of breath, she treaded in place. Back at
the dock, Ava strutted toward the empty chair, her bad arm
hanging lamely at her side without her sling. Despite Lenore's
concerns, she'd been so lucky, though Desi highly doubted
she'd ever set foot in the woods again.

Desi dipped her head back to push her hair off her face and
emerged to the crack of a scream. She shielded her eyes, startled, as everyone in the water squinted toward the dock. Ava
dropped down next to her mother, who was slumped over in her
chair.

Oh no.

Everyone hurriedly swam back toward the dock, but Desi knew before she even got there that Lenore had passed.

She was the last to pull herself up onto the dock, her hands shaking as she wrapped herself in a fluffy blue towel. William Sr. would never forgive himself for being away, but maybe that's what Lenore would have wanted. Maybe they'd already privately said goodbye.

Ava wrapped her healthy arm around her mother and sobbed, while Will stood off to the side, tears in his eyes.

"I need to call my father." His voice shook as he excused himself. Jules and Peter went after him.

Tommy moved in next to Desi, crossing his arms. "Are you okay?"

No, she wasn't okay. She moved away from Tommy and gently enveloped Ava in a hug. She stroked her hair.

"I'm so sorry, sweetheart."

Losing a parent was something you never got over, no matter how old you were, or how many years had passed. Ava clung to her and cried uncontrollably. Had Lenore known when she sent her into the water that her time had come?

She shushed and rocked Ava, who sobbed louder. When she glanced at Lenore, she was surprised to find her lips bent into the slightest smile. No more suffering. No more pain. No more wondering when or how.

She was finally at peace.

14

Desi

THE funeral was quick.

Lenore didn't want a typical church service. She wasn't religious and refused to have some stranger botch her life's details to a room full of neighbors. She also didn't want her family bothered with endless casseroles and tears, overwhelming them with grief and Tupperware. She'd made her peace with the people she wanted to make peace with, so the aftermath would be fleeting and painless.

After the cremation, they clustered at a nearby park to say a few words. Will looked like he was playing dress-up in his oversized suit. Jules stood beside him, her cuticles bloody from anxiety, unsure of how to act or what to say. Ava was beside herself—having almost lost her life and now her mother within a month. Even though they'd all been preparing for this day, Lenore's presence had been the biggest constant in their home, and now she was gone. There was never a true way to prepare for a loved one's death.

William Sr. carried the silver urn, which glinted in the sun. He'd been overly attentive the entire day, tending to everyone else's needs. Desi figured he'd fall apart soon, and it wouldn't be pretty. She wondered who would be strong for him.

Under the shade of an oak, he loosened his tie and produced a letter from his pocket. He tapped it against his open palm, waiting for Ava and Will to join him.

"What's that?" Ava eyed the letter.

"It's from your mother." He sighed. Will hung back, but then released Jules's hands to stand next to his father.

"Open it," Will demanded.

Desi felt like she was intruding on a private family moment, but William Sr. had wanted them here. Emotion surged as she studied Will, his face stern and impassive. She hadn't seen him smile since that day on the dock. A hardness had pushed in to replace his sweet, kind heart, and she hated it—for him, of course, but also for Jules. No matter what her daughter said or did, he would shrug her off, and Desi could sense the insecurity swarming through Jules's heart. She, of all people, knew exactly what that felt like.

William Sr. removed his glasses from his lapel, put them on, and opened the letter. It was a single sheet of paper.

"Dear William, Will, and my darling Ava,

I know this is hard. I know none of you have experienced death, but I do know that wherever you go, I will find ways to connect. (So be prepared!) I want you to move on with your lives, to hold my memory high in your heart and not drown with grief. Promise me, my loves. Promise me you'll find ways to move on.

Besides that small matter, I have just two requests: Ava, I want you to scatter some of my ashes in our favorite place. I don't have to tell you where. And Will, on the biggest snowfall of the year, take Jules and scatter the rest from the sky. Let me sift over my beloved mountain and mingle with the snow. You know how much I loved the snow.

And my dearest William. You have been my truest partner, confidant, and friend. Keep flying, my love. Know that I will be waiting for you when you are ready to rest. To you all: live bravely. I will miss you every moment of every day.

Love always, even when I am no longer here,
Leni"

William Sr. faltered and sniffed deeply to clear the emotion from his voice.

Desi wiped her eyes with a handkerchief and watched the grief ripple through the group, herself included. Above, the leaves swished with the wind.

She'd never gotten to share the same kind of sentiments with Carter, when she'd had all these years to make him understand how much he was loved. They'd just started to open themselves up to each other before he'd disappeared.

Will sighed and looked up to the sky. "How am I supposed to wait until winter?"

Ava took the urn from her father and cradled it in her good arm. "I'm going to do mine soon. She'd want me to."

Will's jaw hardened, and he walked away. Jules looked to his family for help. Ava leaned into her dad, who fumbled with his glasses to blot his tears with a trembling fist. He reread the letter, silently this time, and then stuffed it in the envelope. Peter hung back. Jules looked tormented, stuck between staying put and following Will.

"Why don't we go into town? Walk around for a bit?" Desi offered.

Jules fidgeted with a bloody cuticle and finally agreed. They all said goodbye to Ava and William Sr. and followed the path around the pond back to the car. As they neared the gravel lot, Will sat on a park bench, elbows perched on his knees, staring at the water. A few ducks waddled by, quacking.

"Will, honey, we're going to go." Desi placed a hand on his shoulder. "Let you be with your family."

He stood and shook hands with Peter and gave Desi a hug. Life was so cruel. She'd lost her mother to breast cancer and her father shortly after. The pain lingered even now, like a bruise.

Desi walked a few paces with Peter, desperate to smother her final moments with Carter, which were permanently seared into her brain. The kiss. His eyes. The tenderness. Desi searched for something to talk about, but there wasn't much to say. The last few days, Peter had kept to himself, and she didn't have the energy to pull anything out of him.

A moment later, Jules quickly asked for the keys. Peter tossed them to her, and she jogged ahead, her cheeks stained with tears.

"I hate this for her."

Peter sighed and jabbed his hands into his pockets. "I know, but the boy just lost his mother. Being a good boyfriend probably isn't on top of his priority list right now."

Desi pondered Lenore's request about Jules going up in the plane with Will. Maybe she'd assumed Will would want support, or she wanted Jules to get over her fear of flying. Either way, she knew Jules would have anxiety about getting into a plane to fulfill Lenore's dying wish. And she would have months until winter to obsess over it.

At the car, Jules was already in the backseat, arms crossed. Before Peter climbed into the driver's side, Desi stopped him.

"Can you wait here for a second?"

She asked Jules to come with her and they began walking back in the opposite direction around the pond. Birds glided low until their reflections mirrored the placid water. Trees arched overhead, shielding them from the sun. Jules's face was red and raw, her eyes agitated from emotion. Desi again hunted for the right words. "This is hard."

Jules snorted. "Yeah, Mom. Death is hard."

"No." She stopped and really looked at her daughter, examining her face. "It's hard when the man you're in love with starts to pull away. To shut down." She kept her voice steady, but inside, she was peeling open, layer by painful layer. She'd never really talked about how agonizing it was when Peter had retired from the military and just seemed to emotionally withdraw. How he stopped talking, stopped smiling, stopped interacting. The energy in their house turned heavy and claustrophobic, and she'd felt like her only option had been to endure it. She often wondered if his behavior had been the ultimate punishment since her heart was with another man.

Sometimes, it was hard to grasp the totality of her marriage, how it swung from young and naïve to seasoned and bitter. When she closed her eyes and thought of herself in happier times, she could recall nights of being wildly intimate, of talking for hours about what she wanted from life, of a whispered "I love you so fucking much" into the nape of her neck. Adventurous, sweaty nights tied up in caution tape when they couldn't find rope. Laughing attacks that left her giddy and breathless. Staring into each other's eyes until she cried. But those memories weren't with Peter.

They were with Carter.

The truth surged through her memory until she was almost breathless. She'd sacrificed a happier life with a man she loved to stay loyal to her husband—and what did she have to show for it? Carter was gone. Peter was emotionally unavailable.

She blinked into the sunlight that filtered through the tree branches and assessed the shoreline stippled with bleached pebbles. She didn't want her daughter to wake up twenty years from now with *any* man and not have voiced her opinion. To not stand up for what she deserved, no matter how shitty the timing. When you stayed quiet, nobody won. Again, the image of Carter's smile surged through her body, forcing her to remember.

Surprisingly, Jules curled against Desi's chest and began to cry—big, racking sobs that vibrated her entire body. Desi guided her to a patch of grass and sat down, letting her cry. There was so much she could say, but even more she couldn't.

While Peter had spent all these years teaching her how to survive in the physical world, who'd been teaching Jules how to survive emotionally? Certainly not her. But it wasn't too late.

"Listen," Desi finally said after Jules had quieted down. "Grief isn't linear. It's going to be hard. Will is going to have ups and downs, but you need to encourage him to talk, even if it isn't to you. Okay? Events like this . . ." She stared at the glassy water, her mind on her own personal losses. "They can change people. And I want you to be there for him, of course, but not at the expense of your own happiness."

Jules swiped the tip of her nose and nodded. "It's not just about him. I really miss Lenore." She broke into a fresh round of tears, and Desi nodded.

She missed Lenore too. That tiny stab of guilt she'd first felt that Lenore was a better mother had instantly dissolved once she got to know her. Lenore wasn't better, she was just different, and Desi was thankful her daughter had gotten to spend any time with her at all.

"I've just never felt so"—Jules fanned her arms toward herself—"unglued. I feel unglued. Like I'm feeling every emotion all at once and I don't know how to control any of it."

Fully human. Desi used to feel like that all the time, but over the years, she'd numbed herself with wine, work, fear, excuses. She'd succumbed to the circumstances of her life instead of fighting for what she really wanted and needed. She'd buried how she wanted to feel, chalking it up to a fantasy—nothing she could ever have for real. She'd become so moored in her own small, unfulfilled life when what she really craved was something simple and deep. Something she'd had and forced away because she thought there was no other choice.

"I know, honey. But you don't have to control any of it. You've just got to feel your feelings and communicate."

"You and Dad don't." She looked at her with wet, swollen eyes. "You and Dad walk around like silent partners. You don't laugh. You don't talk." She shrugged, then drew her knees to her chest and rested her head on them. "It's sad."

Desi almost denied it, but reconsidered. Though they'd had a few good moments this summer, she was right. She couldn't protect her daughter by pretending her marriage was fine, because it wasn't. Jules was opening up to her, so it was time to be honest too. "It *is* sad. I'm sad about it." She hesitated, trying to form the words. "I've tried to talk to Dad, but as you know, he's not much for talking." She suppressed her own urge to cry. "This is why I want you to make sure Will talks to you, okay? It's a practice, like anything else. I should have pushed your dad to open up more, made more space for him in our marriage."

To be fair, Peter had been gone during a large portion of their marriage. After she'd had Jules, he'd gone on several more tours, each time promising it would be the last. In his absence, Desi had stepped up as both parents. When he returned, that gap was wiped clean. To Jules, Peter was the hero who'd returned; it didn't matter that *she'd* been the present parent. While Jules fought with Desi about simple things—brushing her hair, flossing, getting dressed, trying new things—she and Peter got along famously and rarely fought. It was maddening.

As a result, Desi had gone from primary caretaker to task driver, nag, and workaholic, when she'd really had no other choice. Somewhere along the way, she'd forgotten how to speak up and had adopted Peter's silence as a way of life. It hadn't been fair to him, her, or Jules. She realized that now. All that time they couldn't make up. "This summer has been good for us though," she finally added. "We're figuring it out."

Even as she said it, resistance strained her heart. *Really, what was there left to figure out?*

"Well, don't stay together for my sake," Jules suddenly said. "Don't be those parents who stay for their kid. You deserve to be happy too." She studied her mom's face, then turned back toward the water. "So does Dad."

Desi appraised her eighteen-year-old with newfound respect. Her child was so much more emotionally capable than she'd realized. It was important for her not to be some mommy robot who got everything done; it was important to be a woman who stood up for what she wanted. Otherwise, how else would Jules?

"How's everything else been with Will?" Desi asked. "Besides Lenore."

She shrugged. "He's been concerned with Ava and her physical therapy, and now this." Her voice crumbled and she turned her head the other way, resting her left cheek on the tops of her knees, so Desi wouldn't see her cry.

"Oh, sweetie. I know. I know how hard this must be." She rubbed soothing circles along her spine. She didn't want to put more pressure on her, but they still hadn't finished the college conversation. She didn't want to drive home the fact that it was too late to back out, as they should have let the school know by now and offered her position and dorm room to another applicant. But they had to have the conversation, no matter the timing. Isn't that what she was sitting here saying in the first place? "I have a question for you."

Jules rotated her head and Desi smoothed the tearstained hair off her face.

"Have you thought about when we leave? What that looks like for you?"

Jules sighed. "I knew we were going to have to talk about this." She groaned and sat up, pulling her legs beneath her. She gripped a handful of grass and sorted through each jade blade, one by one. "I've thought so long and hard about this, and I want to stay. Uncle Tommy said he'd stay with me through the fall, help me enroll for EMT classes."

Desi processed this new information. Her fury began to rise, but she kept her expression unruffled. "Well, that sounds like an interesting plan." Desi calculated what that would look like: her daughter riding around in an ambulance, staying stuck in the same position with no upward trajectory. But hadn't she just saved Ava's life because of her natural skill set? Wasn't that proof that she was on the right path?

She gazed out at the water and beyond, the expansive beauty evident everywhere her eyes landed. She knew in her bones Jules belonged in a place like this, but she didn't want her to rush into anything. "What about a compromise?" she asked.

"Like what?" Jules's face was hardening, and Desi rushed to speak before she ruined the moment entirely.

"What about if you did just one semester at Columbia? That way, Will can grieve, you can both get some time and space, and then you can make an informed decision about your future. Not to mention," she added, "it's really too late to back out. We should have let them know sooner."

"I don't want to go to Columbia for a semester. No." Jules crossed her arms, a barrier.

"Honey, think about before we came here this summer. How excited you were when you got the acceptance package in the mail."

Jules looked at her and laughed. "I was excited because I had nothing else to look forward to, Mom. Until now. This is where I want my life to be." She gestured around her. "Plus, I'm an adult. It's my choice."

Desi wanted to remind her that being eighteen was about the furthest thing from being an adult, but she swallowed that knee-jerk reaction and just nodded. "You are technically an adult, Juliette. This is your future. But if you stay here, you will have to pay your own way. Food, bills, groceries, everything. You'll be on your own."

Jules swallowed, licked her dry lips. "And the house?"

"You can stay at the house, but that's it."

"And Uncle Tommy?"

She rolled her eyes. "I'll deal with him." How typical of Tommy to think he could just freeload at her house without even asking.

Relief washed over her daughter's face.

"There's just one more thing," Desi said.

Jules stood, wiping the bits of grass stuck to her dress.

"You have to tell your father."

Jules nodded, and they began walking back to the car. Yes, Jules would talk to Peter.

And Desi would talk to Will.

15

Desi

SHE arranged to meet Will in town for coffee while Peter, Jules, and Tommy were busy in the woods.

They met at the diner. Will looked tired and drawn. They both ordered coffee, and when the waitress removed their menus, she folded her hands on the table. "How are you holding up?"

He offered a sad smile. "It's a lot harder than I thought it would be."

Desi thanked the waitress as she set two steaming mugs on the sticky table. She took a tentative sip. "My mom died of breast cancer several years ago. Even though we knew she was sick, once she was gone . . ." She twisted the mug. "It didn't really take any of the pain away."

Will nodded. "Exactly. I thought I would feel relief, but . . ." His jaw twitched and he cleared his throat, burying the emotion. "Anyway. What did you want to talk about?"

Desi didn't want to seem insensitive, but this was her daughter's future at stake. "You know Jules doesn't want to go to college."

Will nodded, revealing nothing as he nursed his coffee.

"While I totally respect her decision, I'm not sure if Jules has talked to you about her academic life before coming here."

He stirred cream into his mug. "We don't really talk about school."

"Well, Jules is very humble." She sat forward and looked intently into his eyes. "She's also completely brilliant. I'm not just saying that as her mother. She's always been insanely gifted, naturally talented." She peered out the window. "She graduated top of her class. Everything she's been working toward . . . I'd just hate to see her throw it all away in a rash decision."

Will seemed to consider what she was saying. She hoped he'd understand where she was coming from.

"Jules seems pretty capable of making up her mind."

"Oh she is," Desi said. "Of course she is. But I know what it's like to be eighteen and think you've got everything figured out." She was talking about Carter. She'd met him when she was just twenty. She hesitated before driving home her point. Because hadn't she known what she wanted even then, just like Jules?

Will sighed and slung an arm across the red leather booth. "I remember. I had some pretty wild ideas at eighteen. I didn't really know what I wanted." He studied her and then nodded. "I'll talk to her, okay? Make sure she's thinking it through."

"That's all I ask," Desi said. "She has her whole life to be here and to explore this relationship and town. But college matters, now more than ever." She didn't want to push too hard, but she hoped she was getting through to him.

"I got it," Will said. His eyes darkened slightly, and Desi hoped this conversation wouldn't have the opposite effect and make him do something spontaneous, like propose marriage.

They finished their coffee chatting about various places he'd flown to and what he would do now that he didn't have to arrange for Lenore's constant care. She paid the check and then walked around downtown, perusing the shops. She searched for new information about Carter, but still found nothing. The lack of updates was maddening. She couldn't help but think the worst. She imagined Carter lying dead in a ditch somewhere; Carter committing suicide; Carter having random flings with women; Carter flying to Mexico and starting all over without her.

Every time she tried to grasp an image of him, something didn't add up. She had given him hope that last night. He wouldn't just leave unless he'd had a hard dose of a strong conscience—or worse. She froze in her steps, wondering, not for the first time, if Peter had done something like what she'd just done to Will—gotten to him somehow, convinced him to walk away because it was better for everyone.

Her heart thudded in her chest. If Peter had done anything of the sort, that meant he knew about them in some capacity, though he couldn't possibly know *everything*.

She stood her ground in the middle of Main Street and debated what to do. She couldn't keep calling him obsessively. She wasn't dumb enough to leave a voice mail or send urgent text messages, but this had gone too far. If he was playing some sort of game in order for her to realize how much he meant to her, well, he'd won. She got it.

She'd thought the real terror had been the possibility of Carter showing up in her life, when, in fact, it was wanting him and not being able to find him. That was the worst fate.

Back at home, she emptied the bag from her stop at the market and found Tommy nursing a scotch by the fire. She glanced around. "Where's the gang?"

"Peter and Jules are doing some father-daughter thing. Didn't want to intrude."

She collapsed next to him and poured herself a drink.

He eyed her. "You okay?"

She wanted to say yes and pretend everything was fine, but she couldn't. She had to talk to someone or she would burst.

Desi stared into her glass and suggested they go out by the pool. She removed her shoes and let her feet dangle in the water. The pool was clear and calm, a bundle of gnats swarming the surface. She still hadn't answered Tommy's question, but he waited patiently.

"It's Carter," she finally said. Even saying his name out loud was a relief.

Tommy's face screwed up under the harsh sun. "Carter?" He knocked back his drink and poured himself another. "That's the last thing I thought you'd say."

She shrugged. "I'm worried about him."

"What? Because of that missing thing? He's not missing." He smacked his lips together, and Desi's heart jumped in possible anticipation.

"How do you know that?"

"Because he's Carter. He's unpredictable. Plus, his girlfriend's crazy."

Desi sipped her drink and tried to appear casual. "How so?"

"They're engaged," Tommy said simply. "He probably just wanted to get away from her."

Desi's world went completely still. She couldn't move. *Engaged*? A punch of heat spread throughout her body. While she'd been kissing him, thinking about tearing up her life, he'd already promised himself to someone else?

"I need to go lie down," she said. A small sob rumbled up her throat but she quickly suppressed it. All this time, in the back of her mind, she'd wondered if they'd ever get a second chance. And now, when she finally thought they had, another wrench was thrown into the plot. Carter was engaged. Her mind was a flurry of grief, sorrow, and disbelief.

She stumbled down the hall, already woozy from the alcohol. Shutting the door, she fell into bed, more conflicted than ever.

Where was Carter . . . and even if she found him, was it already too late?

16

Jules

JULES hadn't seen Will in days.

She wanted to give him time with his family, but tonight, she'd arranged something special, just like he had at the waterfall. At the pond behind The Black House, she'd cleared dead leaves and underbrush from the shore and found a spot near several giant, gnarled trees. A bouquet of wildflowers surrounded the blanket she'd laid gingerly over the dirt. She'd strung solar lights between the trees, looping the ends around the knotted branches. When she looked at them, it was like being invaded by fireflies. In the corner, on a patch of cool grass, rested a cooler of Will's favorite foods and another folded blanket. Music streamed from her phone.

While Jules waited, she watched the black water dance under the creamy cone of moonlight. She took a full belly breath and exhaled, feeling for the first time in a long time that everything was going to be alright. When she'd told her father about deferring college, he hadn't said much. Tommy had told Peter their plan, and if she wasn't mistaken, she saw something like envy cross her father's face. She almost told him he could stay too, but she knew he would never go for that. He had a life back in

Chicago, a business, a marriage to figure out. Though she was glad Tommy would be around, part of her wanted to experience The Black House all for herself.

A few minutes later, rustling parted the thick, heavy leaves. Will stepped through, a flashlight in hand. She'd left markers the whole way, and when he glimpsed the scene, he flicked off the flashlight and came over, dropping his backpack at the edge of the blanket.

"Hi." He leaned over and kissed her softly on the cheek.

He smelled like the woods. Her belly stirred, and she was dying to know every thought he'd had over the last few days. It seemed like it had been a year since they'd been together. She patted the empty space beside her. "How are you feeling?"

Will shrugged as he sat.

She waited for more, but when he said nothing, she pressed forward. "How's your dad and Ava?"

"How do you think they are?"

"I'm sorry. I was just asking." Tears threatened, but she blinked them away.

Will gripped both sides of his head. "Fuck, I'm sorry. None of this is your fault. I'm just . . ." His voice trailed off. "Lost." The word landed, and she reached across the space between them to grab his hand. The drumroll of insects consumed the silence. She strained for something to say that would make him feel better, but came up empty.

"I thought I was prepared to say goodbye, but clearly, I wasn't," he finally admitted.

"No one is ever really prepared." She thought about losing her own mother: how she might feel before, during, and after. All the regrets she'd have. She couldn't fathom it. She leaned into the silence and also wondered what would have happened if she'd had to say goodbye to Will next week. That loss, in her world, eclipsed all others. At least she could bring him some good news tonight. She reached behind her and opened the cooler to reveal big slices of sausage and olive pizza dripping with grease, and a Caesar salad from the local pizzeria, Grins. To finish, she'd baked a carrot cake from scratch, studded with raisins and walnuts and heaped with cream cheese frosting. "Hungry?"

He shook his head again and looked at her. His eyes seemed to jab her soul. "Not for food," he said. He reached for her.

Jules eagerly pushed away the food and straddled his lap, kissing him deeply. They hadn't been intimate in at least a couple of weeks, and Jules was desperate for his touch. Their clothes came off in a furious tangle, and afterward, Jules could barely catch her breath.

Instead of lying together, Will hurriedly dressed. Disappointed, Jules rolled away and did the same. He'd been so attentive just now, when they were breathing and staring into each other's eyes, when their hands were clasped above her head, when their bodies climaxed at nearly the same time. But the moment it was over, he'd erected his walls again. She reminded herself it wasn't *her* fault; he was just grieving.

When she was dressed, she dragged the cooler over and handed him a slice of pizza. She bit into her own, which was now cold, but still delicious.

They chewed in silence, and Jules suddenly felt like they were strangers. She finished her piece, wiped her mouth, and turned to him. "So I have news."

"Oh?" He picked lamely at his piece and then tossed it back into the cooler, uneaten, and sighed. "What's that?"

She faltered. "I'm—I've decided to defer college. I'm staying here with Uncle Tommy and am going to take EMT classes in the fall. So, you know, I'll be here. Like, permanently." The news landed, but he didn't react. In her mind, she'd imagined him breaking into a grin and smothering her in a surprised hug.

She felt foolish about her daydream, because the reality was harsh and cold. Will just stared into space and then, to her surprise, uttered a single word: "No."

Jules recoiled. "What do you mean, no?" Her heart began to pound.

"No." He shifted to face her. "You're not throwing away your future, Jules. You've worked too hard."

She opened her mouth, but was literally speechless.

He lay back, crossed his hands behind his head. "Your future is bigger than River Falls."

"*You're* my future," she insisted. "I want to stay here. I love River Falls."

He sighed again—this time, an irritated sound that flew up from his throat in an exasperated hiss—and scoured the sky, freckled with stars. "You're just a kid, Juliette. You don't know what you want."

"A kid?" Jules felt like she'd been slapped. Her heart kicked up another notch, thudding manically in her chest. "Our entire relationship, you've never even brought up our age difference, and now I'm a kid?" She trembled with fear, rage, and anxiety, all balled in the center of her chest. She replayed every moment of their relationship. They'd already talked about their future, made plans. Why the sudden change?

"You should go to Columbia." He sounded rehearsed, no emotion behind the words. "At least try it out and then you can make an informed decision."

Jules snapped her head his way. "What did you just say?" Before he could repeat it, Jules let out a frustrated scream. "Oh my God, did my mother talk to you? Is that what this is all about?" Her mother had used those same exact words during their talk at the lake. Her mother had pretended to be open and to listen, to agree that she was an adult and could make her own decisions. And then she'd gone behind her back to convince her boyfriend to persuade her to go to college? A white-hot rage coursed through her entire body, but she calmed herself enough to turn to Will. "Will, look at me. Please."

Finally, he turned, his face stony, unreadable. Every feature she'd kissed, touched, or memorized seemed just out of reach.

"Do not listen to my mother. This is *my* life. I know what I want. I promise." She took his hands, which were warm and limp. "My future is here, with you." She squeezed his fingers. "I know it just like I knew when I saw you for the first time. Remember?" She shook his hands in an effort to jog his memory. "I was just leaving the diner and you were getting out of your truck. You were talking to someone and I literally crossed the street and almost got flattened by a car because I wasn't paying attention. One glimpse of you and that man bun, and I was smitten."

Will cracked a smile.

"And then you came over and helped me out of the street, and I knew. I knew the very first moment we touched." She continued, embarrassed by the romantic admission. "This is really what I want, Will. You need to trust me. I'm not making this decision for you. I'm making it for me."

He searched her eyes. What was he thinking? Finally, he released her hands and returned his gaze to the sky. "If you decide to stay, that's your decision. But I think we need to take a break."

Everything in Jules seized. She couldn't speak. She couldn't breathe. "Why?"

Will stood, locating his backpack in the dark. "Because I just need some time, okay? I need to figure out what I want too."

Jules scrambled to her feet, and the world tilted beneath her. "I thought our relationship was what you wanted."

Will started toward a stand of trees, avoiding her in his swift exit. "Well, things change." He took a few more steps, turned. "Take care of yourself, Juliette." His eyes found hers, and they looked as gutted as she felt.

When he pushed through the trees, she dropped to her knees, her world growing black and cold. She curled into a ball and wailed.

FALL

17

Jules

JULES followed the signs for car rental returns at LaGuardia.

She nervously searched for the Avis sign. After twelve hours on the road, she was in dire need of a shower and some coffee. She snaked through the confusing airport roads, which were crammed with dormant, grimy construction equipment, idling cabs, rideshare vehicles, and impatient travelers. The air was clogged with cigarettes and marijuana. She pulled up to the Avis kiosk, dropped off the car, and hoisted her bags from the trunk.

Because she'd only agreed to attend Columbia for one semester, she was treating this as a three-month hiatus from her real life and had decided to only pack a few bags. She'd buy necessities if and when she needed them. She walked toward the long line of Lyft cars, now too tired to ride the train, and waited for her app to tell her where to go.

When the silver Toyota Camry arrived, she dropped her bags in the trunk and climbed in. The car was hot and pungent with body odor. Jules stabbed the back window down and sucked in muggy air. God, she missed the mountains. She missed waking up in River Falls, knowing she had the entire day ahead to explore or work with her hands. She closed her eyes, seeing Will's face when he told her goodbye. She'd been reliving that moment every single second of every single day. Finally, she'd agreed to go to Columbia just to ease the pain of his easy dismissal of their relationship. She hated to give her mother the satisfaction, but she wanted to be away from her entire family. She needed time to think.

"Student?"

She glanced at the driver in the rearview mirror. Thick, black eyebrows arched in question as he revealed a precious gap between his front teeth. A set of New York Yankees bobbleheads gyrated on his dash.

"Columbia."

"Smart girl." He nodded. "First time to New York?"

"No, I've been here before." Her first trip to New York was when she was eight, for the Macy's Thanksgiving Day Parade. She'd marveled at all the floats and had so thoroughly exhausted her legs by jumping up and down waiting for Santa that she could barely stand. For the big finale, her father had scooped her onto his shoulders. It had been unusually warm that Thanksgiving, and she'd forgone mittens in favor of warming her hands against her father's jaw. Her palms had scoured his scruff while they waited. He'd whistled under her hands, puffing his cheeks to "Jingle Bells."

As she got older and more interested in art, she and her dad had made the long, arduous road trips into the city. She'd already exhausted every art program and museum in Chicago and wanted to see new and interesting ideas. She loved working with oils and pastels and aimed to spark new inspiration in her own work.

They'd spent two full days wading through tourists to ogle ancient and modern art—the Whitney, MoMA, the Met, the

Guggenheim, and even the Tenement and Skyscraper Museums. Before they headed back, they always stopped at Central Park, eating street meat, and climbed onto the rocks. Below, tourists would pass by in knots, but up on the rocks, the city would shift into view, with its clumps of buildings rising like mountains. Her dad would sit beside her while she sketched, so certain that she'd have a future as an artist.

Her mother never joined those trips, always too busy with work. She'd only dropped everything when Jules had announced she wanted to go to Columbia. When they'd toured the campus, her mother butted in every five minutes to tell her what a good school it was and how studying biomedical science—not art— could really define her future and set her up for a better life.

Now, the driver asked if she was left-handed (she was) and spouted off facts about how left-handed people used both parts of their brain and are naturally smarter, which is why she probably got into Columbia. Jules didn't argue and reminded herself to tell Tommy about that, since he was left-handed too.

They looped onto the Grand Central Parkway, then the BQE. They passed tall buildings with trash-lined curbs, and the dark, choppy waters of the Harlem and East Rivers as they entered Manhattan. Swarms of people clustered on sidewalks and street corners, slick with sweat from the early September heat. Some wore fanny packs, others were dressed for the office. Models waited at crosswalks, getting catcalls from teenage boys and ad- miring looks from impressionable girls who snapped photos to post to Instagram. Bike messengers dipped in and out of traffic, banging on car hoods if they got too close. Jules waited for the excitement to take hold, but every time she searched her feel- ings, there was a black void where happiness should be.

Twenty minutes later, the driver turned onto West 114th Street. The dorm sat directly across from the Hudson River.

She thanked the driver, retrieved her bags, and added her tip before he drove away. She shoved her phone into her bag and craned her head to take in the nondescript brick building with bulky window units. Adjacent to her dorm was Lerner Hall on the Morningside Campus.

She could glimpse the water from where she stood—New York on one side, New Jersey on the other. At least she could stare at the water, even if she wouldn't be swimming.

She pushed through the revolving door to check in. A large man with ham hands gave her a welcome packet and offered her a map. He stabbed a pudgy finger on the small red circles that represented the lounge, mezzanine, and the unisex public bathroom on the first floor. He worked his finger up to the third-floor block of rooms and tapped hers, room 309A. She thanked him and bustled through the lobby with the map in hand. She smiled politely as supportive parents helped their children haul comforters and sloppily taped boxes toward the banks of chrome elevators.

She hustled into one, standing at the very back, all alone, and waited for the elevator to reach the third floor. As she exited onto the carpeted hallway, she spotted her communal bathroom, which she would share with three other people. She moved past the bathroom and approached her room. The door was ajar. Voices converged inside, and she edged open the door with her foot to find her roommate, Melanie, chatting with two adults. Her curly brown hair was swept up into a messy ponytail. She moved from foot to foot as she talked, in constant motion. As Jules eased farther into the room, she realized the two adults weren't Melanie's parents—they were hers.

Jules hesitated in the doorway, shocked and confused. Why where they here?

Melanie turned. "Jules! Look who showed up to surprise you. Is that, like, the sweetest or what?"

She glanced at her parents, who stood, poised and uncertain, on her side of the room.

Melanie hopped over to give her a hug, her head barely clearing Jules's chest. Her face was doused with freckles and she was sturdy and short, like a gymnast. She and Melanie had been texting for a week—a small bright spot during such a brutal end to summer. Melanie was also majoring in biomedical science, and Jules was relieved to have an instant connection in such a massive, anonymous city.

"I'll give you guys some privacy." She squeezed Jules's arm and zipped into the hall. Jules dropped her bags, avoiding eye contact with her parents, and glanced at Melanie's side of the room. A simple double bed with crisp white linens sat next to a plain wooden wardrobe and a small desk. As Jules stood in the tiny, square room, her face warmed, and she fanned herself.

Everything had already been set up: expensive linens in a rich, royal blue, the standard-issue lamp having been swapped for imported gold and a matching alarm clock. Some of her homemade art even hung on the plain white walls along with a photo she'd taken of The Black House at the start of summer. Beside it, a photo of Lenore, taken at the lake the day she died, rounded out the set, and she almost gasped when she saw it. Her mother noticed and smiled.

"I wanted you to have it. I sent one to Will too."

She didn't even acknowledge her mother, as if a photograph made up for what she'd done. Jules continued scanning the tidy space. A compact easel stood in the corner with all of her favorite paints and brushes arranged beneath it—some sort of consolation prize for her chosen major instead of the one she'd really wanted. She wavered between being annoyed that her mother was inserting herself into her life once again and feeling relieved that she didn't have to find a Target and load up on bedding and other essentials.

Her dad crushed her in a hug. "You look like you've been through a war, kiddo."

"Well, it was a long drive." She envied her parents' ability to just buy two first-class tickets, drink champagne, and enjoy the short flight from Chicago to New York without a second thought. She could never do that—could never just purchase a plane ticket and follow through. Over the years, she'd tried but then, days before the trip, she'd be struck with insomnia, anxiety, and insane heart palpitations. The mere thought of stepping into an airport would fill her with such crippling dread that she'd cancel whatever trip she'd booked and immediately experience a flood of physical relief. Now, she knew not to even pretend that she could make herself fly. She couldn't. How ironic that she'd picked a pilot to fall in love with, a pilot to break her heart.

Her mother hung back, busying herself with tidying a bed that didn't need tidying. She'd barely spoken to her mother since they'd left River Falls, but this was her mother's love language: buying and arranging possessions to show that she cared.

Jules decided to extend a small olive branch, if only for the sake of her dad.

"Looks good."

Her mother flushed in surprise. "I just thought it would be one less thing you had to do."

Surprisingly, Jules's eyes filled with tears. She quickly cleared her throat and excused herself to the bathroom. The door was unlocked. She slipped inside and cringed at the cramped corridors. How would four girls share this tiny space?

She assessed herself in the mirror, splashed water on her face, and walked back toward the room. The hall was teeming with excited freshmen hauling boxes and oversized bags. She wished she could have that type of enthusiasm. She should be invigorated after a summer away; instead, she felt like her college career was coming at the end of an emotional roller coaster.

She pulled her hair into a bun and entered the room. Melanie was still nowhere to be found. Jules shut the door behind her.

"What do you think?" her mom asked.

"It's fine," she said. She hauled her suitcase onto the bed and unzipped it.

"Let me," her mom fussed.

Jules knew if she argued, she wouldn't win, so she let her mother sort through her personal items, hanging clothes and refolding others. Her dad scratched the back of his neck.

"You excited?"

She shrugged and busied her hands with unpacking her laptop and cosmetics.

"How was the drive?"

"Long."

Jules put some music on her phone and busied herself with getting organized. Forty-five minutes later, her parents asked if she wanted to get some food. Jules agreed and they walked down the street until they found a small bistro with open windows and outdoor seating.

"Isn't this lovely," her mother commented as they took a seat.

Jules wiped the sweat from the back of her neck and kept her sunglasses on. Horns, sirens, and people's laughter grated her nerves. The new soundscape of her life.

"So when do classes start?" her mother asked, though Jules was positive she already knew the answer.

"Next week." She poked her straw into her ice water.

Her dad cleared his throat. "Remember when we first visited Columbia? You were so excited."

"Things change."

That shut both of her parents up. She audibly slurped the last of her water and chomped noisily on a piece of ice.

The waiter took their order, and then she pushed her silverware away and folded both arms. "Why did you guys even come?"

Her father leaned forward and braced his elbows on the table. "We just wanted to make sure you were okay."

Jules studied him, but said nothing.

"We know you wanted to do this by yourself, but it's an overwhelming thing to be in a brand-new city, so we thought we'd help." Her mother swirled her wine. "And we didn't really have a proper goodbye, so . . ."

There were so many things she could have said to that. No, she didn't want to do this by herself. She didn't even want to be here. And she certainly didn't want her parents' help. "How long are you staying?"

"As long as you need us," her mom said.

Jules wanted to laugh. Yes, she needed her parents, but she also needed Will. She needed River Falls. She needed The Black House, the mountain. She needed someone to saw open her chest and suck out the pain.

"Melanie seems nice," her mother offered.

"Yeah."

"You girls are going to have so much fun. I remember my freshman year of college. It was life-changing."

"Ah, the good old years," her dad joked.

Jules rolled her eyes as they started reminiscing about the years before they met. All she could think about was getting through these three months as fast as humanly possible and heading back to River Falls for winter break.

She kept imagining it in her head, but she couldn't quite foresee Will's reaction. Would he have moved on by then, or could they pick right back up where they'd left off before her mother had interfered? Already, she couldn't wait to be alone in her room so she could try and call him. She just wanted to hear his voice.

The waiter brought their food, and the three of them ate quietly. Jules chewed and swallowed, but her stomach instantly turned sour. She pushed her food away and stared at the street.

"Honey, I really wish you would give this a chance," her mother said.

"I wish you would have given Will a chance."

Her mother's mouth hung open, but she quickly shut it. "I did give Will a chance. I like Will."

"Bullshit."

"Hey, go easy," her dad warned. "Your mother said she's sorry. And you're here now. So you need to make the best of it."

Actually, her mother hadn't said she was sorry. But he was right. No one had physically forced her to come. But here she was anyway, doing as she was told like a good girl. Jules swallowed the lump in her throat. She took a deep breath and tried again. "I will."

Once this semester was over, she was heading straight back to River Falls to start her real life.

18

Desi

NEW York had been painful.

Desi was glad to be back in the office. She shut her glass door and eased into her chair. This morning, she'd jogged to and from her Pilates studio and grabbed a green juice and turmeric oat milk latte from her favorite café. Oh, the joys of city conveniences.

On the way into work, she'd smiled at everyone she passed, that urban energy seeping into her bones and reminding her of where she truly belonged. Here, she could forget about what happened this summer and try to scout out some shred of normalcy. At her desk, she hammered out a few emails and organized her three main tasks for the day.

Her team was relieved to have her back and had thrown her a small welcome party, complete with a cake, though they were now past the fanfare and deep into work mode. She had so many homes out on bids and a few others she needed to close. She couldn't believe how much she'd missed the art of the sale, of walking into someone's home or company and showing them that with a new design, they could have a better life.

Desi spun around in her chair to grab a set of plans. On the bookshelf above was a photo of her and Peter at their wedding. She retrieved the photo, squinting at the two of them. Peter had never looked better, in his three-piece suit, his lips stretched into a genuine smile. He was dipping her during their first dance. Her head was thrust back, her ivory lace gown flowing behind her. They'd gotten married at the Four Seasons in front of all their family and friends.

She placed it back on the shelf. What a farce. Every time she looked at the photo, she felt foolish and naïve. She'd had such high hopes for the woman in the photo, but she'd disappointed herself and those around her over and over again.

She spun back around, plans in hand, and lost herself in work. But her thoughts kept slipping back to New York and how angry Jules had been with her—how angry she still was. She wished Jules understood that college could be the time of her life. She didn't need to be tied down, and sooner or later, she'd come to understand that she was right.

Since they'd gotten back, Peter had turned even more silent and moody. He'd barely said two words to her on the plane ride home. She understood that Jules leaving for Columbia was a loss. They both needed time, but especially Peter. While he had his work too, it didn't fulfill him as much as hers did. At least she had her company.

By the time Desi looked up, it was lunchtime. She removed her glasses, stood and stretched, and told the team she'd be back in an hour.

Her office was right in the middle of River North, and anything she wanted was at her fingertips. She decided to pick up a quick lunch and clear her head.

Once she got her salad, she walked to Washington Square Park, which was right by the library, and scouted out a bench. As she settled, her cell rang: Tommy.

"What's shaking, sis?"

Tommy's voice was spotty and she strained to hear him. "How's the house?" She refrained from jumping to her next question.

"It's great. How's Chi-town?"

Desi bit into the mixed greens, her mind wandering straight to Carter. She'd been obsessively scouring for new clues about his whereabouts, assuming he'd come back home. There was no new information. "It's good. Everything okay?"

Tommy's voice broke up. "Des? You there?"

"I'm here. You cut out."

"I said that Jules is doing well, though she sounds like a little lovesick puppy, if you ask me."

Desi sighed. It seemed her main point of communication with her daughter would be through Tommy. She chatted with him about how Jules was settling in and then changed the subject. "Have you heard from Carter yet?"

"Jesus Christ, Desi."

She kept her voice neutral. "He's a family friend. And he's missing. How is that not a concern?"

"He's not missing," Tommy said.

"How do you know?" Her heart thudded with possibility.

Tommy broke up again and then the call disconnected. "Perfect," she mumbled. As Desi chewed, her thoughts were sucked back to so many memories of her and Carter. They used to roam all over the city, their affection on full display as two young people madly in love.

Once they'd restarted their relationship after Peter deployed, she'd been more cautious. The guilt plagued both of them, so that they kept their relationship confined to random, obscure places.

She glanced around the neighborhood, realizing this is where they'd often come. They'd head to Tempo for omelets, grab coffee, go to the library, and wander around this park, avoiding pigeons, and planning their future. Neither of them had lived downtown, so they'd felt safe here, anonymous in a city of millions.

Desi tossed her container into the trash, and began walking the short distance back to the office. She tipped her head to the sky, taking in the heat. She knew the city would start to cool as winter barged in. She'd already promised Jules they would go to The Black House for winter break. She hoped they would at least be on speaking terms by then.

She wanted to make the best of these next few months, to get up to speed with clients, and to figure out next steps with her marriage. In all her worrying about Carter and Jules, she hadn't given much thought to what would happen next for her and Peter.

Desi pressed the crosswalk button at Oak and State and waited. When the light turned green, she began to cross and saw a familiar-looking man on the corner. She kept walking and glanced back, realizing it was Peter. She stopped on the corner of the sidewalk. He was talking to a woman she didn't know, and every hair on Desi's body sprang to attention. He laughed, kissed the woman on the cheek, and walked the other way. He shoved his hands in his pockets and whistled, looking lighter than she'd seen him in years.

Desi's mouth literally fell open. Who was this man so unencumbered by his own darkness? She searched for the woman, who was walking the opposite way toward the lake. Desi jogged closer and trailed behind her. Was she a client or someone he worked with?

Desi racked her brain to think through the other tactical strategists, but honestly, she paid so little attention to that part of his life. This woman was too polished for that kind of work. She was fit, her calves flexing in her high heels. Her skin was dark and smooth and her arms were perfectly sculpted in her sleeveless Chanel dress. Suddenly, the woman stopped to answer a phone call, and Desi rammed right into the back of her. The woman's perfume wafted into the air. It smelled like lilacs.

She dropped her phone, and Desi apologized and reached down to retrieve it. She heard a man's voice saying "You there?" before she handed it back.

Desi's hand shook as she handed it over. "Sorry about that."

The woman inspected her phone for damage and waved a hand. "No worries." She put the phone to her ear.

Desi's heart hammered so violently in her chest, she felt physically ill. She must look like a lunatic, standing there, watching this woman in the middle of her private conversation. The woman's eyes scanned her face, and she hesitated. "Let me call you right back." She hung up and pocketed the phone.

"You're Desiree, aren't you? Peter Wright's wife?"

"And you are?"

The woman stuck out her hand, devoid of jewelry. Her nails were short and polished. "I'm Phoebe Hamil. Your husband's divorce attorney."

Desi's world tilted, and she refrained from reaching out to the woman to right herself. She was literally speechless. Not only had her husband gone behind her back to hire a divorce attorney, she somehow knew what she looked like.

"Do you want to go somewhere and talk?" Phoebe pointed down the block.

Desi nodded, still hunting for words, and followed the woman into a nearby Starbucks. They found a table by the window. Desi collapsed into a chair, her thoughts spinning. She waited for Phoebe to speak, but when it was evident she wasn't going to say anything, Desi located her voice.

"When did he hire you?"

Phoebe made a production of folding her arms across the table. "Two weeks ago."

Two weeks ago was when they'd returned from The Black House. But they'd been so busy getting Jules ready for college, not to mention the trip to New York. How had he had time to go out and get a lawyer?

"Listen, he wants this to be civil. He'd like to start with a legal separation."

"Don't you think he should be telling me this?"

She smiled. "He was planning on talking to you tonight, actually." She spread her arms. "I guess fate intervened."

Desi was stunned. The reason her husband was so lighthearted wasn't because he was having an affair—it was because he was finally going to be free.

She was confused, but knew that she wasn't in the proper mental state to have a logical conversation with this woman. They'd never signed a prenup. He'd be entitled to half her fortune that she'd sacrificed the best years of her life to build. Now she'd have to get a lawyer as well, which she had zero time to do.

"Look, there's a way for this to go smoothly."

"Is that right?" Desi sat back and crossed her arms. "In that Peter will take half of what I've earned? I don't think so."

"Peter's not after your money."

"Oh really? Then what is he after?"

Phoebe eyed her and sighed. "He just wants to move on with his life. Don't you?"

Desi blinked back tears. Yes, she wanted to move on. She wanted to move on from what had happened twenty years ago. She wanted to move on from what had happened this summer. She wanted to move on from her husband's torturous silent treatment. But she couldn't. She'd never be able to until she had some sort of resolution around Carter.

She gauged Phoebe, and some of her anger deflated. She had nothing to do with this. This was simply her job. "I'm just caught off guard," she explained. "Even though we've discussed the possibility of separating, this makes it real."

"I know." For a moment, Desi thought Phoebe was going to pat her hand, but she kept her fingers firmly in place. "But we will make this tidy, I promise."

Could a divorce be tidy? Sensing the conversation was over, she stood. "Thanks for your time." Desi pushed through the revolving door, paused, and turned back. "Can you please not tell him we talked?"

Phoebe gave a curt nod as she gathered her bag. "Sure thing."

Desi exited and walked numbly back to her office. She wanted to call Peter right then and demand he tell her what was going on.

It wasn't even the divorce she was mad about—it's that he hadn't even thought to discuss it with her first. Both of them had always acted so separately in their marriage, doing what they felt was best. They were so rarely a team. Again, her thoughts floated back to Carter. Had something triggered his disappearance and Peter's final decision to end their marriage?

She entered her office, drained of all energy, and told James to hold her calls. She collapsed on her couch by her big open window, staring out at the city's jagged skyline. Everything was changing. Peter was slipping away. Jules was in college. Her twenty-year marriage was ending.

It was time to figure out what she wanted too—not in spite of her secrets, but deep down, when she searched her heart.

And when she did, she knew just who she found waiting.

19

Desi

THAT night, Desi beat Peter home and had a meal fully pre-pared: roasted duck, fingerling potatoes, stir-fried greens. A bottle of their favorite wine—8 Years in the Desert—chilled on the table.

As Peter dropped his bag and walked into the dining room, he paused, surprised. "What's all this?"

"Just thought it would be nice for us to connect," she said. She made a production of pouring him a giant glass of wine and fixing his plate. She smiled as he sat across from her and took a heaving gulp.

She expected him to come clean, to feel so guilty that he'd just blurt the truth, or that Phoebe had gone against her word and warned him. However, she knew Peter didn't operate that way. His expression was always wiped clean, no indication of what thoughts were festering. Desi had been so self-preoccupied, she'd never paid much attention.

Their lives were always such a whirlwind of activities: pickups, drop-offs, swim meets, track meets, art shows, galas, fundrais-ers, weekend trips, endless client meetings. He was the silent partner, getting things done, taking care of laundry, dishes, and cooking, taking Jules to and from her appointments or meets when she was caught up with work. Had she just been entitled and blind throughout the majority of their marriage? It was no wonder he wanted to jump ship.

With that realization, her anger slipped, though she still clung to bits of it. Maybe they could have an honest conversation for once instead of playing head games. He thrust his fork into the edge of his duck and slid the knife through the tender, pink meat.

"I ran into someone you might know today," she began. The callous words were out of her mouth before Desi could shove them back in.

Old habits . . .

"Oh?" He chewed loudly—one of her ultimate pet peeves—and swallowed.

"Yeah, Phoebe Hamil. Your divorce lawyer, right?"

Peter choked and grabbed his napkin as his face turned an alarming shade of purple. For a horrifying moment, she wondered if she was going to have to give him the Heimlich, but after a few painful beats, he swallowed the wad of meat and rubbed his chest. It was childish of Desi to take pleasure in his discomfort, but a small part of her wanted to catch him off guard too. The silence grew thick and messy, but she bit her tongue.

Finally, he spoke. "I was going to tell you." He let out a round of short, rough coughs and downed more of his wine.

"You don't think the dissolution of our marriage is something we should have discussed together?"

Peter set his glass down, composed himself, and nodded. "I'm sorry, Des. I just feel like there's no getting back to where we need to go, you know?"

She nodded. "I do know. I just would have liked to discuss it before you hired a lawyer. This is something that affects both of us. And Juliette."

All the tension drained from his body. "You're right. I'm sorry."

Desi replayed their summer—the random, unexpected sex, the small signs of affection that had completely disappeared now that they were back in their natural habitat. Never mind Lenore dying, Ava's arm being ripped off, and Carter's untimely dis-appearance. She didn't know what she'd been expecting, but it hadn't been divorce. She didn't feel like she could handle one more thing—not yet anyway.

"I've thought about it too, you know," she said. She jabbed a bite of the greens and sawed through it. "For a while now. I know you're unhappy." What she meant was that they were both un-happy. She just covered hers up better.

Peter's eyes found hers, and she didn't look away. He hadn't looked her in the eye without animosity in so long, but there was nothing there but understanding. "It's not fair to you ei-ther," he said. "I know I haven't been the best partner."

She nodded. He hadn't, but neither had she. He'd funneled all his energy into Jules, into being a good father. But that didn't sustain a marriage. She'd never thought she'd be the kind of woman who stayed just because of a child.

"Before we jump to any decisions, would you be open to talking to someone?" Her therapist hadn't gotten them anywhere, but she figured it was worth one more try. "Just so we can get on the same page and maybe work through logistics? I'd really like us to be amicable. Since we're going to be coparenting." She rolled her eyes, attempting to make the situation lighter.

She fully expected Peter to say no. He hated therapists and

had only obliged attending a few sessions because she'd bad-
gered him into it. He always preferred to be the one asking
questions. Instead, he surprised her when he said yes.

"Do you want me to find someone new? I know you have a lot
on your plate," he said.

She was shocked. "I actually have someone in mind. My therapist recommended him."

"Him?" Peter took another sip of wine.

"Yes, him. Would you be more comfortable with a woman?"

"It doesn't matter," Peter said. "I owe you this."

She moved the food around on her plate. Even if they didn't
work through any old issues, perhaps they could both get closure. Whatever that meant.

They ate in silence. She glanced at Jules's room down the hall,
missing her energy, her enthusiasm, and her kind spirit. Peter
caught her looking and reached across the table to cover her
hand with his own.

"I miss her too," he said. He quickly removed his hand, cleared
his throat, and went back to eating.

Desi wavered between wanting to cry and wanting to scream.
With Peter, she would show neither emotion, instead remaining composed as she always did. She had to show him she was in
control, that even her daughter leaving for college and him asking for a divorce wouldn't be her undoing, just as he wouldn't
reveal that it would be his.

They finished dinner, did the dishes, and separated. Peter
went to his study, and Desi took a hot bubble bath and then did
an hour of work in bed. When she turned off the lights, Peter
wasn't beside her.

For the first time in a while, she didn't mind.

20

Jules

THE party was too loud.

She realized she sounded like a grandma for complaining about the noise, but she couldn't hear herself think. She'd already been in New York a month. While the city seemed to energize most people, it drained her and made her constantly want to take a nap.

Jules did her schoolwork and stayed mostly to herself, though Melanie encouraged her to go out and meet new people. She thought there was no point in making friends since she wouldn't be coming back next semester, but she kept that thought to herself.

The weekends were hard, and after an especially brutal week of core classes, Jules had agreed to go to a party—a decision she immediately regretted as they walked into the three-story house with the Greek letters nailed to the front door.

Jules stayed close to Melanie, until some guy in a backward ball cap and khakis asked Melanie to dance.

Dubstep blasted through the house. People danced and screamed random words into each other's faces. She thought about Will, how they'd first met after she'd literally fallen in the street. He'd asked her for coffee, and they'd talked for hours—real conversation about city life versus mountain life. As the music thumped through her entire body, she realized she'd trade places in an instant to get that moment back.

Jules found the kitchen and poured herself a drink. She sniffed it and took a small sip, thumbing through her phone out of boredom. She'd tried to call Will so many times over this past month, but he never answered. His dismissal was humiliating. She stayed up nights wondering why he didn't answer, if he was over her, if he'd already moved on.

After a few more unanswered texts, she'd taken to stalking him on social media. She pulled up his Instagram now and saw he had no new posts but a few new Stories. She clicked his circular profile photo and watched Will standing on a diving board. He was still tan and strong, and her stomach leaped at the sight of him, bare chested, in fitted swim trunks. He placed both hands in the air, asked for silence, then bounced three times before doing a perfect front flip into the deep end. Jules's stomach lurched as he sliced through the water. She wanted to crawl through her phone and never come back.

He surfaced to a chorus of cheers. In the next frame, he pulled himself out of the pool and some blonde wrapped him in a towel. Jules's stomach dropped. The frame disappeared and the next video was from Will as he talked briefly into the camera. The blonde in the background appeared behind him, giving him bunny ears.

Her breath felt sticky. She rewatched the videos two more times before she pocketed her phone and then ran to the bathroom. She fell to her knees in front of the toilet. The seat was already cocked halfway up, the lip of the bowl splattered with old urine. She retched until her stomach was empty and then sat beside the toilet, her mind twisting and turning with worst-case scenarios.

It had only been a month. How could he have moved on already? Jules grabbed the roll of toilet paper, wiped her mouth, and stared into the mirror. Her face was puffy, her eyes swollen and bloodshot. She didn't think she could feel worse after their breakup. She never should have left.

She stumbled out of the bathroom, the music's bass thumping beneath her shoes. She found the kitchen again and downed cup after cup of the mysterious punch. When a guy started talking to her, she considered kissing him, but thought better of it. To kiss anyone would be a betrayal, even if Will was back in River Falls doing the same thing. When her stomach bucked again, she knew she needed to go back to the dorm and sleep it off.

She searched for Melanie, but couldn't find her. She texted that she was leaving. Outside, a few people were making out on the front steps.

She imagined Will kissing that other girl. A jealous rage swept through her body, sending a fresh wave of nausea rolling through her gut. Desperate, Jules texted Ava. Her voice had been on those videos too. She waited, gnawing on a fingernail, and was surprised when she texted back immediately.

His ex. Lacey. She sucks. Ha. They're just friends. Don't worry, J. Still rooting for you 2. When r u coming back???

Jules read the text again and typed a quick reply before figuring out which way Carmen Hall was. She took a left and walked a few blocks before she realized she'd taken a wrong turn and was on a side street, alone. She pulled out her phone and checked Maps, when a group of boys, probably around her age, appeared around the corner. She moved back against the brick wall to get out of the way, but one of them stopped and turned to her.

"You lost?" one of them asked.

Jules looked up and saw five guys of varying weight and ages. Rather than hurry away, she pushed off the wall and looked him right in the eye as she'd been taught. "No. Are you?" She thumbed her Skeletool in her pocket, as well as pepper spray. Though she'd had too much to drink, her thoughts cleared as adrenaline kicked in.

"Ooh, look at that, boys. We got a feisty one," the shortest one said. His face was pale and freckled, and his shirt squeezed his oversized frame. He slapped a friend on his chest as they circled around her. Jules was almost a head taller than most of them.

"No, not feisty," Jules said. "Prepared." In one move, she brought out the pepper spray and Skeletool. She began spraying the two to her immediate right and gripped the knife in her left hand. The two she sprayed fell to their knees, screaming, while the other three looked at each other uncertainly.

"Let's go, dude."

"Fuck that, man! Look what she just did." One of them lunged at her, and she swung her knife at him, but he caught her wrist. He drove her back against the brick wall, and being drunk, her reaction was too slow. The back of her head slammed against the brick, and she heard a sickening crack. She immediately slid down to the sidewalk. The guy released her in surprise, and the others told him to run.

Jules reached up and felt the warm rush of blood before she saw it. Her head throbbed.

"Hey! Hey, stop!" A man and a woman were walking toward her down the street, and the man took off after the boys, his dress shoes clacking against the pavement. The woman snapped photos and yelled for help. She dropped to her knees.

"Are you hurt?" She wore a beautiful green dress and had eyes that reminded her of Lenore's.

She tried to reply, but couldn't. Her entire body began to tremble, and the woman called 911. Jules couldn't catch her breath.

"Hi, I have a young woman who's been assaulted," the woman explained. She gave the dispatcher the address and rubbed soothing circles on Jules's back. Her world began to spin, and she felt sick. She vomited on the sidewalk again, as the woman yelped in surprise and moved around to the other side.

"It's okay. Help is on the way."

Jules crawled to her hands and knees, and the pain in her head made her gasp. Nothing felt okay. She closed her eyes. Her vision blurred. She reached out a hand to steady herself, but collapsed forward on the pavement. Her cheek scraped the dirty concrete, her teeth clicking together. She fought to stay conscious, then slowly slipped away.

21

Desi

"Do you still want your marriage to work?" The therapist asked the question again.

Desi waited. She certainly didn't want to answer before Peter. He scratched his jaw, which was covered in dark stubble. She was annoyed that he hadn't even shaved for this first meeting.

"I don't think so."

"That's fair," their therapist, Robert, said. "And what are your feelings, Desi?"

She picked at a pillow in her lap and considered her answer. Her eyes roamed the plush space—the comfortable leather couch, the giant window behind them that allowed in a steady stream of buttery light, the rich, dark, wooden bookcases perched on either side of an art deco desk. The lighting was dim, and the room smelled of cinnamon and coffee. It was the perfect environment for confessing her darkest secrets, but for some reason, she'd clammed up the moment she walked through the door. She'd always cared what strangers thought of her, and this was no exception. She wanted to be seen as thoughtful and fair in her marital decisions.

She searched the recesses of her heart for her truest feelings—

not just what she was supposed to feel, do, or say. Finally, she shrugged. "I feel the same way."

"Then you're both on the same page, which is a strong start." Robert scribbled something on a legal pad and flipped the yellow page. "What do you think are the biggest issues facing your marriage today?"

Desi and Peter looked at each other. In the entire season of their marriage, she knew her biggest issue was attempting to knock down the fortress he'd built, which caused her to fixate on her relationship with Carter. She didn't mean to compare them, but she couldn't help it. As the years passed, instead of knowing Peter's every quirk, or being able to finish his sentences, she felt more and more like she lived with a stranger. This summer had shown her flashes of the way things used to be, but even now, those were just fleeting memories that had already started to fade.

"When Jules was little, she used to tell me I had five smiles," Desi suddenly blurted. Both Peter and Robert looked at her, curious. She set the pillow between her and Peter and folded her hands in her lap. "I would be doing random things—washing the dishes, folding laundry, even distractedly listening to something she said, and she would ask: 'What's wrong, Mommy? You have your worried smile.'" Desi's voice wobbled, and she cleared her throat, embarrassed by the sudden emotion. "I would say, 'What do you mean, sweetheart?' And then she would count my smiles off on her little fingers." Desi paused. Her throat burned as she held back tears. "She knew my every mood, what certain expressions meant . . . She paid attention because she cared," Desi explained. She turned to Peter, the rust-orange pillow a barricade between them. "If I asked you about my smiles, you wouldn't be able to tell me." She shrugged. "Somewhere along the way of being parents and running separate businesses, we've lost track of each other." She glanced at Robert. "Like so many marriages, I think we are logistical partners, reactionary even. We don't think of each other as romantic partners first. We coexist, and now that Jules is out of the house, our distance is the loudest thing between us."

Robert nodded, his black glasses sliding a bit down a long blade of nose. "That's perfectly typical of long-term marriages." He pushed them into place. "Peter, how does that make you feel hearing that?"

Peter took a beat, then looked straight ahead at the clock on the wall. "Desi actually has four smiles: one when she's truly excited and isn't thinking about work, one when she's cooking and listening to music, one when she's interacting with clients, and one when . . ." His voice faded and he glanced at her. "One when we're alone, and I touch the tender spot right below her jaw. That smile is my favorite."

Desi looked at him in stunned silence, a knot of longing exploding in her chest. It had been years since something that romantic had come out of his mouth. Why didn't he ever show that he was paying attention or that he cared?

"How many do I have?" Peter asked. His face shifted from engaged to cold, and any warm feelings she'd had instantly dissolved.

Sadly, Desi didn't know the answer. She paid attention to details of her work and so rarely to the people in the room. She felt bad about that. But instead of leaving him with the satisfaction of being right, she responded, "None." She turned her attention back to Robert. "He doesn't ever smile."

She thought of the smile he had given his divorce attorney a couple of weeks ago, and how that had gutted her. But at home, he never smiled. She was so sick of the heaviness, of the dark cloud that followed her no matter where she went. Just once, she wished he would roll out of bed, tell her a bright good morning, and give her a kiss. But no. He walked around as if the world owed him something, as if his burdens were the heaviest to bear. And no matter what she did, it was never right. If she worked too hard, she wasn't being an attentive enough wife or mother. If she tried to be more present, she was high maintenance and didn't like the same things he liked, so he'd get frustrated and tell her to forget it. Neither of them could ever just be themselves.

"Ever?" Robert asked.

"He won't even look at me when we have sex," she said suddenly. "He makes me face the other way."

Peter inhaled and stood. "I think we're done here." He stormed out the door, and Desi clutched her purse and stood.

"Same time next week?" Desi had been the one to push for therapy and here she was, acting like an infant. Maybe she wasn't capable of being open and honest with Peter. Didn't that tell her everything she needed to know?

Robert nodded and showed her to the door.

In the hallway, Peter paced, and stabbed the elevator button three times in a row.

"You know that doesn't make it come faster," she said as she checked her phone. "I don't know why people do that."

"I don't know why *you* just did that," he snapped. "You made me sound like a complete asshole in there."

"I didn't make you sound like anything," she said. "I told the truth." The elevator doors parted and she stepped in and held the door. "Coming?"

Peter grudgingly stepped inside, and all the fight deflated from her body as quickly as it had filled. "I just want to know why you're so angry all the time, why you never seem happy," she said.

"I am happy."

"Not when I'm around."

He shrugged.

They stood on opposite sides of the elevator as it lowered toward the lobby. Desi had the sudden urge to pull the emergency button and trap them both inside until they could work this out. But she didn't, because this wasn't some movie where everything worked out in the end. This was life, and their marriage was complicated. When the doors opened, Peter stormed ahead of her. She followed behind, her heels clicking on the alabaster tile.

When she got outside, Peter had already disappeared. They'd arrived here separately. Desi checked her watch. She didn't want to go home and thought about calling Beth for a drink.

She walked for a bit, wandering around the jammed Chicago streets. A nip was in the air, indicative of the winter weather to come.

She walked east until she hit the lake and slipped off her shoes to step onto a grassy patch near the water. She watched the glittering blue, wondering why she didn't come here more often.

She texted Beth, and they decided to meet at a nearby pub. She tried to ignore the fact that she was in Carter's neighborhood. Immediately, her nerves began to fray, and she almost texted Beth to cancel. Outside the bar, she waited, thumbing through her work emails.

"Desi?"

She looked up to see a somewhat familiar-looking blonde. She had that raw, worn look of someone who'd lived a tough life. Her clothes were shabby chic and she smelled like cigarettes. Desi pushed away from the wall she'd been leaning on and dropped her phone into her purse.

"I'm sorry. Do we know each other?"

"Haley," the woman said. "Carter's fiancée."

Fiancée. Desi tried to keep her face calm, but her hands began to shake. "Have we met?"

"No." The woman fished a cigarette from her cross-body bag and lit up, exhaling into the clear sky. "But he talked about you a lot, so I looked you up on social." She said it without any self-consciousness, then squinted at her as she inhaled, the end of the cigarette burning orange. She pointed to her, a thick puff of smoke trailing past her face. "He was crazy about you, you know."

Fuck. Desi considered what to say. If Carter had told his current girlfriend they'd had a relationship, who else knew? "Well, that was a long time ago," she said. She feigned looking in her purse so she wouldn't feel the intensity of Haley's gaze. "How is he, by the way?" She blinked at Haley, everything inside her screaming what a liar she was.

She snorted. "Took off. Typical." She waved a hand through the smoke. "Easier to run away than to face the fact he didn't want to commit." She flashed a tiny diamond on her left ring finger. Her nails were chewed and painted a deep purple. "We were engaged. Guess he got cold feet."

Desi opened her mouth, the knife twisting deeper. "Congratulations," she said. She shifted from foot to foot, practically willing Beth to appear and rescue her. "So you haven't heard from him at all?" She didn't want to reveal she'd seen the missing person report.

"I reported him missing actually." She laughed again and propped her arm with the cigarette above the other, as if she was a genie about to grant a wish. "The bastard. He probably gets off on the attention." Now Haley leaned against the wall, digging a combat boot into the brick. "It wasn't going to work anyway."

"Oh?" Desi could barely swallow, could barely breathe. "Why's that?"

"Because he's still in love with you." She flicked an inch of ash at her feet. Desi jumped back, avoiding it. "Maybe you two will live happily ever after. If he ever comes back," she added.

Before Desi could respond, Beth trotted up, lifting both hands. Her sleek bob rustled in the wind, her silken blouse showing off her curvy frame. "Sorry I'm late! Twin emergency." She rolled her eyes, kissed Desi on the cheek, and eyed Haley. "Oh, I'm sorry. Am I interrupting?"

"Nope." Haley stood upright and ground her cigarette beneath her boot. "See you around, Desiree." Haley walked off, her slim hips swaying.

Desi felt dizzy and clung to Beth's arm to steady herself.

"Whoa, are you okay?" She assessed Haley. "Who was that?"

"That was Carter's girlfriend," Desi said. "Or should I say fiancée." Even though she'd heard they were engaged, she'd foolishly hoped it might not be true. "Did you know they were engaged?"

Beth shook her head and snorted. "Maybe that's why he disappeared?"

Desi faked a smile. "Maybe."

"Come on. Wine is calling my name." Beth held open the sticky wooden door and Desi stepped inside the dimly lit pub.

"Will you excuse me for a moment?" Desi walked briskly to the bathroom, washed her hands, and stared at her reflection. Could Haley see the longing in her eyes? Her words repeated in her head: *he's still in love with you*. She balled the stiff paper towel and tossed it into the trash. So he hadn't hidden his feelings for her the way she had for him all these years. Even his fiancée knew he loved someone else.

Yes, she'd had more at stake than Carter ever did, but she didn't care anymore. She wanted another chance.

She just had to find him first.

22

Jules

"LOOK who's awake," the nurse said. "How are you feeling?"

Jules tried to swallow. Her mouth was dry and had a funny, rubbery taste. She reached up to touch the back of her head, and the nurse interjected.

"Don't touch it, sweetheart. Ten stitches. It's going to be sore for a while."

Ten stitches? Jesus. She rested back on her pillow and tried to piece the fragments of the night together.

"You're lucky. The couple who was walking caught all those boys. Other bystanders restrained them until the cops came. Whoever raised you certainly taught you how to take care of yourself, young lady."

Jules attempted to nod, but couldn't. Had they pumped her stomach too? She no longer felt drunk, just woozy. Was she going to get in trouble for underage drinking? She wondered if they'd already notified her parents. *Shit.* She groaned and tried to sit up.

"Doc will be in in a second, sweetie. Hang tight."

Jules adjusted the pillow behind her. Her entire body hurt.

She closed her eyes and must have drifted off when a booming doctor's voice shook her awake.

"Ms. Wright, I'm Dr. Standler." He grabbed her chart and scanned it. His large belly protruded from his open doctor's coat, and his skin was ruddy and pocked, most likely an unpleasant reminder from teenage acne. "Quite the night you had, I see."

"Something like that," she croaked.

He clicked his pen, checked her vitals. "I'm going to write you a pain prescription, but no refills." He ripped off the page and handed her discharge papers. "I don't have to tell you that you're not of legal age to drink. Just be careful, okay? You've got plenty of time to party."

She almost rolled her eyes and took the paperwork. "So I'm free to go?"

"The police have come to take your statement. They're right outside."

She nodded, waited until he was gone, and changed out of her hospital gown. A few minutes later, Melanie burst into the room, her eyes glassy, the tip of her nose bright red.

"Oh my God, are you okay? What happened?"

Jules was too tired to talk, but gave her the basic details.

Melanie crushed her in a hug, which made her head throb even more. She reeked of booze. "O-M-F-G, I am so sorry! I never should have asked you to come to that stupid party."

"Melanie, it's fine. I shouldn't have walked home alone. I went down a side street." Ever since Will had broken up with her, she'd been acting recklessly. She knew it wasn't safe to walk home alone, but she'd done it anyway. She had to start thinking more clearly.

"But New York has become, like, the safest city in the world or something. I just can't believe this *happened* to you!" She rubbed her arm, and Jules politely pulled away.

"I'm fine," she said again. She pulled on her shirt, which brushed the tender part of her head. She winced and looked around the room to make sure she had everything.

"There's a major scene out there. You're, like, famous. It's all over the news."

"The news?" Jules looked at her, confused. "Why would it be on the news?"

"Because you fought off five total douchebags with your cool knife and pepper spray. You're, like, a goddess, Wright! Wait until everyone at school hears about this. Holy shit. Queen Bee for life."

Jules didn't want any more attention. She didn't even want to press charges, though she knew she should. No woman should ever be approached by guys like that. Still, she didn't want to relive what happened. She just wanted to go back to her room, pack up her stuff, and call it a day. But she had eight more weeks to hold up her end of the bargain before she could get back to River Falls.

Back to Will.

Her stomach tightened thinking about that Instagram Story. She trusted what Ava had texted and only hoped what she'd seen on that video was innocent. Still, it wasn't like Will to even post on social media. At first, when he'd started posting, she'd thought it had been for her benefit—a way they could passively see each other. But maybe it wasn't.

In the hall, two police officers and the couple who'd helped her were in deep conversation. They turned when she exited, and Jules offered a smile under the garish lights. She answered the police questions, happy to send Melanie to get snacks from the vending machine to get her to stop talking, and then personally thanked the couple. She was just signing out when her nurse waddled toward her, her shoes squeaky on the waxed linoleum.

"Ms. Wright, can I see you for a second?"

"Sure." She paid her copay and walked a few steps to the left.

"We're going to have to rewrite your prescription," she said.

"Why?" Jules asked. She knew so many kids who got addicted to opioids, but she probably wouldn't even take them. She hated medicine.

"Because we just got your bloodwork back," she said, distractedly. She ripped off a new prescription and pressed it into her palm. "You're five weeks pregnant."

WINTER

23

Desi

DESI stood in her penthouse kitchen and fidgeted with her Cartier watch.

The encrusted diamonds erupted in a radiant explosion from the overhead pendant lights. She downed her second cup of coffee and slipped the stack of design books off the edge of the island and fanned them back onto the coffee table in the living room. She assessed the order. Her phone vibrated with a work email, disturbing her solitude, and she cringed at the time.

"Peter! We need to go!"

Down the hall, his deep voice belted an off-key tune in their oversized steam shower.

She crossed the living room, bypassed the kitchen, and entered their master. "Peter, we're late." She adjusted her blouse in the bathroom mirror and gave herself a once-over. She'd lost her tan from summer, but it felt good to have regained her city pace these last few months.

He peered around the wall of beveled glass, beads of water marring her clean floor. "Late for what? It's our house, Des."

She rested one manicured hand on the vanity. "I hate to drive with snow on the way. Especially with all those winding roads."

"It'll be fine." He went back to singing.

She focused on his freckles, leftovers from early summer. They scattered across the arc of his deltoids, down his spine, and stopped a few inches above his ass.

She padded down the concrete hall, appreciating each light fixture picked by hand, the Ralph Lauren paint, Silver Plated, RL Number: RM13, the Kartell furniture she'd curated, bought, and staged. She cleared her throat and knocked on Jules's door.

This was the first time Jules had been home since she'd left for Columbia in the fall. After her attack, Desi had called her almost daily, but Jules never answered. She still blamed Desi for the breakup, and much to her disappointment, time away hadn't lessened her anger.

Jules had already been home for a week, and her open-door policy was now closed; her normally chatty recaps at dinner had morphed into stabbing whatever was on her plate and swirling it around like soup. Desi knew she was still angry, but she hoped River Falls would put her in a good mood again.

"Jules?" She knocked again lightly and waited.

Jules's feet thumped on the shag before she slid open the pocket door. "It's open."

"You ready?" Her question knifed the empty room, and Jules grabbed her suitcase and rolled it into the hallway. She studied her daughter. She'd gained a little weight and was paler than usual. All that vitality she'd had in River Falls seemed to have been sucked away.

Was it entirely her fault?

A few minutes later, Peter emerged in pressed jeans and a well-worn sweater, slightly pilled. "Everyone excited?" He fastened his watch.

Desi considered the question. Below them, city life bloomed. There was something about walking down the city streets, latte in hand, that made her feel electric. All those people around her, with their dreams and tasks, even if they weren't saying a word. She needed the energy of this city, but it was clear Peter and Jules did not. She tried to remind herself that winter was coming, and with it, lots of gray days and brutal wind. At least in River Falls they'd be on top of a mountain and get to enjoy the snow.

When it was clear no one was answering Peter's question, Jules slipped off the gold-plated barstool Desi had flown in from France and looked between them. "Are we doing this or what?"

They all rolled their suitcases into the elevator, which led down to their reserved spot, number 517, in the cold, cavernous garage.

The cooler air screamed through the interior as doors opened and smacked shut. The bags stowed, Peter revved the engine and pulled out onto Fulton Market, past the string of niche businesses: Google, Publican Quality Meats, Summit Design + Build, Facebook. Desi remembered when they'd bought their loft before this area had become so popular, when it was just the fish market and a few delis. The neighborhood used to stink, men in stained aprons spraying fish guts from the blood-slicked streets. Now, it was full of hipsters, techies, and multimillionaires.

Desi flipped down her passenger visor and caught Jules's reflection in the back. She was listening to music and seemed so pensive. Lost. Sad.

As they drove, she unpacked the last few months. While Jules rarely called from New York, she had been chatting with Tommy, since he'd been staying at The Black House. Desi got her weekly downloads from him and from spying on social media. Though it looked like Jules was taking an active part in college, she never looked as happy as she'd been during the summer with Will. She'd been doing other sorts of spying too—desperately trying to find out about Carter. He'd disconnected his phone. She assumed he'd gotten a new one. It was evident, from his silence, that he didn't want to be found. Still, she couldn't help worrying that something bad had happened to him, though his missing person report had long since grown cold.

Hours into the ride, Desi turned down the radio. "Does Will know you're coming?"

Jules gazed out the window, headphones on. Desi turned around in her seat and gently waved a hand to get her attention. Jules cocked one of her headphones away from her ear.

"I asked if Will knows you're coming?"

Jules gritted her teeth and sighed. "Why do you care?"

Desi thought about letting it rest, but pressed on. "Of course I care. It's not like I thought you two would never see each other again."

Jules shot her a cold, hard look, then snapped her headphones back into place, signaling their talk was over.

Desi turned around. She thought they'd made such progress that day at the funeral, and then she'd ruined it by talking to Will. How might things have panned out if she'd just stayed out of it? Did she really know what was best for her daughter?

She adjusted her legs in the seat. Already, she was itching to stretch. She glanced over at Peter, who was lost in thought, his hands firmly at ten and two. Gone were the days of road trips where they would talk for hours about their plans, or sing songs with Jules in the back, or answer that ever-annoying question: Are we there yet? There was no use pretending anymore.

She flipped through the radio until she found something to take her mind off the silence, closed her eyes, and reclined her seat. "I'm going to try and take a quick nap."

Her thoughts shot back and forth, from concern to panic to curiosity. She opened her eyes and peered at Peter. She studied his strong profile, his square shoulders, the firm line of his mouth.

She was so tired of being in limbo. It was time to move forward with their lives. They were technically separated, though, due to the sky-high Chicago rent, they'd been living together and operating on separate schedules. She'd made a deal with herself that they wouldn't leave The Black House until one of them had decided to file for divorce.

She didn't know why they were stalling, as it was clear their marriage was beyond repair. For some reason, Desi didn't want to be the one to file. Somewhere, in the recesses of her brain, she thought Peter would use that decision against her; that he would spin the story to tell all their friends she was the one who wanted out. She was the one who wanted to break up their family. She was the one to blame.

But wasn't she?

Exhausted by her own mental combat, Desi shut her eyes and surrendered the worries. She had weeks to figure out what to do next.

She just needed a little more time.

24

Jules

JULES carved ribbons on the ice.

The mountain air cleansed her lungs. After spending a semester in New York City, she felt dirty, like she needed to be scrubbed clean from the inside. She opened her arms, her red mittens reminding her of something a little girl might wear. She rotated backward and heard the steady scrape of her blades as she flew across the ice. Her cheeks were frozen, but she felt more alive in that moment than she had during the last few months. She'd missed this place, the air, the *space*.

She turned again and skated to the middle of the ice. As a kid, she'd taken figure skating lessons. She'd loved it, but when her coach told her mother she had real promise, Desi hadn't been able to take her to the early-morning practices before school. Jules used to blame her mother for that, but now she realized her mom had essentially been a single parent and done the best she could. By the time her father retired from the Marines and was around to help, Jules had lost interest and moved on to other things. She always seemed to move on to other interests, mastering what she could before trying something new. She placed a protective hand over her belly. But a baby . . . a baby she wouldn't be able to quit.

She launched into a combination spin and lowered into a sit spin. Her ankle wobbled and she landed on her butt. She slowed her breath and lay back. The fuzzy white sky was crammed with oversized snowflakes. She closed her eyes as they peppered her cheeks. Her clothes warmed the frozen pond beneath her.

She thought about her mother's question: *Does Will know you're coming?*

Not only did he not know she was coming, he didn't know what she had to tell him. Her hands once again rested lightly on her stomach. She was still not used to the idea of being pregnant and hadn't made up her mind about what she wanted to do. The idea of becoming a mother this young frightened her, but the idea of giving up something she'd made with Will seemed preposterous.

After a few more futile attempts to get in touch with Will, he'd made it clear he needed space. She could have pulled her trump card and told him she was pregnant, but she wanted him to *want* to talk.

She longed for their drawn-out lazy summer afternoons, their time at the waterfall, their long walks and talks, or even drifting asleep in each other's arms. Sometimes she wondered if she'd imagined it all, or if she'd ever feel that way again.

She'd kept everything inside for the last few months and now . . . now, she needed to see Will. She needed to know if that last day they'd spent together had been a product of her mother's doing—if Desi had scared the shit out of him, or even lied—or if breaking up with her had been what he actually wanted.

She caught a few snowflakes on her tongue, flapping her arms up and down to make a snow angel on the ice. Something about this movement cracked apart her sorrow, and she bit back tears.

She was tired of being so unhappy. She'd done what her mother insisted she do, and now it was time to do what *she* wanted. Jules pulled herself up, made one more lap around the pond, and then stepped off the ice and retrieved her shoes hanging from a sturdy tree branch.

She quickly changed, the cold soaking into her feet, and tossed her skates over one shoulder to trek back to the house. The land looked so much different in winter. Whereas Chicago seemed peaceful when it first snowed, the city would immediately turn gray and slushy, bundled commuters braving the vicious wind to get to their destinations. Here, the rich greenery of summer had morphed into an even richer white. The ivory-tipped trees sagged with snow. No matter how heavy they got, the branches would still hold themselves up, resilient, strong. The silence roared, filling her with peace.

As Jules trudged through the snow, she thought again about Lenore's request. Had Will already scattered the ashes? Though it made her sick to think about flying, she'd do it for Lenore.

She neared The Black House and thought about Ava. She felt terrible that she'd pretty much stopped talking to her too beyond a random text, but it seemed awkward to continue their relationship once Will broke it off.

Hadn't she learned that from her parents? Just sweep it all under the rug and hope it went away?

She didn't want to be like her parents. She didn't want to pretend. She didn't want all the sacrifices that came with a life like theirs. She wanted real, messy, honest, complicated love. And that meant having hard conversations.

She approached The Black House and shook the snow from her parka and boots. Inside, Tommy, Desi, and Peter were having their morning coffee. She could see their profiles in the kitchen, talking. Jules closed the front door silently behind her. The fire crackled from the living room as a mountain of white pushed up against the windows. She removed her boots, dropped her skates by the door, and headed straight to her room. She showered, changed, and fastened Will's necklace before assessing her reflection.

She was going to get her life back.

In the hall, she scribbled a note, swiped Tommy's keys, and stuffed her feet into her boots, still damp from the march through the snow. She crunched through the gravel and climbed behind the wheel of Tommy's Chevy Silverado. She hadn't yet driven down the mountain by herself, but she couldn't wait.

Carefully, she turned on the truck, flipping on the heat and waiting for it to thaw. Snowflakes attacked the windshield, turning it downy white. When the truck was warm, she flicked on the wipers and slowly navigated down the gravel toward the paved path. At the end of the driveway, she waited as the gate groaned open. She peered in her rearview, almost expecting someone to chase after her.

She took a right and drove to the main road, which sloped in a lazy circle down the mountain. She used caution on every curve, holding her breath. The roads were slick in spots. Her anxiety tensed her hands on the wheel as she continued down, mile by mile, until she came to the mouth of the mountain and exhaled.

She drove the short distance toward downtown and parked in front of Lenore's boutique. The city was already decorated for the holidays, with a congested web of lights strung over the main strip, extending from one side of the street to the other. Red bows, oversized bells, and garland clung to most storefronts and made Jules think of a Hallmark movie.

Jules glimpsed the frosted OPEN sign in the boutique window. She took a deep breath, locked the car, and went inside.

A woman behind the desk greeted her. Not Ava. She stepped farther into the boutique, sifting through the racks of clothes, dragging her fingers along garments Lenore had chosen to stock. She missed her so much, even though she'd known her for such a short time. Lenore had believed in her, and right now, she needed that kind of courage.

She perused the empty shop. Maybe Ava didn't even work here anymore? She was just about to give up when Ava emerged from the back with a rack of clothes in her left hand. Jules watched from a distance as she hung the clothes in their appropriate places. Her hair was longer and was now dirty blond instead of purple. Her earrings had been removed, her face wiped bare. Jules's gaze drifted toward her arm, but she was wearing a furry rainbow sweater.

"Ava?"

Ava turned, distracted, and her entire face changed when she saw Jules. She went from stunned to elated in a second and crushed her in a fierce hug. "You're back!" She held her at arm's length and Jules laughed. God, she'd missed her energy.

"Oh my God, tell me everything about New York. Patty, I'm going on break!" Ava was a hummingbird, flitting around the shop, grabbing her coat and hat while talking a thousand miles a minute. They walked in the bitter cold until they came to the diner, and Ava waved to the owner, Johnny, as she steered Jules to a booth in the back.

Ava had yet to take a breath. She only stopped when the waitress came over to fill their water and take their drink orders. Jules pushed her menu aside and folded her hands in her lap.

"You look so great, Ava." Jules was relieved to see she'd returned to her same bubbly self.

"Thanks. So do you."

Jules said thanks, though she felt washed out and overly tired. Jules asked about her arm, which was slow to improve, but getting there. Ava pumped her for details of college and New York. Jules filled her in on the campus, the people, her classes, if she had any cute professors (two), and then she asked about Bricks, Lindsay, her boyfriend, and the twins. It seemed nothing had really changed, which made her feel comforted somehow. She stared out the window while Ava ordered food. How had her mother ever convinced her to leave this place?

Jules waited until the waitress walked away to ask about Will. Ava glanced at her watch. "Fifteen minutes until you asked about my brother. I'm impressed."

Jules sighed. "How is he? Really?"

Ava folded her hands on the table. "He's . . . sad, Jules. He's really sad."

Jules was gutted to hear it. She didn't want Will to be sad. "Lenore?"

Ava nodded and rotated her coffee cup on the table. "Of course, Mom, but mostly you, Jules. He misses you."

Jules felt something crack open in her chest: pain, longing, desire, uncertainty, fear. All of it oozed into her body like white-hot energy, a full-on resuscitation. "Has he actually said that?"

Ava narrowed her eyebrows. "Jules, he's been moping around since the moment you left. He hasn't been the same. So . . ." She leaned forward and wrapped both hands around her mug. "Now that you're here, can you please fix it? You guys are meant to be together, so stop Romeo and Julietting this situation and just get married and live happily ever after already."

Jules laughed. "Did you just use my name as a verb?"

"Duh, dude." She leaned back as the waitress brought twin

platters of eggs, toast, and bacon. Jules stared out the window again, wondering if what Ava said was true.

"But I tried to contact him. A bunch. He never responded," she finally admitted. What she didn't admit was how many nights she'd cried herself to sleep because of it.

"Look, your mom scared the shit out of him, okay?" Ava took a heaping bite of eggs and washed it down with coffee. "She made it seem like he'd be single-handedly responsible for fucking up your entire academic career if you stayed. You know Will. He would never do anything to mess up your life."

Jules winced. So this truly *was* her mother's doing. "Will wasn't messing up my life. He gave my life purpose."

Ava mimed throwing up and then crunched into a piece of bacon.

Jules's stomach bucked. "So if I call him . . ."

She chewed and swallowed. "I'll make sure he answers."

"And your mom's ashes . . ."

She wiped her mouth and took another swig of coffee. "He hasn't done it yet. He'd never say it, but I think he was waiting— or rather *hoping*—that you'd come back. Plus, this is techni- cally the first big snowfall of the year. And you're here. So." Ava smiled. A bit of egg was lodged between her front teeth. Jules pointed it out, and they both started laughing.

"A true friend. Thanks for not letting me walk around like a complete asshole."

Jules's heart felt like it might explode, from both happiness and relief. "Where is he now?"

"Working, unfortunately. He got a job flying private planes for North Carolina's elite, so he's been gone a lot. But he's sched- uled to get back home tomorrow for like a week or two, I think? He's getting his own place, but he keeps postponing it."

Will was getting his own place? An entire fantasy unraveled

in her head, but she knocked it away. Tomorrow. She would see Will tomorrow. No matter what.

They finished and paid. On the way out, Jules swiped a book of matches and stuffed them in her pocket.

"Did you take up smoking?" Ava joked.

"No, I collect matches from all the places I've been." She shrugged. "My nana used to be a collector." She remembered when she was little, her nana had kept giant fishbowls full of matches from all the places she and Gramps had traveled together. Jules used to shake them up and reach her hand in with eyes closed, vowing to visit the same faraway places someday.

Jules walked Ava back to the shop, the locals going blissfully about their day. Cars loaded with snowboards and skis parked in town, their passengers running into a cafe to grab coffee before making the arduous climb to the slopes.

"I'm really glad you're back," Ava said. "River Falls hasn't been the same without you."

Jules pulled her into a fierce hug. "I'll see you soon." She climbed back into the truck and drove back up the mountain.

No longer was she fueled by anxiety.

Instead, there was only sheer anticipation.

25

Desi

DESI curled up in the armchair adjacent to the fireplace.

The fire roared, and she stared at the snow outside. It collected in great clumps and blanketed the yard, the pool, and even the patio. Her thoughts had quieted from the drive up, and she was beginning to sink into the solitude of this place once again. Peter and Tommy sat across from her, reading the paper and sipping coffee.

Suddenly, Jules banged through the front door, Tommy's keys in her fist. He turned around in the recliner.

"Hey, kiddo." He eyed his keys. "Go for a ride?"

Jules stood in the foyer, snow sloughing onto her clean floors. Before Desi could tell her to clean it up, Jules's eyes turned razor sharp as they focused on her.

"I needed to see Ava," Jules said.

A small pit began to form and blossom. Desi had been waiting for this conversation for months. "And how was that?"

"It was really interesting, Mom." Jules practically spat. "She pretty much confirmed what I'd thought about your little conversation with Will being the *entire* reason he broke up with me."

Peter and Tommy looked at her. Desi had never told Peter

she'd gone to see Will, or that she'd convinced him to break up with Jules. Now, it was all coming out, yet another secret she'd been unwilling to share.

Desi adjusted to look her daughter in the eye. "You're right. I did have a conversation with Will. But I didn't tell him to break up with you. I simply told him to consider what was best for your future."

Jules smacked her hand on a side table, sloshing a tepid cup of coffee that rested there. "Bullshit!" she screamed. "You have no idea what's best for me or my future." She gestured wildly around The Black House. "This place is what's best for me! River Falls. My friends. Will." She took a step farther into the living room and dropped her voice. "I've been miserable in New York. I got attacked. I hate . . ." She started to say something, then reconsidered. "I hate it there."

What she really meant was that she hated *her*.

Jules had never spoken to her this way. Desi searched for something to say. But what could she say, really? She wasn't one for a public scene, even if the spectators were her own family. "We can talk about this later," she finally said.

Jules laughed. The sound was bitter rolling off her lips. "You know, you talk such a big game about being open, but you guys sweep everything under the rug. You think I don't notice?" She stared between her parents. "Your marriage is shit, and you don't even care. Just end it already!"

"Watch your mouth, young lady," Peter warned.

She ignored him and pressed on. "You think I can't make my own decisions, that I can't possibly know what I want because I'm only eighteen? I know the time I spent with Will's family was the most loved I have *ever* felt. They didn't judge me, or pressure me, or make me into some sort of survivalist freak." Immediately, Jules looked remorseful and glanced at her father, who was clearly wounded. "They weren't obsessed with making everything around them so perfect and cold. They were warm and real, and I wish I had a family like that, not stuck here with you." Jules directed those last words at Desi, and Desi felt their impact like a bullet to the heart.

Is that what they had done? Was Jules simply the product of her and Peter's demented realities?

"Alright, kid. That's enough." Tommy hopped up and guided Jules to her room. The bedroom door shut, but Jules's voice reverberated, still riled, through the walls.

Desi sat in stunned silence. Was Jules right? Peter stared at his lap and finally sighed and ripped a hand through his hair. "Desi, why did you do that?"

Desi crushed a hand against her chest. "Me? Did you hear her?" She gestured toward her room. "I didn't do anything."

"With Will." His face was cold, and she could already sense more resentment building, yet another marital strike. "You never told me you went to talk to him. You had no right to do that."

"I had no right to keep our daughter from making a monumental mistake? Peter, listen to yourself. Can you honestly tell me you were okay with her giving up her entire future to stay here and play house with her brand-new boyfriend? She's eighteen, not twenty-eight! Her life is just beginning. Why am I the villain, when I know you were thinking the same thing?"

"You don't know what I think," Peter said.

"You're right!" Desi stood, her entire body trembling. "I don't, because you never fucking talk. You never say what's going on." Desi bypassed him and stopped at the entrance to the kitchen and turned. "Jules may be eighteen, but she is brilliant. She has an exceptional mind, and she's not going to waste it. She could do anything with her life, and she needs to explore her potential."

"Maybe this *is* her potential," Peter said. "Don't you see that? She's not you. She's not me. She gets to choose. Not everything has to look the way you want it to."

"Nothing looks the way I want it to," Desi said.

Tommy slipped into the room, sensed the tension, and bypassed them both, going into the kitchen. She followed after him to refill her coffee. Tommy eased onto one of the kitchen island stools, hands folded. "Want my two cents?"

She topped off her cup and turned, blew the steam away, and leaned against the counter. "I'm going to get it whether I want it or not, right?"

"Yep." He paused. "Look, the more you try and dictate her life, the worse it's going to be. Remember how Mom was with you?" He whistled. "She couldn't have kept you away from your boyfriends if her life depended on it. You were so certain of yourself, of what you wanted, even back then."

"But I didn't know," she said. "That's the thing. Love is blinding. You think your whole life is wrapped up in this person, and then you wake up twenty years later, and realize you could have had a different life." Her voice faded, and she was embarrassed by her own admission. Carter flashed through her mind. She might not have known what she wanted at eighteen, but she had at twenty. Was there really such a difference?

"Look, if you want a relationship with her, you have to actually listen to what she's saying. Even if it's what you don't want to hear."

"It's never what I want to hear," Desi joked.

Tommy drummed his fingers on the table. "You're playing the wrong game, Des."

Desi studied her brother. "Is this a game?"

He was quiet and shrugged. He'd shaved off that God-awful mustache and instead had the hint of two-day stubble. He scraped his fingers along his jaw, then hopped up, patting her on the shoulder. "It's all going to be fine."

She scoffed as he exited the room. Dumping the rest of her coffee in the sink, she attempted to clear her mind. But she was too jittery and didn't need something else to make her anxious. She stared out the window into the woods, all of the trees immovable white sticks.

"You need to go talk to her, Des."

She bristled at Peter's sudden presence behind her. She gripped both sides of the sink and squeezed. "Please don't tell me what I need to do. I'm her mother." She whipped around. "And what she said is right. About our marriage." She motioned between them. "We need to figure this out once and for all."

He was silent, per usual, but nodded. "First things first." He jerked his head toward Jules's room.

She padded down the hall and knocked on her daughter's door. She waited but heard nothing. She tried the knob, and to her surprise, it twisted open. She cracked the door and saw Jules curled up in bed, a purple pillow hugged to her chest.

Desi's heart tugged. No matter how old she got, she still had the terrible habit of seeing Jules as that same little girl whose every problem she could solve with a hug or a kiss. But she wasn't six anymore, and Desi needed to step back and give her child space before she lost her completely.

"Can I come in?"

Jules remained silent. Desi sat on the corner of her bed. "Look, I never should have gone to Will behind your back. I know that."

Jules rolled over, her face tearstained. Her skin was pale and bloated, and she didn't look anything like her strong, confident daughter.

Desi's heart lurched. "Oh, honey. I know this is hard, and I'm so sorry if I pushed you into doing something you didn't want to do. I guess I just thought that deep down you wanted to go to college, because you'd worked so hard. And that even if you were tired from high school, that once you got there, you'd realize it was the right choice."

Jules sat up and dragged the pillow into her lap. "I never really wanted to go to college," she said. "I tried to give it a chance, but it's not for me, Mom."

Desi bit her lip and wanted to tell her she had no idea what she wanted. She'd only given college three lousy months. That wasn't enough. Every freshman had to find their footing, carve out their own path. It took years to gain that kind of self-awareness. Then, after four years, she'd come away with knowledge that she would never gain playing house in a place like this.

She looked at her impressionable daughter and wanted to scream that what she thought she wanted at eighteen would change so rapidly by the time she was twenty-eight and then thirty-eight. Teenagers weren't blessed with the foresight to know how they would feel years from now. It's why it made it so impossible to convince them otherwise. She'd raised Jules to be an independent thinker, and here she was, exerting that in the biggest way possible, which also meant throwing everything away for a summer romance.

"Look, we can figure out what happens next, but I just need you to know how sorry I am for coming between you and Will. That's all I care about right now. That you hear my apology."

Jules crossed her legs and pulled the pillow over her stomach. "Thank you for saying that."

"And also, what you said about me and Dad . . ." She hesitated, then pushed forward. "You're right. We haven't been in a good place for a long time." She scratched her head, then dropped her hand. "I thought the time alone might be good for us. We saw a therapist for a while." She didn't tell her that was due to Peter hiring a divorce attorney, but she wanted her to know they'd been putting effort into it.

"Did that help?"

She laughed. "Not really. I think we're leaning toward divorce."

Desi braced herself for the impact, but Jules only nodded. Of course she wasn't surprised—she probably felt relief. Desi reached forward and ran her fingers over the pendant Will had given her. "Are you going to see him?"

"I hope so."

"You should call him."

"We'll see." She sighed, and in that sigh, Desi glimpsed all the pain she'd caused her daughter, just by needing to be right.

Desi needed to focus less on her daughter's life and get a grip on her own before it spun out of control, and she was left with no one. She kissed Jules on the forehead and then left her room, feeling utterly drained.

She searched for Peter in the kitchen, but didn't find him. She stood in the center of her house, alone. A piece of wood from the fireplace popped, and she moved to throw another log on.

As she pushed the embers around with the poker, she wondered how she'd gotten here. This was not how she'd pictured *her* life turning out when she was just eighteen. Her current reality served as the ultimate cautionary tale, but Jules would have to travel her own path.

Hopefully Jules's journey would be one filled with more truth and honor than hers. Maybe that's what this was really all about—

wanting her daughter to choose differently, to be more honest, to let her secrets fly.

To not make the same stupid mistakes.

She knew to move forward, she had to let Carter go for now. She couldn't fixate on where he was or why he'd disappeared.

Give up the ghost.

The words ballooned in her heart, along with the actual truth no one knew. There'd been more than one reason she'd kept Carter away all those years . . .

As long as he was gone, her real secret was safe.

26

Jules

I need to see you.

Early the next morning, she typed the text and chewed on her cuticle.

She waited for Will's reply, tearing through the flesh around another nail until she tasted blood. She grabbed a tissue and dabbed her sore cuticle. The text bubbles appeared, then vanished. She held her breath, waited. Nothing.

Frustrated, she threw her phone on the bed and paced her room. She stared at the drawing of the old farmhouse and sighed. She'd been such a naïve girl at the start of summer, taping her drawings to the walls and hoping to just unwind before college. Who knew she'd fall in love and get her heart broken? And then spend the last three months wishing she could turn back time?

She rotated back to her bed and stared at her phone. She should just call him. What was she so afraid of?

She was afraid of being rejected as easily as he'd rejected her in August. It was like Will and her mother could crawl into her heart and see what was written there. They'd already determined what she needed, when only *she* understood what she wanted. Even with the time away, Will still burned in her heart like the brightest ember.

Her phone buzzed from the duvet. She lunged for it.

There's a big snowfall headed our way. I was thinking of taking Mom's ashes up before it hits. If you want to come, we can talk then.

She studied his words, confused. He owed her a real conversation. Why couldn't they go to his house or the diner first? She didn't want her first exchange with him to be thousands of feet in the air.

She sat with the phone in her hand for a while, uncertain of how to reply. She wanted to tell him so much: That she'd written him a letter every day. That she'd taken a million pictures to chronicle everything about New York. That she'd gone on long hikes upstate and searched for waterfalls. That every time she passed a diner or an old Chevy, she thought of him. That she wore his necklace every single day.

She wanted to type back OK, but hesitated. Could she get on a plane? Even the thought made her nauseous. She weighed her options and settled for a compromise. *I'd really like to talk to you first. You owe me that.* She pressed send before she could change her mind. The text bubbles appeared and disappeared in their agonizingly slow march before he finally replied.

Be there in 30.

Thirty minutes? Anxiety throttled her system. She jumped off her bed and rummaged through her clothes. It was freezing today, so there was no disguising a cute outfit under her snow clothes. She packed a bag with random objects, tools, snacks, water—always a habit no matter where she was going—and tried not to think about her last time on a plane.

She dressed in layers until she looked like a puffy version of herself. She knew from her dad that prop planes could be cold, and she'd be right up front in all the action. Her stomach flipped again. Or, maybe after they talked, they could decide to fly another day. Either way, she felt like she was going to be sick.

She calmed herself, brushed her hair, and pulled on a black beanie. She thought about writing her parents a note, but she was out of time. She'd text them after she and Will talked.

She crunched down the gravel drive to wait for Will, her legs stiff beneath her layers. She walked all the time in New York, but it was about sheer street survival there, dodging bodies, climbing in and out of grimy subways, trying not to get hit by wild cars in crosswalks.

She definitely wasn't going back after winter break.

She could already imagine her mother's icy response—how, if she wanted to live on her own, she'd have to pay for everything, which is why she'd been working to save. She'd taken extra shifts at the café by her dorm, and she'd squirreled away every cent she could. She was serious about this. Taking the bus back to Chicago from New York had given her ample time to think. And, as if to solidify her decision, when they'd pulled up to The Black House, she'd instantly felt validated. This was her home.

Jules smoothed a hand over her hair and checked the sky. The snow was coming, always announcing itself in starts and stops in a place like this. She was used to snow, but without all the Chicago buildings to insulate her, she shivered beneath her clothes. Right on time, Will pulled up in his truck, and her heart kicked. Suddenly, she had the urge to run, but she took a breath and opened the cab door.

Inside, the heat was on full blast and his familiar smell consumed the entire truck. The Cinematic Orchestra crooned one of her favorite songs, "To Build a Home," and she immediately wanted to burst into tears. Had he played this on purpose? This was one they'd listened to many times. Just thinking about it cracked her heart in two.

"Hi," she finally managed to say as she tamed her thoughts and fastened her seat belt.

"Hey." He hesitated and then looked over at her. His eyes lingered at her throat, and she involuntarily touched the necklace.

He'd shaved his head, that gorgeous dirty-blond hair she used to run her fingers through all gone. He'd lost weight and his eyes looked tired, but there he was. The boy she loved.

I miss you. I love you. Why did you break up with me?

"Thanks for picking me up," she said.

"I'm surprised you said yes." He put the car in gear.

"Me too." A tear slipped down her cheek. She turned her head and looked out the window. They bumped over the dirt path outside the gate in silence until they approached the main road and began to snake down the mountain. She had so many questions she needed answered, but now that they were alone, she felt insecure. She didn't know where to start.

They continued to drive in silence as the music drifted from one emotional song to the next. She was losing her resolve, losing her ability to stay strong. No matter how hard she tried, she was helpless when she was around him. Twenty minutes later, they were at the tarmac, and he put the truck in park, but left the engine running. He opened his mouth, closed it. "Jules, I need to apologize," he said.

Her heart pounded in her chest, but she stayed quiet.

He ran a hand over his buzzed head. "When you left, I wasn't thinking clearly. With Mom's passing, I was just a mess. I needed time." His eyes found hers. "But I shouldn't have taken your mom's words to heart, and I shouldn't have broken up with you like that. You didn't deserve that."

"Why didn't you say something? I tried to contact you so many times."

"I know." He knocked his head rhythmically against the headrest and then turned to her. "I started to call you a million times. You know I hate texting." He smiled. "But I didn't know where to start, or if I even should. If there was a chance you were happy in New York, I didn't want to mess that up."

Tears carved a path down her cheeks and he reached out to swipe a few away. Chills traversed her skin from his touch. "You couldn't mess anything up. I'm not going back to New York. My home is here. My life is here." She locked eyes with his and witnessed the pain, contained, like hers. "I've missed you so much," she whispered. "Every day."

Before she could think about it, she unfastened her seat belt and flew into his arms. He held her shaking body, her face smashed against his neck. She breathed him in, cried harder, let all the tension of these last few months fade away.

"I'm here, Jules. I'm here now. I've got you." He let her cry and stroked her hair.

She never wanted to move. She wanted to stay like this, in his arms, nothing complex between them. Finally, she pulled away and sighed. "I'm a mess."

"You're beautiful." He swallowed, smoothed her tears away, and took her hand in his, brought it to his lips, and kissed it.

"I was so hurt when you just cut me out of your life. I thought . . ." She'd thought so many things.

"I know." He lowered her hand, but held on to it, rubbing his thumb over and over the web of skin between her thumb and index finger. "I haven't moved on. I won't. I was just trying to figure out my life. Everything seemed so great this summer, and then it just all fell apart. I didn't want to drag you down with me."

"You won't." She thought of the girl in the video and felt almost foolish for asking, but she had to. "Are you seeing anyone?"

He held her gaze. "No."

A seismic weight lifted from her shoulders, but then the truth slammed into her, and she felt tense all over again. Should she tell him now?

She took a shaky breath and situated herself on the warm seats. "I have something to tell you."

He waited while she formed the words. She hadn't yet said them out loud.

"I'm pregnant."

The statement hung in the air, and for a moment, she wasn't sure he'd heard. She gauged his reaction, fearing terror or disbelief, but then he broke into a grin and whooped, gently pulling her into another hug.

"I can't believe it," he whispered. He pulled back, took her face in his, and kissed her softly. "Are you sure?"

She nodded. "Completely. No one knows. I wasn't sure how you'd react, so I haven't made any decisions yet."

"Juliette." He swept the hair from her face and looked at her. "I'm in this with you, okay? You don't have to make any decisions alone."

She nodded. Relief came in giant, cleansing waves. It was all going to be okay.

They discussed logistics and telling their parents, which Jules had zero idea how to do. Her mother would be so disappointed, but it wasn't really about her anymore. The more she talked about the baby, the happier she felt. People started families young all the time. She could still accomplish her goals and be a mother.

She looked out the windshield. "Do you still want to go up?"

He assessed the clouds and then her. "Jules, you don't have to do this. My mom would understand, especially now that we have a baby to think about."

The out he was giving her made her want to scream yes. But Will was a pilot. If they were going to be together, she had to get over this fear. She shook her head. Lenore would want her to do this, and it would mean even more with a grandchild. "I want to go." She looked at him. "Is it safe?"

"Storm's not due to hit until ten. If you're sure, we can just get up to cruising altitude, spread her ashes over the mountain, and circle right back. Ten or fifteen minutes tops." He looked at her. "Are you sure?"

Was she sure?

She nodded, sucked in a deep breath, already anxious about what was coming next. "I'm sure."

This was important. She had to get through this. Once the ashes were scattered and they were safely back on the ground, their real lives could begin.

27

Jules

ARCTIC air charged through the cockpit of the prop plane, and she double-checked that her belt was secure before glancing over.

She gently touched the silver urn she squeezed between her legs. "Are you sure this is safe?" She wasn't one to fear the elements, but he knew how nervous she was. Outside the smudged window, snow clouds gathered on the horizon in clotty reams of white.

"I promise," Will said. He flipped a switch. "Up, down. Quick. You'll see." He checked and rechecked buttons she had zero knowledge about. He'd gone over the details with her. Once they got up to cruising altitude, they'd open her window first, and she'd scatter some ashes and then it would be his turn. Lenore would be imprinted along the mountains she loved.

"Ready?" He offered a tight-lipped smile.

She searched his eyes, which had darkened to the exact color of the turbulent sky. She wanted to ask what this meant to him, if scattering Lenore's ashes would bring some sort of closure, or if that void would always be there, hollow and black.

The news about the pregnancy whirled between them. It had

infused both of them with a giddy excitement for the future. She settled back into her seat, not wanting to appear afraid. She'd always been told she was fearless, and she tried to grasp that image of herself now, but it was slippery, just out of reach.

The engine stuttered and gathered strength, and she forced herself to stare straight ahead. She pressed her hands around the urn, which felt icy in her hands.

The small plane charged down the short runway. Will squeezed her knee and the electric current danced through her body. As long as she was with Will, she'd be safe.

"It's going to be fine!" he shouted.

Suddenly, they were airborne. Her stomach kicked as the plane wrenched sharply to the left. She clutched the door. Her fingers burned from the frigid metal. She focused on the sights below, the small town she'd come to know and love, studded with random, sprawling homes, trailer parks, shops, acres of mountains carved with wide trails and ski lifts. They rose above River Falls. Her stomach lurched again when he swerved and straightened.

She directed her thoughts elsewhere, but they kept coming back to the same daunting fears she always had in a plane: death. She told herself to breathe, to relax, but her heart beat viciously in her chest. Perspiration gathered under her arms, despite the cold temperature.

Miles away, snow clouds hovered like blimps, but she knew how quickly they could descend over the mountain and drop anchor. She attempted to envision herself safe at The Black House, in front of a roaring fire with a good book. The very thought made her long for home.

The engine wheezed as they lifted higher. She squeezed her eyes shut, then forced them open, told her fingers to uncurl and relax.

When they reached cruising altitude, he pointed out some of the landmarks below. The city center, the waterfall, even her house. Her heartbeat thumped in her head, drowning out his remarks. The peaks of the mountain were scrubbed of the rich green of summer; now, they were mostly bare and brown, capped with ice. When they cruised over her house, she gazed longingly over it, nestled in the tangled forest like a glossy black rock. They rose higher. The choppy air bounced her up and down. She gripped the door again and slowed her breath.

"You okay?" he asked.

No, she wasn't okay. She hadn't been okay since the end of summer. But with one text and a quick conversation in his truck, it seemed her life was back on track. She opened her mouth to answer, but his pensive face froze.

A whiny alarm pierced her eardrums, and the plane bucked violently to the left. Gray smoke billowed in front of the cockpit window. Will cursed, jaw firing.

Ahead of them, a cloud, thick as a pearly white wall, swallowed them whole. One moment, she could see, and the next, they were encased in white. She lost all sense of the horizon. The plane dropped, steadied, then dove again.

"What's happening?" Her voice floundered under the wail of the failing turbine engine.

The fibrous muscles in Will's forearms flexed as he gripped the yoke. "Hold on!" They plummeted and a flat mountain face zoomed into view.

The plane capsized. Smoky spirals mixed with inflated clouds. Her mind couldn't catch up with the wicked assault on her body. She dared not look over at Will, because she didn't want to see it written all over his face too.

They weren't going to make it.

The regret cracked across her back, as something from the

plane shifted and pierced her between the shoulder blades. If only she'd listened to herself. If only she hadn't felt the need to sneak away because she'd needed to see Will. Now, here they were.

Going down.

"Brace for impact!" Will yelled.

She obeyed his commands, making her body work. She bent over and tucked her head between her knees, but the seat belt bit into her stomach and made her nauseous. She couldn't breathe. Instead, she unbuckled and crammed herself into the footwell.

"Jules, get out of there!" Will barked at her, but she stayed put. She knew that in commercial-sized planes, being toward the back of the plane was safest. For props, she had no idea.

The plane plummeted, miles of altitude eaten in seconds as the clouds parted and the tops of her beloved trees thrashed the belly of the plane. The engine screamed. They hurtled toward the earth, angry branches and rocks peeling away the plane's exterior. They lifted up for one glorious moment, evened out.

She curled tighter. The air was damp and cold, but they coasted steadily. Above her, Will yelled sharply into the walkie-talkie, but his voice was drowned out by the anguished whine of another siren. Then, they were diving again, free-falling. She held her body in place, but her mind roared.

Only a miracle would save them.

28

Desi

DESI stared out her kitchen window.

Snow fell steadily, making mounds of her outdoor furniture. She considered waking the entire household and demanding they go outside and play. She was reminded of her nightmare last summer, when she chased Peter and Jules before he plummeted through the ice.

She shook away the image and listened to the steady hiss of coffee filling the pot. She gripped her sweater, rubbing her arms against the freezing air seeping through the cracks of all the windows. She replayed the conversation with Jules. No matter how many steps she took forward as a mother, she always seemed to regress. They were at a tipping point, and if she pushed too hard either way, she could lose her daughter's trust completely.

"Morning." Tommy walked into the kitchen. He yawned and made a beeline for the coffeepot.

His hair stuck up at odd angles, just as it had when they were kids. He ran a hand through it now, taming it into place, and slid onto a barstool.

"How'd you sleep?"

He took a healthy gulp and nodded. "Good. You?"

She shrugged. "Just worried about Jules."

Tommy traced the lip of his coffee mug and considered her statement. "She'll come around."

"Hope so." She slid her elbows onto the kitchen island, her own mug firmly cupped in her hands. "You're lucky you're not a parent."

He rolled his eyes. "Yeah, but I'm fully invested in all *your* drama, so . . ." He loudly slurped his coffee.

Before she could retort, Peter waltzed in, freshly showered. A small dot of toilet paper still clung to his jaw where he'd nicked himself. "Morning, troops," he said. He pulled down a mug and poured himself a cup. "Is Jules still asleep?" He sounded surprised.

Desi motioned to his face, and he pinched the bloody paper between his fingers and threw it in the trash. It was true Jules never slept this late, but who knew what kind of hours she'd been keeping at school? Guilt wormed its way in. If Jules had stayed in River Falls for the last three months, things would probably look very different.

Desi swung between torment and satisfaction. She had hindsight her daughter couldn't possibly have, even though Jules felt like she was ruining her life. She knew how every decision felt so detrimental but actually wasn't. What her daughter did at this age mattered. She needed a solid career and a degree. Desi made a mental note to check out the colleges in town as a possible compromise. Maybe there was some program that would be worthy of Jules's talent. Even as she mulled over the idea, doubt creeped in. Jules would hate it.

Desi nodded outside. "Pretty spectacular, isn't it? I'm so glad we stocked up on food. There's no way anyone can get up or down this mountain today."

"Depends on the plow situation." Peter sipped his coffee. "But yeah, I'd say we're stuck here for a while."

Desi's heart broke for Jules. She wouldn't be going anywhere in this weather. Not for a few days at least.

Peter deposited his dish in the dishwasher. "I'm going for a hike."

"What?" Desi said. "A hike? In this?" She pointed outside, as a big hunk of snow slid down the window.

"I'm going to check the shelter." Peter turned to Tommy. "Interested?"

Before he could reply, Desi shot him a look. They weren't done talking.

Tommy waved him away. "Nah. You go. Report back."

Peter gave a small salute and packed up.

They moved to the living room and Tommy started a fire. Today would be a perfect day to read books, watch movies, and eat popcorn. When Jules was little, they would grab every blanket and sheet in the house, creating one massive pallet on the floor. They'd watch movies and eat snacks until they drifted to sleep. Desi would wake hours later, back aching, and stare down at her little family unit with a sense of gratitude and pride.

She glanced around the house now, at all of the expensive furniture and personal touches she'd slaved over. She knew Jules was embarrassed by their wealth. How ironic that she worked so hard for two people who could care less about material possessions. Case in point: her husband would rather explore a snowstorm than spend a morning snowed in with her.

Tommy crouched with the rod in hand and nudged the logs. Finally, he replaced the poker and sat on the couch next to her.

"I heard from Carter, you know."

Desi's entire world sloped. She kept her game face in place. "When?"

"A few days ago. I knew how worried you were about him and I wanted to let him know."

"But his phone's disconnected." Desi blushed from the admission that she'd been calling him, but at this stage, she didn't care. She just wanted to know he was safe.

"He got a new one."

She waited for him to say more, practically dying to hear. "So where is he? What happened?"

He avoided her gaze. "He just wanted a change. He moved to Oregon."

"*Oregon?* Why?" Desi sat up, sloshing a bit of her coffee. She sopped up the mess as tears stung her eyes. Had he really felt the need to move across the country to get away from her?

Tommy looked at her so intently, it was as if he knew the truth. Lately, her nightmares about Peter had morphed into nightmares about Carter. In her most recent one, she'd been in Fulton Market back home, the main strip bustling with endless restaurants, shops, and bars. In her dream, she'd looked longingly in each window, then miraculously appeared in front of her favorite bar. Through the frosted window, sitting at the dark bar, nursing a whiskey, was Carter. She'd pressed her hands to the glass, wondering if it was really him.

Before she could move, he'd turned and caught her eye. She'd waved sheepishly and he'd rushed out into the night and thrown his arms around her. They just held each other there like that, for minutes, saying nothing. When he'd finally pulled away, a small wound in his forehead had spread until he vanished in a puddle of blood.

"Are you in love with him, Des?" Tommy asked.

Desi faltered for words. She thought about lying, about telling him he was ridiculous, but she was so tired of lying. "Why would you ask that?"

"Because it's obvious," he said. "I know you guys dated. I'm not blind. And guys talk too. Carter was wild about you. When you chose Peter, he just shut himself off. Over the years, I've tried to bring it up, but he's always been respectful. But when he showed up here, I figured something had happened. And since you and Peter are splitting up, I just thought . . ."

Desi's mind spun with this information. Why had he never uttered a word? "Did he say anything to you? Why he left?"

"I can't say."

"What do you mean, you can't say?"

"It's between him and Peter."

Desi froze. So Peter had talked to Carter that night. Of course he had. Otherwise, Carter wouldn't have left. She ripped the afghan away and stood, unsure of what to do. "Give me his new number." She extended her hand, practically demanding his phone.

Tommy scoffed. "No. I'm not getting involved."

"You already are involved. Give it to me."

"No," he said again. "Carter wants you to figure out what's going on with Peter. Then, you can call him."

Desi wanted to scream. All this time, Carter had patiently waited for her. He didn't want this decision to be about him. He wanted Desi to make the right decision for her.

The fire popped and they lapsed into silence again.

A sudden thought made her stomach jump. "So Peter knows we dated?"

"What do you think? They were friends."

The truth bit into her heart. They *were* friends. And now that friend had moved to the other side of the country to keep his distance. She sat there for what felt like hours, wondering how long Peter had known and why he'd never confronted her with the truth.

Suddenly, Peter banged through the side door and stood at the edge of the kitchen, shrouded in snow, his face as stricken as she'd ever seen it.

"What is it?" Desi sat up.

"There's been a plane crash in the mountains," Peter said. "I saw it go down."

"Oh my God!" Desi covered her mouth with both hands. "Will they be able to get anyone out in this weather?"

Peter walked to the landline and picked up the receiver. "Dead." He removed his gloves, warmed his hands. "I'm assuming most lines are down from the storm."

Tommy was sitting stiffly, tracking Peter's movement. "How far?"

"Couldn't tell. A few miles maybe?" Peter blew into his hands, looked between them. "I'm going to go and try to help."

Tommy was already on his feet. "I'll get my supplies."

Peter looked at Desi and then at Tommy. Some sort of understanding passed between them.

Desi stood, heart pounding. "What are you not telling me?"

Peter hesitated. "It looked like Will's plane."

Terror seized her heart. She pressed a hand to her chest. Jules wouldn't survive losing Will, especially before she'd even seen him again.

"Peter, do you really think . . ." Her voice trailed off. This couldn't be happening. Not after everything with his mother and Ava.

Tommy returned a few minutes later, layered up, pack secured on his back. Peter loaded up food and water, and tightened the straps on his own bag.

"Desi, is Jules up yet?"

Desi shook her head. She didn't want to wake her. Not with

this news. Not until they knew for sure. "No." She checked her watch and saw it was well after nine.

"Have you checked that she's even here?" Peter stormed past their stunned faces and pushed into Jules's room.

Of course Jules was here. Where else would she be?

Peter emerged a second later, his face unnaturally pale.

Desi knew before he even said it.

Her daughter was gone.

29

Jules

"HOLD on!"

The prop plane's left wing crunched and shattered. Something snapped, and she wasn't sure if it was bones or branches. The metal screamed, loosened, then shredded, and for one horrifying moment, she wondered if Will had been sucked away.

She didn't have time to understand what was happening. She clung to the tender moment between them on the ground, the look on Will's face when she told him she was pregnant. The way his lips had felt on hers. Would those be her final memories from an agonizingly short-lived life?

She peered up from the footwell. He was still there, fists clenched on the yoke, his clothes flapping in the wind from the missing door. They plummeted off a rock face and tumbled, bumping like a skipped pebble along rough terrain. The windshield fractured. Jagged shards launched through the cockpit. Will screamed, an inhuman cry that pierced her heart. Glass jabbing skin, then bone.

Jules squeezed her eyes shut, suspended in space. They coasted up, then crashed down. Her ears burst with sound. She could barely breathe and had no sense of direction.

She wanted to reach out to Will, but she was afraid. Tucking herself tighter in the footwell, she prayed harder than she'd ever prayed. After one more roll, the remainder of the plane burrowed to a shuddering stop under a few feet of snow.

Her brain hummed with terror. She hunted for sounds, but was met with silence. No screams. No crunching metal. No more tormented howls.

Am I dead?

Outside, the wind slowly cranked into a persistent, audible whine. She tried to move, but couldn't. The snow continued to pour into the open windshield and missing door.

They were buried.

The air burned. She listened for the crackling of flames or stench of gasoline. Was she on fire, or was it just so cold, it hurt? She waited for her brain to stop slamming around her skull, for her messy thoughts to solidify into something finite.

Get out.

She counted to ten, then punched her entire body through the snow. Her head thumped against an immovable object and was tossed back. She tried again. Snow clogged her nose and throat. She chomped on dirty ice, knew not to swallow it, because it would dehydrate her. When she thought her lungs would burst, she gathered every ounce of strength and clawed toward the surface. Finally, her fingertips whipped into the piercing, bitter air.

The cold bit her extremities, reminded her of a world beyond the crash. She struggled for air, kept climbing toward that narrow mitt of space. She punched wider, then heaved her body up until her torso broke through. Her rib cracked, and she screamed. She collapsed and rolled to her back. The snow lashed in every direction, a frenzied alabaster halo.

Her world was bleached: white trees, white mountain, white sky.

She cradled her rib and felt its jagged point stab her palm beneath layers of clothes. She tried to sit up, couldn't. She pawed the air, as if waving an invisible white flag at the pearly mountains. Slowing her uneven breath, she took inventory of the rest of her body. Rib, broken. Knee, possibly torn meniscus. Head, concussed. She couldn't grasp the rest of her injuries beyond the shock of the crash, the way it had tossed her around in its arctic fist.

She flipped to her belly, and a spasm of pain roared through her middle. She rotated and began a cocked army crawl toward the pilot's side.

Stay alive.

Those two words repeated in a vicious loop with every inch of space eaten beneath the rising dome of white.

Stay alive. Stay alive. Stay alive.

30

Desi

"PETER, what do you mean she's not here?"

Desi pushed past him into Jules's room. She searched the dresser for a note and then the small table by the front door. No one's keys were missing. "Maybe she went ice skating?"

Tommy disappeared to the mudroom and came back, her figure skates in hand.

Desi began to violently tremble. She grabbed her phone, checked for unread texts, and then sent a frantic one to Jules. She waited for it to go through, but it failed. She tried again. "Does anyone have service?"

The men tried their phones and sadly shook their heads.

"It's the storm." Peter was eerily calm, as was Tommy. She reminded herself they were trained to stay calm in a crisis. For years, their lives had literally depended on it. But this wasn't war. This was family.

She wondered if there was a way to drive down the mountain and cross over to where Peter first saw the plane, but he reminded her they'd never get down the mountain in these conditions, and so the fastest way wasn't around—it was through.

"Des, did she say she was going to see Will?"

"She talked about trying to reach out today, but she'd never go up in a plane in weather like this." Even as she said it, she knew that Jules might have done anything—even fly—in order to see Will.

Tommy checked his watch. "Peter, we need to go."

The men continued to gather supplies, but Desi stopped them. "I want to come."

Peter shook his head. "It's too dangerous."

Tommy zipped up his parka. "You should stay in case she comes back."

Desi searched her brother's face. How could he possibly understand? If there was even the slightest chance her child had been in that plane, she was coming too. "Give me two minutes."

She ran to their bedroom and ripped open her chest of drawers and shrugged into a base layer, thermal underwear, and snow gear. She hesitated as she hunted for her thickest pair of socks. Could she keep up with Peter and Tommy? She slammed the top drawer, her hands icy with nerves. She considered the alternative of staying and pacing her living room, stuck with her own thoughts. She had to go.

When she was ready, Peter tossed her a black ski mask and a pair of his gloves. He'd doubled the size of his pack, and she felt guilty for the extra supplies he now had to carry because of her.

"What can I bring?"

"Nothing. Let's go."

She shoved her keys in her pocket, as well as her phone, and stepped outside. The biting wind stole her breath and gave her pause, even under all her layers.

Tommy turned back and yelled through the wind. "You good?"

She gave him a thumbs-up and put her head down, slogging

through the snow that was already calf high. Terror rampaged through her body with every step. They had to find Jules.

She bowed her head to her chest as they reached the trail at the back of the house. Jules dominated every inch of her mind. She once again replayed their conversation, how upset her daughter had been these last few months. She was an adult; yet somehow, Desi's dominion over her daughter's life held fast.

The wind eased under the cover of trees as they stepped onto the familiar trail. Her stomach grumbled, and she realized none of them had even eaten breakfast. They were fueled by coffee and adrenaline and not much else.

She caught up with Tommy. "What do we do if we can't get anyone on the phone?" Her voice was muffled behind her ski mask. Tommy's and Peter's faces were bare, used to all types of conditions and terrains.

"Peter's probably not the only one who saw the crash," he reminded her. "And Will most likely radioed for help."

But how many other people on this mountain would have been out during a snowstorm? If someone from the tower had heard him, could they even send help? She left all these questions unasked as they trekked farther from the house.

"What if she comes back to the house?" she asked suddenly. "We didn't even leave her a note."

"Desi." Peter's voice was sharp from the front of the line. "Stop worrying and just move. You're burning energy."

Desi fell to the back of the line and did as she was told. It seemed to be her full-time job to worry. That's what she did best. The cold made her lungs work extra hard. She attempted to clear her mind, but she'd never forgive herself if something happened to Jules.

She struggled with her darkest fears as they waded deeper into the whitewashed forest. She needed to keep her mind busy so she didn't focus on the worst-case scenario. She mentally sorted through things to think about, but everything seemed meaningless compared to Jules and Will.

Desi glanced up at the trees, heavy with snow. Tommy's and Peter's strong legs sliced expertly through the foot-high powder, carving a direct path for her to follow. How had she just been at home, drinking coffee, when her little girl could be dead?

She buried the morbid thoughts. Her maternal instincts told her that her child was very much alive, but uncertainty still gripped her in its fist.

After a while, the crunch of fresh snow became melodic. She hadn't been in this much snow in years. She thought back to the last time a snowstorm like this had hit Chicago, when Peter first deployed. The snow had been at least six feet high, muting the loud city and turning it into a winter wonderland.

The whole city was theirs. Because of the storm, she'd foolishly thought he wouldn't be able to deploy. She envisioned the two of them stuck in their little apartment, eating by candlelight, making love, and shutting out every care in the outside world.

Two days later, he'd left for Iraq.

They were newlyweds. Though Peter had promised to retire when they got married, as a sniper, his options were endless. Since most Marines retired in their twenties, she was relieved he'd have the rest of his life to figure out what he wanted to do. But Peter had asked to move up in rank. The military was what he knew and loved, and he hadn't been able to leave it. Even when he'd promised her he would.

She didn't let her mind go back to that time often, because it reminded her of all her broken dreams about their marriage, all the ways it had failed. Funny how Peter always reminded her that she'd put her career above her family, but really, he'd chosen first. He'd chosen to serve his country rather than honor their brand-new marriage. She knew, for him, it had been an easy choice.

When he deployed, Desi was still working at a local design firm. She was hungry for her own business, but didn't yet have the knowledge or funds to branch out on her own. That winter, once the storm had passed, she lost herself in work and stayed away from their apartment as much as she could.

Tommy had deployed with Peter for their second tour, so she was doubly worried. She had no way to reach either of them. For weeks straight, she searched the news for casualties and then decided she had to cut herself off, if only to maintain her sanity. It was part of being in a military family—death was imminent, if not probable. Worrying was part of the territory.

One night, when she'd been feeling particularly anxious, she'd wandered into one of her favorite bars in Old Town after work.

She'd sidled up to the bar, ordered a whiskey, neat, in honor of Peter. All the anxieties of the past few months, all the stress, all the loneliness—she just let it drain, shot after shot. She kept telling herself she was a Marine wife, so she had to be strong, though she had no idea what that even meant.

Before she paid her tab, she'd glimpsed a guy at the end of the bar, watching her. Her whole world froze as he limped over.

"Hey, Des."

She could hardly breathe. She hadn't seen Carter since their breakup. Looking at him was like slicing open a fresh wound. "Carter." She breathed his name, and his entire face broke into a smile. It was blinding and such a stark contrast from his dark, brooding eyes.

"Rough day?" He nodded to the empty shot glasses around her.

"You could say that." She sipped her water self-consciously, wondering if she reeked of booze. She peered at him. "How's your leg?"

He hiked up one pant leg to reveal his new prosthetic. "Better every day," he explained.

She nodded somberly. She knew losing his leg had been a horrific process, full of surgeries and trials. She'd never understand how young men went to other countries, killed strangers, and then returned without pieces of themselves. She wasn't sure how anyone survived that kind of mental or physical terror.

"How have you been?" she asked. She wasn't sure if she was referring to his life in general or his life without her.

He laughed. "Taking it a day at a time."

She knocked back more of her water, started to feel her head clear. He studied her wedding ring, and she covered it self-consciously. "Do you miss it?" What she really wondered was if he missed her.

"Every damn day." He locked eyes with her, and she resisted the urge to look away.

Instead, she nervously twisted her glass on the bar. She was still young and naïve and should have known better than to enjoy the company of her ex-boyfriend. Finally, she broke their gaze and signaled to the bartender for her tab.

"Can I walk you home?"

She'd said yes before she could say no. As the cold air shocked her sober, she reveled in the familiarity of Carter, of how they always seemed to pick up without a beat.

"Des, this way." Tommy barked at her, ripping her back to the present. She realized she was looping left to go on her running trail instead of forking right past the shelter. Were they not even to the shelter yet?

She jogged to catch up to Peter. "How far away do you think you saw the plane go down?"

"Maybe two miles? Could be farther. I'll know more once we're out of the woods."

Two miles. Desi could run two miles in twelve minutes flat, but hiking through a snowstorm meant it would take . . . what? Hours? She had no idea how to convert the time.

Desi tried to clear her mind on the walk. Why had she been thinking of that night with Carter? That was almost twenty years ago.

She fell back in line. Peter never really looked at her the way Carter had. With each tour, he withdrew a little more. He lost his voice. He became introverted and cold. He wanted to spend time honing his skills, alone in nature.

Maybe that's why she'd started seeing Carter after that night. She told herself it was only to see a friendly face, to have a drink, to keep each other company. At first, they'd talked about Peter and military life, and it helped her feel more connected.

But then, they started meeting for an entirely new reason, and before long, Desi was in too deep.

31

Jules

FINALLY, Jules heaved herself on top of the snow.

She rolled to her back and assessed how badly she was injured. She tenderly touched the tip of her rib, making sure it hadn't protruded through her skin. She gripped her stomach, praying the baby was okay. Every breath drove a knife of pain through her torso. She switched to nose breathing and rolled over to crawl a few paces forward toward the wreckage.

Will.

Only half the plane was left. The pilot's side was completely buried under white, the metal squashed under the foot of Mother Nature. She blinked at the stark image, wondering how she was still alive. She shuffled forward and cried out from the fresh spasms of pain.

Jules forced herself to stand and gasped at the intensity. She pressed a hand over her torso again, thumbing through the thick layers of clothing until she felt the notch between her second and third ribs. Her feet were numb, but she limped to the pilot's side of the plane and lowered to her knees. Her right kneecap throbbed where it rested in the snow.

The cold and adrenaline shocked her body awake. Before she reached in, she zipped up her parka and hood and put on her gloves. Then, she began digging through the snow.

"Will!" She screamed his name, which was barely audible over the vicious wind. Their story couldn't end like this. They'd only just reconnected. She dug harder, bits of snow sliding into fragments of space between her gloves and wrists.

She scooped away the ice until she could make out streaks of blood. She wasn't sure what she was looking at, until she realized she was staring into a large gash at the side of Will's head.

"Oh God." Her stomach bucked and she vomited into the snow. She swiped a hand along her mouth and gingerly gripped his shoulders and pulled. His head lolled backward and she gagged again.

Deep, gaping wounds marred his cheeks, forehead, and chin. She wildly eyed the cockpit for her bag. Had it survived the crash? She rummaged through the plane until she found a few small towels in the console. She applied pressure to the cuts. Blood spurted between her gloved fingers, but she held strong. She leaned in and listened for his heartbeat. His breaths came in slow, shallow sips. There was no telling how much time he had, if he had internal injuries, or what other monstrosities lay beneath the snow.

While she held the towel firmly in place, she hunted for familiar landmarks, but the snow whipped too ferociously to gain clarity. She needed to get them someplace warm if they had even a slim chance of survival.

Thanks to Tommy, she knew face and head wounds could be slow to clot, but she held pressure until her fingers ached. She then tied the two remaining small towels together and made a tourniquet for his head. She tied it as tightly as she could,

screaming from the agonizing effort. Electric jolts of pain prod-
ded her body. She steadied herself, then, with his head resting
back, balled snow in her gloves to pack his face wounds.

She knocked the loose snow from her hands and searched
for trees to erect a shelter, but she couldn't see more than a
foot or two in front of her. She racked her brain to remember
if she had a flare in her pack, but her thoughts were jumbled
and unclear.

First things first. She had to dig Will out of the snow, drag
him to safety, get the bleeding to stop, and figure out where they
were. If there was a blizzard, no chopper would be able to safely
land. She searched for the telltale smoke that would signal a
crash, but the storm had literally snuffed it out.

The panic swirled in her chest, a tiny tornado of doom. She'd
forgotten to text her parents on the tarmac. Why hadn't she just
left them a note? She slowed her breathing as tears froze to her
cheeks. She had to stay calm.

She dropped back to her knees again and began heaping the
snow away from the rest of Will's body. Out of the corner of her
eye, she glimpsed the edge of Lenore's urn, poking up from the
footwell. Her tears fell harder, and a sudden desperation took
hold.

They'd gone up to honor Lenore's last request and now, here
they were, crashed and stranded. Possibly on the way to their
own deaths.

Jules struggled to remember everything she'd learned, seen,
or been taught by her dad and Uncle Tommy. The snow fell in
clusters, burying them deeper.

Once the footwell was clear, she gathered Will under his shoulders and gave a firm pull, but nothing happened. She tried
again, groaning with the effort. A fistful of snow entered her
mouth. She spit it out and leaned forward in the cockpit, trying

to release his legs. One was wedged in the footwell, his foot cranked the wrong way.

She freed one foot and then the other, then swung his legs over the side, searching for signs of life, but he was completely limp. Her father had made her do dead man's carries at boot camps for his trainees. Even with her rib and other injuries, she had to find a way to get him to safety.

She maneuvered his broken body into the snow, forcing her heart to calm as the fresh powder turned pink. How many wounds did he have? She knew he could bleed out before she even had a chance to help.

Behind them, as the snow momentarily lifted, she spotted a row of mature spruces in a singular line one hundred yards out. She squatted and braced herself, hooking her arms beneath his armpits. She counted to three and began to drag Will backward, the heavy snow bunching against her calves and forming a white wall behind her. She made it a few steps, had to stop, readjust. Her rib made a sickening clicking sound, but she kept going. Behind her, the trees seemed to grow farther away. She tried again, made it a few feet, then lowered his lifeless body to the earth. Her lungs burned. The wind pierced her ears and stole her breath. She regained what energy she could, dug her heels in, and pulled him backward through the snow, counting in her head. Her legs quivered as she backed up to the spruce and collapsed under its heavy branches, panting. Her body trembled from adrenaline, and she took a moment to gather herself.

The trees were set several feet apart, which would make for a safe shelter underneath. A trail of blood marked their path and then was immediately buried by the furious snowfall.

She dug out the snow around them and pulled down leaves and anything she could find to make padding for Will's back.

She trudged back to the plane and almost cried from relief when she spotted a stack of blankets and a first-aid kit in a hidden compartment. He used to joke that she had influenced him to prepare for the worst, and she'd never been more grateful. Back at the trees, she laid down a fresh blanket, then rolled his body on top of it, lifting him in thirds and setting him down as gingerly as a baby.

"You're going to be fine," she said. Her shaky voice defied her words. Her teeth chattered. Her fingers were already numb, even with the gloves on. Her nose ached, her eyes watered. She opened the first-aid kit, grateful for the gauze and tape. She disinfected her hands and scraped the snow from his wounds, applying packets of ointment and then placing the few bandages on his larger cuts.

She willingly slowed her breath. Will remained unconscious. She prepped herself to examine the rest of his body. Part of her didn't want to know, but she had no choice.

She started at his feet, the one that faced backward. She hesitated. She didn't know what to do. Were you supposed to leave it alone or try and set it? Did she relieve the pressure by taking off his shoe or keep it on?

Her thoughts scrambled, her brain struggling to find order. She snaked up his legs. His left femur was jagged and poking through his skin at an odd angle: broken. She pressed lightly on his abdomen, and he moaned. She immediately let go, afraid of making anything internal worse. But she was heartened just to hear his voice, even if it was involuntary. His right shoulder hung limply at his side. She felt around his head and found something sharp and metallic, right beneath the major cut. Her hands froze.

She must have missed it. She gently rolled his head toward her. A small triangle of shrapnel edged out of his scalp. Her heart dropped, and the intensity of the situation settled in. Will needed medical attention. She looked around, the snow rising, blocking them in.

All of those years of prepping for life-threatening situations had carried her here, and she didn't know if she could make it. She cried silently into her hands, overwhelmed with what to do next. She cried for the life she might never get to have with Will, for these last few months that had terrorized her day and night. If he died . . .

No.

She wiped her nose and took a cleansing breath.

She needed to focus on what she could control. She gauged the trees and decided this was a safe spot to build a fire. She made sure Will was as comfortable as possible and then stalked the area around them for broken branches or fallen logs. There were a few she was able to drag back to their site, all of varying sizes and shapes. She focused on building a direct barrier for the fire, so the wind wouldn't kill the flame. She used her hands and dug out a space, removing the snow until she hit bare land. She arranged a few damp logs she'd found for the base, then snapped thinner branches and twigs to lay on top of the wet wood. She hunted for some sort of dry grass, which seemed impossible in this weather.

She pulled down the leaves of the spruce, wiped them dry, and made a nest at the top. She knew how flammable spruces were and wanted to be careful to contain the fire. In her jacket pocket, she retrieved her matches, thankful for her recent souvenir from the diner. She clutched the matchbox in her frozen fingers and struck one, which immediately blew out. She struck another, willing the fire to light, but one after another, they caught and instantly extinguished.

She steadied her hand and cupped the other one around the

nest, protecting it from any excess wind. Finally, what seemed like hours later, with only a few matches left, the pile lit, and she gently blew until the flames reached a steady blaze. She placed a few fresh branches on top and readjusted the logs behind them to brace from the wind.

She moved Will closer to the fire, keeping his chest as warm as possible. That's where people lost heat the quickest. The snow continued to build around them, and even with the fire, she was freezing.

She glanced up and wondered if she could make a roof with one of the blankets, but knew it would get too heavy with snow, since she didn't have twine to secure it. Her rib ached and made it hard to breathe, but she needed to get to work.

She grabbed a crumpled bottle of water from her bag and cracked it open. She took a greedy sip, then gingerly grabbed Will's head and opened his mouth. She dribbled water into his parted lips, but he was lifeless, and the spare drops leaked out. She checked again for his pulse, digging her fingers into the flesh of his neck. It thumped weakly against her index and middle fingers. She sat back in relief.

"Just hang on," she said. "Please hang on."

She tossed the water in the bag, warmed her hands by the fire, and headed back out. She searched for any loose logs or branches she could snap from trees. She lost track of time as she worked, building a wobbly fortress around them and packing snow on the outside of the branches for extra insulation. It wasn't much, nothing more than a slightly tilted A-frame, but maybe it would keep the wind at bay.

She made endless trips back and forth. She hunted for signs of other life, a helicopter braving the weather, some spark that would give her hope. She wasn't worried about food, but dehydration and hypothermia happened fast out here.

She calculated how long it would take her parents to know where she was. They would ask Ava, who would hopefully realize Will was gone too.

She thought about who he'd been talking to on the radio on the way down. Had anyone heard him? Had anyone even known he'd gone up in the first place? She rushed back to the plane and searched for the walkie-talkie. It hung loosely in the floorboard, and she foolishly gripped it and pressed the button, hoping to hear static or some form of life. She waited, but of course, it was dead. She rested her head on her forearm and climbed back out of the plane.

32

Jules

ONCE the shelter was built, Jules stoked the fire, removed her gloves, and thawed her frozen hands.

The adrenaline was starting to wear off, and an intense fatigue rattled her body until she wanted to curl up and go to sleep. But she couldn't. Their survival depended on what she did next.

When her hands were warm, she ventured back to the plane, disturbing what wreckage remained to search for anything she'd missed. Still in the footwell, tipped on its side, was the urn. Her heart kicked, and she picked it up, making sure the top was still firmly screwed on. She tucked it under her arm like a football and trudged back to their shelter.

She sat the urn between them and moved it closer to Will, as if Lenore could somehow help. "Your mom is here," she said softly. She felt silly saying those words out loud, but she thought it was important to communicate. "We'll fulfill her wish one way or another, right?" Her lips trembled as she talked. She let the sentence dissolve between them. If only she'd insisted they do this another time, none of this would have happened.

She sighed and wiped away her cold tears. Will's body

remained so still she wondered if he'd stopped breathing. She pressed her fingers beneath his nose, the slim stream of air still evident.

She had no idea where they were and hadn't been paying close enough attention when they went down. She didn't know whether to try and get help or to stay with Will. If she could figure out where she was, maybe she could make a path back to a house or to town. She pressed her hands to her stomach again as a dull cramp spread through her abdomen. It wasn't just her and Will she had to think about—she had to consider her child.

Jules fashioned a face mask out of a blanket, tying it firmly in place. She gave Will some more water and made sure their makeshift shelter was secure before slipping out the wedge of space in the back.

The wind had picked up and pierced any slivers of flesh that were still exposed. She tucked her chin toward her chest and pulled out her compass. She headed north and decided if she didn't get anywhere in ten minutes, she'd turn back.

Each step was a slog, the snow soaking her boots and calves and, in some areas, all the way up to her knees.

She pushed forward for what felt like miles until she came to a small clearing on a bluff. She was able to peer down, but everything was misty and white. Was that River Falls? She waited for the wind to settle, searching for any familiar buildings or landmarks. She glanced behind her. Her footsteps had already disappeared with the fresh powder.

Frustrated, she realized she was going to have to wait until the snow lessened. She walked back toward camp, the compass a guiding comfort. The icy wind abated her injuries, blocked out her physical pain, and guided her to more pressing issues: What if they froze to death?

On the way to Will, one tree bled into the next. The wind and snow reminded her of a shaken snow globe. During any other circumstances, she would have marveled at it.

Once back at the shelter, she slipped inside and removed her phone from her bag. The screen was cracked, and of course, there was no signal, but she typed out a text to her parents anyway.

I've been in a plane crash with Will. Somewhere on the mountain. Please help.

She pressed send and saw the Text Fail alert over and over again. If only her phone would work, she could share her location. She could get her dad and Tommy here. They would know just what to do.

She tried until her fingers throbbed and threw the phone back in her bag. She dropped down and curled into Will for body heat, but she was afraid to put any pressure on him.

The fire crackled, dwindling, but Jules kept it stoked. A throbbing headache robbed her of her usually sharp wits, and then she remembered that she'd just survived a plane crash. What happened in the following hours would tell her how serious both of their injuries were. Her stomach ached. They both needed more water. She closed her eyes and tried to work through her next moves: water, fire, explore, rest.

She peered through the cracks in the freezing walls of branches and moss, willing the snow to lighten. Time was not on her side, but she would do everything she could not to let it run out.

She turned to face Will and propped herself up on an elbow. Even with his bandaged and cut face, he still had the same effect on her.

"I never should have left you," she whispered now. If she had stayed, would they even be in this situation? She thought about the conversation they'd started back on the ground and moved in a little closer. "I wanted to tell you the moment I found out

I was pregnant," she admitted. "But I didn't know if you'd be relieved or scared." Another flush of relief danced through her body at the memory of his face when she'd told him. There'd been no fear there—just joy.

Her words gained steam as she talked. She told him about college, about how living in a small, cramped dorm with a window unit was her version of hell. She told him about Melanie, and how she *never* stopped talking, so much that Jules couldn't study at the dorm and spent most of her time in the cavernous library. She described the stench of the New York City subways, that underground lair that breathed fire and grit. She told him how New Yorkers piled their garbage on curbs, and that she'd counted more rats than birds. She told him how every street corner was crammed with people of all different backgrounds and cultures—which was the part she liked. It reminded her of Chicago. She told him about the amazing food, the obscure diners she'd found, the small pockets of green, the museums off the beaten path with incredibly weird art.

She told him she wanted to go back with him someday, that they could pack a picnic and sit in Central Park and marvel at the concrete jungle around them. And then they could come back home to River Falls.

"This is my home, Will. You are my home." She tenderly pressed her palm to his chest, rooting around for his heart. "I think I love you more now than I even did this summer, if that's possible."

She sighed and rolled to her back, the tears flowing freely. She closed her eyes, opened them, and stared at the roof of their makeshift shelter. She rotated toward him again, wondering if there was anything she could say to somehow wake him, but he lay still.

She gripped his limp, cold hand in hers and squeezed. "You're going to make it through this," she said. "I need you. *We* need you." She squeezed his hand again and held it firmly.

She almost let go when she felt the tiniest pulse between them, a small flicker of his fingers in hers.

"Will?" She scrambled up to sitting, her rib giving a distinct crunch, then squeezed his fingers again, and waited.

After a few moments, he squeezed back.

Her heart hammered violently in her chest, but she tried to stay calm. "Will, it's Jules. Can you hear me? Squeeze my hand if you can hear me."

His fingers remained loose, but after a few moments, he moaned. She pressed her hand to his head, but her fingers were too cold to gauge his temperature correctly. She moved in closer. "I'm here. I need you to wake up for me, okay? I need you here with me."

She waited but he remained quiet again, no signs of movement. The wind howled beyond the shelter, and she kept her mind focused on staying in the moment. If she let her mind wander for even a moment—to the worst-case scenarios, like freezing to death—then she wouldn't be able to think.

Suddenly, Will groaned again, and his eyes began to move behind his lids, back and forth, rapidly, as though he were dreaming.

Tears streamed down her face, but froze to her cheeks before they fell. "That's right. Come on. You can do it. Just open your eyes." She gripped his hand and held her breath as he struggled to make the most mundane, involuntary movements voluntary. After minutes of struggle, his eyes peeled open, his lids bloated with swiftly forming bruises.

She wept in relief and wanted to tackle him, but she knew she couldn't. He blinked a few times and stared into the windy pocket above them, where she couldn't close the shelter entirely.

"Will, it's me. Can you hear me?"

He opened his mouth, but no words came out. Thoughts toggled in her head. *What if he has brain damage? What if he doesn't know who I am?* She grabbed her water bottle and dribbled a few drops into his mouth. He swallowed and cranked his head, wincing. His eyes locked on hers, and a tear slipped down his cheek. She rushed to brush it away and left her hand on his face.

"We were in a plane crash. I've moved us to shelter, but you're . . . you're badly injured."

Will opened his mouth again, a great, yawning void where his voice should be. Finally, he blinked again, centered himself, and spoke. "How bad?"

His familiar voice, thick with gravel, brought her to tears. She'd forgotten how even the sound of it soothed her. Though they'd been apart for months, the gap dissolved. She was here, with him, and she was going to make sure he survived.

She assessed his wounds and thought about downplaying the severity, but Will would want all the information. "You have a bunch of face lacerations and some shrapnel in your skull. Your ankle is broken, as well as your femur. I can't say about internal injuries, but we obviously need to get you to a doctor. Can you move?"

She waited for the information to compute. Wincing, he lifted an arm and then dropped it. "Check," he said.

She was relieved he could make a joke. "Your legs?"

"I think so."

She waited, but nothing happened. She moved toward his legs and squeezed. "Can you feel this?"

"No."

She tamped down the panic. "I'm sure it's just temporary." But she remembered how limp they'd been when she'd dragged him, how they reminded her of wet noodles. She reached into her bag and broke apart a protein bar. "This is a hell of a homecoming," she offered.

He attempted to roll his head to look at her and gave her a sad smile. "I'm so sorry."

She shook her head. "It was one of those freak accidents." As she said it, she realized that her very worst fear had come true. While she'd avoided planes all these years, the first one she'd gotten on had crashed. What were the chances of that? She bit into the protein bar, suddenly ravenous, and offered him a piece. He shook his head and struggled to sit up, but she kept him firmly in place.

"I'd stay still until we know what we're dealing with. How does the rest of your body feel?"

"Like it's been beaten with a bat." He was quiet for a moment, then spotted the urn between them and sighed. "We didn't . . . get to spread . . . her ashes." He wheezed between breaths.

Jules swallowed the bite and wrapped the rest. "It's not too late."

But wasn't it? Jules understood the kind of pressure Will put on himself, and he'd never let this go.

"Once the snow dies down, I'm going to see where we are in relation to town. I went out earlier, but I couldn't tell." She rubbed her hands near the fire. "Who were you radioing? When we went down?"

"The tower." He attempted to adjust and grimaced as his body failed to cooperate. "No one picked up the signal. Never got confirmation."

"Did anyone know you were going up today?" She thought about air traffic control, though she doubted that was applicable to a private airport hangar.

He barely shook his head. "No."

She let that sink in. "Someone had to have seen us. Someone will find us or send help."

They were quiet. Will closed his eyes and she wondered if he was asleep again. She couldn't handle him going completely under. Just him being awake made her feel like they could do this—that they would survive if he was awake and talking.

The fire cracked and popped as she added a few more sticks and spruce needles. The sound was hypnotic. She wasn't sure how long they sat there, but when the fire grew louder, she realized the wind had died down. She peered outside and saw a gap in the snowfall.

"I think the storm is lessening." She put on her pack. "I need to see where we are. I'll only go out for a bit and be right back, okay?"

He gave a small nod, but he was being pulled deeper toward sleep. She deposited a kiss on his lips and her entire stomach flipped. He opened his eyes and looked at her. He reached a hand—slowly—to grip her face.

"I love you so much, Juliette. I never should have let you go."

Relief stomped away the agony. All those lonely nights in her dorm, feeling lost and helpless at parties, rejecting physical advances from horny freshmen. All of the pain, worry, and concern vanished as she leaned into his hand and kissed him again. "I love you too. I'll be right back, okay?"

"Okay."

She took another sip of water and stuffed the rest of the bar in her pocket. There was one more in case Will got hungry and she placed it, unwrapped, by his side.

"Wait." He took a few shallow sips of air and then tapped the urn with his fingernail. "Take her with you."

Jules hesitated. She didn't feel right scattering his mother's ashes without him, but what if he never got the chance?

"Are you sure?"

He nodded, more tears carving through the dried blood of his face. "Watch her fly."

She scooped the urn from the ground and eased out from the semi-warmth of the shelter. The cold stunned her warmed skin. With the urn in hand, she set out, crunching through feet of snow, right back on the same path she'd gone before.

This time, it wasn't fear that fueled her; it was hope.

33

Jules

JULES retraced her steps north.

It was easier to walk without the wind and swirling snow, but the snow was almost up to her hips. She eyed certain landmarks—trees, rocks, stumps—anything she could reference in case she got disoriented or turned around. With Lenore's urn tucked securely under her arm, she marched through the snow and hunted for the right place to scatter the ashes. Jules struggled to remember what trees Lenore loved best: pines. She scoured the fifty-foot trees, but the more important task was getting back to the edge of that mountain to figure out if what she'd seen earlier was a town or just wishful thinking.

She hadn't worn her watch, and she didn't want to fish her phone from her bag. She wasn't sure if it had been minutes or hours. Her rib seemed to snag on every breath, and another sharp pain throttled through her stomach and made her stop in her tracks. She waited for it to abate and then advanced slowly, rhythmically, toward the edge.

Minutes later, she was there. She almost jumped up and down, but her sore knee prevented her from trying. Down below was a town—though it didn't look like River Falls. A few buildings clustered in the center of a neat grid, and smaller homes dotted the periphery in a distorted rectangle. She searched for a hospital or clinic, but couldn't see with all the snowfall. No cars were on the roads; no snow plows were even out.

She tried to calculate the next town over—Conway Hills or Sunset Valley. Either way, there was life down there, thousands of feet below. As the hope gathered in her chest, Jules swiftly realized she had no way to get safely to the bottom.

She gauged the slope. It was a treacherous descent with jagged edges and areas of complete vertical drops. Even the most experienced rock climber would fumble in these conditions, especially without equipment. She looked east and west and followed her sight line to see if the mountain veered down to a manageable climb in either direction. She decided to travel east for ten minutes, and then turn back and try west.

The urn grew colder in her hands. With every step she took away from Will, she worried. What if he needed her?

Suddenly, she started to run, losing all sense of calm as she moved east. Her rib jabbed her skin. She bit her lip until she tasted blood. The mountain continued to unfold with sharp rises and drops, and the town seemed to grow farther away, not closer. She felt like a caged animal, just out of freedom's reach. She could see it, but she had no way to get there. Dejected and cold, she started the journey back. Her heart still pounded at the thought of something happening to Will in her absence. She traveled west for only a few minutes and decided to cut diagonally back toward camp. Halfway back, she approached a massive pine tree, all alone, its needles still forest green and loaded with snow.

She arched back to marvel at its height. She whistled. "Lenore, this might be your tree." She removed the lid and took a deep breath. What would Will say in this situation? She wasn't one for speeches, but she mustered the truest words she could find.

"To the best mother I've ever known." Her gut clenched with those words, but it was true. She loved her mother, of course, but Lenore had appreciated who she was—not who she wanted her to be. "May you finally rest in peace." She lifted the urn and shook it, the gray, rocky ashes floating high above her head toward the pine with a sudden swoop of wind. She smiled as they swirled around the branches like smoke. Jules shuffled around the tree, sifting more ashes, until her rib emitted such a sharp pain, she had to sit down to catch her breath.

She gasped for air and stared into the urn. A thin layer of ashes remained. She'd save them for Will. It would give him something to live for, a purpose once he was better to fly up and honor his mother's original last wish. Once she caught her breath, she made the rest of the way back toward camp, practically breaking into a run when she saw the shelter, its thin line of smoke filtering through the opening in the top.

She crouched back inside and found Will snoring softly. She collapsed in relief and set the urn to the side. Removing her gloves, she once again warmed her hands by the fire. She needed a plan. She had no way of getting down this mountain, but she had to find a way. However, she understood that every time she went out, she risked burning more energy, and leaving Will vulnerable, in a critical state. The helplessness rioted in her chest, but she snuffed it. Panic wouldn't help.

She tried to think like her father and Uncle Tommy. What would the next logical step be? Try and make the camp optimal and wait for help?

She studied Will again. If she could only assess what his injuries were, she'd know what to do. Broken bones could heal, but a broken femur could be life-threatening if the break sliced through a main artery. Plus, he had shrapnel in his skull. He could get an infection and die within hours. He couldn't feel his legs. What if he was paralyzed? Not to mention any internal bleeding.

Her breathing became labored again. She couldn't seem to clear her head, to get in the right mindset to figure out what to do. If Will was in her position, what would he do?

She knew before she'd even completed that thought: He would stay with her. He wouldn't leave her side.

Firm in her immediate decision, she put her gloves back on and went out to forage for sticks and leaves for a better roof. She didn't know how long they'd be here, but she wanted to make them comfortable. She wanted as much time with Will as she could get.

34

Desi

THE hike seemed endless.

Her thighs ached. Her feet were cold and heavy, and she couldn't feel her face—even under the thick, itchy ski mask. Peter had broken some warming packs to shove into her gloves and around her chest. But she was freezing, scared, exhausted, and hungry. Part of her wished she'd stayed home. What if she became a liability?

Especially when they had no idea what they would find when they got there. *If* they even got there. They stopped to catch their breath, and Desi asked for the time. They'd been walking for two hours.

"What if we don't find anything?"

"Then we move on to plan B." Peter took a swig of water and offered her some. She took heaving gulps, then downed the pack of snacks he offered. She didn't ask what plan B might entail. She wanted to stay focused.

Tommy had gone a few steps ahead to scout the best direction, as the trail had long since disappeared. She didn't understand why Jules, Tommy, and Peter were so called to the wild, when it could literally kill you at every turn.

Desi searched Peter's face, but his mind was on the task at hand. Thinking of Carter had loosened a long-hidden truth in her chest, and she wanted to talk about it—to talk about *them*. Why had she agreed to live in a silent, joyless partnership for so long? She figured it was some sort of self-inflicted punishment for what she'd done, but it wasn't all her fault. She knew that. It took *two* people to make a marriage work, and she'd felt like a party of one for years.

"Peter." She placed her hand on his arm. Snow clumped against his skin, and he brushed the ice away. His ears were bright red, as was the tip of his nose. He was still so ruggedly handsome after all these years, and her stomach knotted a little at what could have been between them.

"She'll be fine, Des."

She hesitated. Of course, she was thinking about Jules, but somehow, she was worried less about her very capable daughter out here in her natural habitat than she was about what would happen after. What happened to Jules *if* she was okay? What happened to them if everyone survived? "We need to have a serious conversation when we find them."

Peter regarded her. She couldn't tell if he was perplexed or annoyed. She'd always had terrible timing. She wanted to start serious conversations when he was running out the door, had just gotten home from a long weekend away, or was ready for bed. She was notorious for it, but once she decided to talk, nothing could stop her.

"Not now." He jerked his head toward Tommy, whose red jacket disappeared around another tree. He whistled and Peter followed after him.

She had to jog to catch up. "Did you hear what I said? I don't mean about Jules. I mean about us."

He glanced at her, definitely annoyed, and clenched his jaw.

"Why do you always do this? We are trying to find our daughter and her boyfriend—who might've been in a plane crash—and you want to talk about our marriage?" His voice rose, a rare occurrence, and she regretted even bringing it up. "Fine then! Let's talk." He planted his feet and turned to her, arms crossed inside his puffy jacket. "Why don't we start with Carter?"

Tommy halted a few feet ahead and rotated, a worried expression on his face. Desi looked from Tommy to Peter. "What do you mean?" she stammered.

He took a step closer. "You know exactly what I mean."

What does he know? She hoped he couldn't hear the thud of her heart bumping against her parka. Now she had a choice to play dumb or let the truth finally tumble free, right here in the middle of nowhere.

"Do you mean the fact that he moved?" Tommy offered.

Peter turned. "He moved?"

Desi shot him a death look. "Stay out of this, Tommy."

Tommy lifted his gloved hands and retreated a few steps. "I'm just going to forge ahead. Don't be long."

Desi envied her brother at that moment, but she also knew they were wasting valuable time. She began walking again, and Peter stalked after her. Her mind spun. Where did she even start?

"What do you want to know?" she finally asked.

Peter stomped through the snow behind her. His silence consumed her, infuriated her. This was just like him to ask and then punish her with silence.

"How long after I deployed did you fuck him?"

She gasped and rotated, almost ramming straight into his chest. "Are you serious right now? *That's* what you want to know?"

He laughed. Bitterness contorted his face. Slowly, the real

truth slid into focus. Peter didn't love her; he hadn't loved her for so very long. Because if he'd known about her and Carter for two decades and had chosen to stay with her anyway, she understood that wasn't love or looking the other way—that was his way of punishing her. In Peter's mind, letting her go for an indiscretion would have meant she could have lived her life, maybe even worked it out with Carter. Staying meant she had to endure his silent fury, his frigidity, his withholding, which meant experiencing a thousand little deaths every single day. She'd driven herself crazy over the years trying to make it better, wondering if what she'd done had caused such a split between them, wondering if she should tell him the truth, when he'd known anyway. What a waste of their lives.

He moved closer to her, so close, she could see tiny crystals of ice clinging to his eyelashes.

"How long?"

She calculated in her head. After she'd seen Carter that first night, they'd met every week. They seemed to understand each other in a way she and Peter never had. It made her sad for not making sure she and Peter were truly compatible before they got married.

"A month." She whispered the words behind her ski mask and stared at her boots, which were dusted with a fresh layer of over-sized snowflakes.

He sneered at her and turned on his heel, but not before whispering, "You disgust me."

The pain was swift, but she knocked it away. She jogged to catch up and grabbed his elbow. "No, you don't get to do that."

"Do what?" He jerked his arm free.

"You don't get to blame this entirely on me." Her words gathered steam. "Carter and I dated way before I met you. He introduced us, remember?" The words were coming faster now, and she couldn't contain them. "Carter was too unpredictable. When I met you, I thought . . ." She trailed off, ignoring the stung expression on his face. "You promised me before we got married that you would retire. But the moment we got married, you left. You *knew* I wouldn't marry you if you were going to be active duty. We both agreed to that, and the moment you got a glimpse of domestic life, you bailed. I felt like you couldn't stand to be near me, that a civilian life was like death."

"So the moment I leave, you fuck your ex-boyfriend?" He moved a few steps away from her, then doubled back with such ferocity, she flinched. "You know why I left? Because you scared me. I never felt good enough for you. You seemed so certain of your life. You didn't even want children. But that didn't matter to me. *You* mattered. And then, when we got married, you just seemed . . . unhappy. I worried that it was me, that I couldn't make you happy. I panicked. I thought one more tour would give us both time to adjust to married life." His eyes bore into hers. "Little did I know, you were already playing house with someone else."

She shook her head. "It wasn't like that." But wasn't it? What she'd done was horrible. She should never have strung Peter along all these years, when they were both so clearly unhappy.

"I could tell something was off when I got back, but then you got pregnant and . . ."

And he fell in love with Jules. He stayed because of Jules, not her.

"Did you talk to Carter?"

He seemed thrown by the change in topic, but he knew exactly what she meant.

"That night you went to pick up Jules. Carter was fine and then he was gone the next morning."

He looked directly in her eyes and almost smiled. "Yes, I did."

She didn't dare ask what he'd said, as he wouldn't tell her anyway. "So you've known all this time . . ." It wasn't a question, and the statement hung between them, damp and untouched. "Why did you stay, Peter?"

"We have a family," he said.

"But our lives could have been so different." They could have still raised Jules and found other people.

"I hate *your* life," he snapped. "I hate how everything has to be a certain way."

She scoffed. "You're a Marine! Everything has to be a certain way."

"That's not what I mean. You spend more time on furniture or designs than people, as if you can take them with you when you die." He paced a few steps again, his back turned. "I wasn't the only one who suffered because of that. Your daughter suffered too. She grew up with a shallow mother. Your whole life has been shallow!" He threw his arms into the air and screamed into the trees.

"Shallow?" She closed the gap. "It's my work! At least I was making my clients happy, making their worlds better, instead of murdering innocent people for a fucking country you're so quick to complain about."

"Watch your mouth, Desi."

She continued. "I'm part of this relationship too. You've been mentally, emotionally, and physically checked out ever since you got back from Iraq. I *tried* to get you to go to therapy. I tried to help you, but you refused. You denied me a life with a husband. You refused to do the work."

His red nostrils flared, his hair lifting and flattening with the wind. "Because you were clearly in love with someone else," he whispered. "I wanted you to pay for that. I wanted to dedicate my life to our daughter—not you."

Instead of stalking off, Peter let those words land, and her eyes immediately filled with tears. As she stared into his eyes, any traces of love hardened to hate. She'd asked herself so many times over the years how she might have been a different mother if she'd been with someone else. The real secret bubbled in her chest, dying to escape. She'd never said the words out loud—never dared hurt Peter so much—but she knew she now had nothing to lose. "It's funny," she said.

"What's funny?"

She moved so close to him that his angry, frigid breath blew into her face. She searched his eyes, spotting the golden flecks she used to marvel at when they'd first started dating. "It's funny that you've dedicated your life to a daughter who isn't even yours."

She turned, heart pounding, and headed deeper into the forest.

35

Jules

AFTER hours of work, Jules was exhausted.

She snuggled in next to Will, thankful for the fire. She'd erected a flimsy roof above them, making sure the smoke had a safe path to escape. She'd never been more thankful for her father's lifelong training, which had prepared her for this very situation. It solidified her future. She didn't want to spend one more second in some small, stuffy classroom, reading textbooks and listening to a professor talk.

She wanted to help people, to use her hands to work each and every day, to do the *real* work that humans had gotten so far away from. This was her chance to claim her own life, to build something meaningful here, with Will and the baby.

She turned to him and traced her hands over his face. The bandages had long since filled with blood and congealed, but the gashes had finally clotted. She tried not to think about the metal at the back of his skull, how it could be leaking poisons into his system. She tried not to think about his legs, and how his back or neck might be broken and what life would be like if he could never walk or fly again.

She batted away the pessimism and moved in closer. Her rib

was unbearable, but she ignored the pain to be as physically close to Will as she could.

"What has life been like for you?" He blinked at the roof. Slivers of light danced over his face like needles.

She propped herself up on her elbow, surprised that he was awake. "You really want to know?"

He rolled his head toward her. Even with his torn and bloodied face, his eyes focused only on her. "I've wanted to know everything."

She shrugged, hiking one shoulder and dropping it. "New York is a beast." She smiled. "I used to pretend you were there with me. Every amazing thing I saw, I took pictures to share with you. But the longer I was there, the more I knew I just wanted to come home."

He knew which home she meant.

"So show me now."

"The pictures?"

"Got nothing but time, right?" He smiled and attempted to adjust, groaned.

She helped him get comfortable, then flipped through photos on her phone. She walked him through those first few days of setting up the dorm, Melanie, and the endless freshman parties held in tight studio apartments or the stuffy dorm activities room. She told him about her attack and even let him feel the bumpy scar at the back of her head.

She'd taken pictures of everything, feeling more comfortable behind the lens than having to truly interact with the people around her. Once she'd acclimated herself to the city, she'd trekked all over Manhattan, snapping hundreds of photos. As she flipped through them now, a small sense of gratitude filled her body. Maybe her mother was right. If she hadn't gone to New York, she wouldn't have been able to really figure out—to her core—what she wanted. She knew college wasn't for her, that New York wasn't for her, that Chicago wasn't for her. She knew that her summer romance with Will hadn't just been a fling—it meant something, and it always would.

Finally, she put her phone away. "What about you?"

He smiled sadly and stared once again at the thatched roof. "I've spent every day figuring out a way to show up in New York and get you back. But I didn't want to screw up your life."

She was hurt that he thought she'd move on so easily, but maybe that had been easier for him. Losing Lenore, almost losing his sister, losing her . . . She gripped his hand and threaded her fingers through his. They fit so well together, as if their hands were made for each other. "I could never move on. This is it for me, Will. There will never be anyone else."

He nodded. These weren't words from a silly eighteen-year-old girl. She was speaking from the very depths of her soul. She was *certain*. She'd always been certain, from the first moment she saw him to right now, with his broken body and his will to live. They would get through this.

She sat up, and another pain ripped through her abdomen. She gripped her belly. This one wasn't sharp like her rib, but a deep cramping. Suddenly, something warm and sticky spread beneath her. She moved away and saw a small circular blood-stain where she'd been sitting.

"Are you okay?" Will strained to see.

She stared at him fearfully as another cramp ravaged her abdomen.

He peered down where she'd moved away and spotted the blood. "Oh God . . ."

Will struggled to sit up, but failed. Tears filled his eyes and a few slipped down his cheeks. His body would not cooperate as he told it what to do. He tried again, but his limbs remained limp and immobile.

She couldn't lose the baby. More pain gripped her stomach, and she doubled over. Before she could say anything, she rummaged through the first-aid kit and found some gauze. It wasn't much but she used it to soak up some of the blood, which was already lessening. Once she was settled, she took some deep breaths.

"I just need to rest." Even as she spoke, she realized the seriousness of what was happening. She was bleeding. She needed a hospital, or she might lose their baby. She'd researched everything about pregnancy, knowing that the first twelve to sixteen weeks were crucial. She was almost fourteen weeks. With the crash, there was no telling what had gone wrong.

Will reached for her hand. "You have to go, Juliette." His eyes locked with hers, and she understood how desperate he must feel not to be able to move or help.

"I don't know how I can get down there," she said. And if she was bleeding, moving would only make it worse.

"You have to try," he said. "You have to."

She gripped his hand as tears flowed freely down both their cheeks. "I don't want to leave you here."

"I know, but I'll be fine. I promise." He turned more toward her, wincing as a thin sheen of sweat coated his forehead. "I'll never forgive myself if you lose our baby."

Our baby.

The cramps intensified, and Jules wasn't sure she could even make it ten feet, let alone thousands. But she had to try. Not only was Will's life in danger, but now hers was too. She hadn't even thought about it as *their* baby; she'd mostly ignored what was happening to her body until she could tell Will. Now she knew this was meant to be. They were going to be a family.

And if she was going to be a mother, she had to think like one. She had to try and save herself, even if it meant leaving Will behind.

She packed her bag, moving the extra bottle of water near Will, as well as the first-aid kit. Her pants were damp from the blood, but she felt like it was slowing enough for her to walk. Her breath seized in her chest as she looked at him.

She kneeled in front of him and took his face in her hands. She kissed him deeply, lips trembling, and studied his face, memorizing every inch.

"I'll be fine," he said. "I love you, Juliette."

"I love you too, Will," she whispered. She crawled back toward the opening, tightened her pack, and headed out into the snow.

36

DESI couldn't believe she'd finally told him.

She quickly caught up with Tommy, who was oblivious to what she'd just revealed. He glanced at her, saw the seriousness of her expression, and knew not to ask. She didn't even care where Peter was. She wanted the shock to tear him apart, just as it had tormented her all those years.

After she and Carter first slept together, she'd felt terrible and wonderful, all wrapped into one. She knew she'd crossed the ultimate line, and she had to tell Peter. She had to ask for a divorce. As she'd literally been wrapped up in Carter's sheets, tracing the line of his shoulder, he'd leaned in, kissed her softly, and said, "I want to work this out."

She'd rolled to her back, nodded, and stared at his popcorn ceiling. A brown water stain patch spread in the top right corner. "Me too. I just don't want anyone to get hurt."

He sighed, folding his hands behind his head. "Me neither. But I love you, Desiree. I want to spend the rest of my life with you. I did then and I do now."

Hadn't Peter just said the same thing not too long ago? How had this even happened? The difference was she felt something when Carter said it—not a sense of obligation because they were married—but because it was wild, unbridled, and deep. They were willingly choosing each other *despite* all the obstacles in the way. It was the tougher choice, but the right one.

She looked at him, her stomach turning flips. Thoughts of Carter consumed her: at work, at home, in the bedroom, and everywhere between. Theirs was the kind of love that kept her up at night.

After that day, she'd considered hiring a lawyer to assess her options, but she didn't have the money and knew she had to tread lightly. When Peter returned, he could be dealing with PTSD, and she didn't want to push him over the edge.

Almost two years after he'd left, Peter came home unexpectedly, when their tour had been cut short. She wasn't ready. She was focused on Carter, on the life they were building, and when Peter arrived, she realized she needed to give him time to adjust before she pulled the rug out from under him.

It wasn't until she'd taken a pregnancy test that she knew she had to rip off the Band-Aid. Peter had been home for two months, and she still hadn't gotten the nerve to ask for a divorce. And now she was pregnant.

She'd decided to do it over dinner, but then, Peter had walked into the living room. The pregnancy test she'd buried in the trash was clutched in his hands. He'd fallen to his knees, wrapped his arms around her waist, and wept. It was the first and last time he'd shown such emotion, but Desi was caught completely off guard. He'd devoured her in kisses, told her that this baby was the only thing he'd ever wanted, and that he would be the best father any child could hope for. He was going to retire and they could finally build the life of their dreams.

Desi had been paralyzed. Peter had never cried in front of her, and she didn't know what would happen if she suddenly broke up with him. That would mean not only admitting that she was in love with someone else—it would also mean admitting that the baby wasn't his. She and Peter had slept together regularly since he'd returned home, but she knew the baby was Carter's.

She felt caught between two relationships, but in that moment, with his arms around her waist, all her feelings for Peter reemerged, and she was more confused than ever.

"Des, what happened back there?" Tommy edged into her thoughts, and she returned to the present, the vault of memory once again closing up.

"I told him the truth," she said, teeth chattering.

"Like the *truth* truth?" he whispered. "That you slept together?"

Should she tell him the rest? She could already imagine Peter's next form of action. He'd request a DNA test, something she'd already done to be sure.

She'd always known that nothing would ever gut Peter more. Jules was his pride and joy, his reason for living, and she wasn't even biologically his. She didn't think through what that rage could do to Peter, how he might destroy anyone and everyone around him as a result. She glanced behind her. What would the consequences of this be?

She saw the flicker of concern in Tommy's eyes, but he stayed silent.

She swallowed and kept charging forward. Not only had she lied, but she'd denied Jules a relationship with her real father. Though Peter was an incredible father, was Jules better off for never knowing Carter?

Once she'd made that painstaking decision to work it out with Peter, she and Carter had severed all communication. Nothing had ever been more agonizing than telling him it was over again.

Suddenly, Peter whistled behind them, and they both turned.

She glimpsed his gloved hands a few yards back motioning to the right.

"Plane!" he yelled.

She and Tommy veered to the right, a tree branch snagging on her jacket, physically holding her back. She snapped it in half and kept running until they reached a flat, snow-filled clearing. Fifty feet out, remnants of what used to be a prop plane were torn and strewn across the white. She searched for the telltale red stripe of Will's plane, but it was impossible to tell from this distance.

"It's Will's!" Peter confirmed.

"Oh my God." She clamped both hands on her mouth and fell to her knees. Tommy ran ahead, and she squeezed her eyes shut.

"Clear!" Tommy yelled.

Peter was already reaching into his bag to send up a flare. She stomped through the snow to get to the plane.

Up close, the wreckage appeared primal, carnage left over from a wild animal attack. She stared into the bucket seats, smeared with blood, and realized, heavily, that no one could survive this. The three of them stared at each other.

"Is there any evidence Jules was here?" Tommy asked.

She searched through the frozen rubble, hunting for what, she wasn't sure.

"There!"

Tommy gripped her shoulder. He pointed west, toward some trees in the distance.

"What?" She followed where he was pointing, and that's when she saw it. A makeshift hut with a whip-thin line of smoke drifting into the sky. Shelter. Fire.

Life.

Peter and Tommy sprinted toward the trees. She tried to keep up, but it was like her bones were made of jelly. She was hyperventilating, afraid to see what state Will might be in, but knowing if there was a shelter, then he must be alive. She didn't know if she hoped Jules was with him or not with him, but either way, she was about to find out.

She was the last to reach the shelter and dropped to all fours to crawl inside. The fire sealed the shelter with heat, and she was instantly flooded with warmth as she huddled inside. Will lay on a gray blanket, his face bandaged but soaked with blood. Desi resisted the urge to scream and searched wildly around them. She glimpsed a bloodstain on the ground beside his body.

"Where's Jules?"

There was too much commotion. Tommy was digging in his bag to tend to Will, who lay unconscious. Her question emptied into the space, died.

"He's burning up," Tommy confirmed.

She scooted back as Tommy analyzed his injuries. Peter stayed by his side, handing him instruments or tools as he requested them. Tommy used his stethoscope to listen to his heart. He shook his head at Peter and examined his head. His fingers stopped and he turned Will's head gently.

"Shit." He worked his way down, feeling his neck and back, examining his leg that appeared bent the wrong way. Desi's stomach bucked. He listened to his lungs again and whispered, "Tension pneumothorax." He whipped the stethoscope away. "He needs a chest tube."

"What does that mean?" Desi racked her brain for what that term meant.

"He's got a collapsed lung," Tommy explained. He put on medical gloves and dug in his bag. "He needs a needle decompression and chest tube." He eyed Peter. "Can you assist?" He tossed Peter a pair of gloves and Desi watched from the corner of the shelter, unable to move or speak.

Tommy gave Will oxygen and then pulled out a 14-gauge needle. Desi used to fear needles until Tommy became an EMT.
Then she soaked up everything she could, surprising herself
with her interest in the procedures. Why had she been so quick
to want a different profession for Jules?

She watched her brother work, his adept fingers grabbing the
surgical scissors and hacking through Will's sweater. Tommy
felt for the second or third intercostal, just superior to the rib.
He drove the needle into the space in one quick motion and
waited for the lung to expand. Desi knew enough to know this
was a temporary solution, that Will would need a hospital immediately, as a collapsed lung was life threatening.

After a few tense moments, Will sucked in a big breath and
began to breathe normally. Tommy removed the needle, bandaged the area, and gave him more oxygen with the small por-
table tank. Tommy listened to his heart again and nodded.

"Good for now."

He started an IV. They all sat silently, morbidly, until Will
blinked awake. Desi wasn't sure how much time had passed,
but she literally couldn't hold the question back the moment his
eyes fluttered open.

"Where's Jules?"

"Jesus, Desi, give him a minute," Peter snapped.

Will struggled to speak, and to her surprise, he began to cry.
She closed her eyes, wondering if she was dead, wondering if
she'd ever get to see her child's face again.

"She left," he croaked.

"What do you mean?" Peter asked calmly. He sat by his feet,
adjusting his blue medical gloves.

"She's . . ." His voice faded, and he tried again. He went under
and Desi wanted to scream.

"Just give him a minute," Tommy said. "He's just now getting oxygen back into his system."

He worked his way down his legs again, removing his boot to assess his foot. Desi looked away at the backward appendage, the massive swelling that didn't even appear human. Tommy whispered something to Peter, and he nodded gravely.

"What?" she asked.

"I think his back is broken," Tommy said. "No natural reflexes. Could be paralyzed. We've got to get him to a hospital."

Desi squeezed her eyes shut and shook her head. *Poor Will*.

"Jules . . ." Will came to again, and Desi shot to attention. They all looked at him, waiting to speak.

"What about Jules?" Desi encouraged. "Was she here? Was she with you?"

Will attempted to nod. "She's . . . she went to get help."

Desi's entire body slumped with relief. If her daughter had gone to get help, then she was alive. That meant she was intact enough to move.

"There's a town down the mountain, not too far, but . . ."

Peter was already on his knees, removing the rubber gloves, and edging toward the exit. He slipped from the shelter and was gone. Desi had no idea how Peter would find her, but if anyone could follow her tracks, he could. She dropped her head into her hands and collected her thoughts.

What she'd just told Peter, how selfish she'd been . . . She didn't think she was capable of hurting another human so much, but as she stared at the physical wreckage of her own decisions as a mother, she knew that *she* was more of the problem than she could even comprehend.

So much of this mess was because of her, and if anything happened to Will or Jules, she'd never be able to forgive herself.

Desi moved back to the corner of the hut, while Tommy listened to Will's breathing again, content with his vitals for the moment. Desi wavered between going after Peter and staying here.

"I know you want to go," Tommy said. "But Peter knows what he's doing."

"But she's my daughter."

"She's his daughter too," he said.

She couldn't sit here with her guilt and shame; she had to help. Unable to sit and wallow, she tugged her ski mask back into place and took off out of the shelter.

Tommy called after her, but she searched for Peter's footprints and followed them deeper into the expanse of intermittent trees. Snow clung to her boots and gathered around her thighs.

Somehow, she had to make this right.

37

Desi

DESI marched through the snow.

Her footprints fit completely inside Peter's, and she snaked diagonally toward his trail, realizing she didn't have anything to defend herself with if a predator suddenly came out of nowhere. She hesitated, but then forged ahead.

She was relieved Jules was okay and was beyond proud that her daughter had not only survived an almost fatal plane crash, but that she'd built a shelter, started a fire, and kept them both alive without professional help. How blind she'd been to the skills her daughter had honed all these years. Why had she been forcing another, duller life on a daughter who was so alive, so fully capable of creating her own future?

She stomped into the headwind, thankful for the tiny break in snowfall and wondered if anyone had seen the flare. She pulled her phone out of her pocket and searched for a signal, but again, nothing.

Her thoughts kept getting pulled back to what she'd told Peter. Would he tell Jules? She'd wanted to sit her down so many times over the years and try to explain, but the wound was too wide, the damage too deep.

She knew the real victim wasn't Jules or Peter, however. It was Carter. Carter, who'd never gotten to know his own flesh and blood. Desi had not only ended their relationship—she'd stolen his chance at fatherhood. Had she ever let herself truly imagine his pain, or was she always preoccupied with the devastation it would cause *her* family if the truth came out?

The first time she'd seen Carter after they broke up had been after she'd had Jules. She was pushing her around the neighborhood in a stroller. She'd been so exhausted, it had taken her a moment to recognize him. She'd nervously fumbled through a light hug and awkward conversation. He looked well, and she hated how she felt in his presence—like a magnet was drawing her in, even when she knew she needed to stay away. Finally, he'd torn his gaze away from her to the stroller.

"Des." His eyes had filled with tears, and she'd tried to push past him, but he gently held her in place. "I'm happy for you. Truly." He didn't even look at the baby, but released her and kept walking in the opposite direction. That was the last time she'd seen him until he'd shown up at the farmer's market. They'd never talked about that day: if he'd suspected the baby was his, or if it had been easier to assume she wasn't. He never asked, and she never told.

Now, as she trudged through mounds of white, she realized what a coward she'd been. For years, she'd known what she wanted, but she hadn't been ready to blow up her life in order to get it. After she had Jules, she'd finally gotten funding to start her own business. She and Peter had friends together, a life together, a baby. Carter had no money, no prospects. He only had the memory of her.

The part of her that wanted to *appear* successful had already wormed its way into her mind, and she chose the illusion of a successful, happy life over what her heart craved. There'd been too much to risk, too much to expose.

She understood now that she'd been trying to inflict the same choices on her daughter. Jules looked at Will the way she'd once looked at Carter. And she'd foolishly wanted her daughter to choose safe and happy over wild and free.

Up ahead, she spotted him.

"Peter!" She called his name, but it died in the wind.

She began to run, forcing her exhausted legs forward until she caught up. He didn't even flinch when she touched his arm.

"Go back, Desi." His voice was flat.

"No. I want to find her too. I have as much of a right to be here as you do."

He snorted, stopped, and turned. His mouth was a hard, white line, but his eyes were ravaged by the sudden truth. "Why did you stay if you knew Jules was his?" he finally asked.

She swallowed the knot in her throat, recalling the day he'd found the pregnancy test. How happy he'd been. How certain of their future. "Because you wanted to be a father so badly. And I wanted to make you happy."

"But that was Carter's choice too. You stole that from him."

"It was between you or him. I chose you." Even as she said it, she knew that by staying, she had chosen wrong. She'd made decisions for everyone: Jules, Peter, Carter, herself. And then she'd built a life on that set of lies, and now look where they were. Carter had moved across the country. Her daughter was missing. Will could be dying. And she'd already lost Peter a long time ago. This was the final stake in the ground.

"Jules is the best thing that ever happened to you," she reminded him. "You've always been an amazing father."

"To a child who's not mine." He looked at her again. "I'll never forgive you for keeping this from me. Ever."

"I don't expect you to."

He turned and kept walking. There was so much she wanted to say. She'd sacrificed her own happiness to let him be a father, but that didn't seem to matter now. Instead, the truth negated everything. She'd ruined them all.

"Juliette!" Peter yelled and charged toward a heap in the snow.

Desi ran after him. Jules was curled on her side, her face ice white, her eyes closed, her limbs tucked in for warmth. For one terrifying moment, Desi thought Jules was dead. Finally, her eyes fluttered open.

Jules looked confusedly between them, her lips parched, and then began to cry.

Desi dropped to her knees. "Honey, are you hurt?"

Jules shook her head. "I need a hospital. I need to get to town." She pointed somewhere behind her, then looked at both of them. "Will?"

"Tommy is with him," she whispered. "He's taking care of him now."

Peter scooped his daughter up as easily as if she were five and began heading back to the shelter. "Let's get you warm, sweet pea."

Desi followed them wordlessly, wishing she could do something to help. Jules clung to his neck, her eyes closed, moaning. A daughter in her father's arms. Her stomach clenched.

What have I done?

When the shelter came into view, she ran ahead to warn Tommy.

"He's got her," she said.

Tommy nodded and made room beside Will to examine Jules. A few seconds later, Peter laid her gently on the second blanket. Will was still unconscious but some color had seeped into his cheeks.

Jules moaned and gripped her stomach.

Desi moved back a few feet. "What's wrong with her?"

Jules was pasty white, gripping her stomach and crying. "I don't want to lose it," she screamed. "Please."

Tommy pressed lightly on her stomach, and Jules screamed.

"Appendix?" Peter asked.

Tommy shook his head and continued feeling her abdomen. But Desi already knew: the bloodstain, her insistence to get help, her daughter's fuller appearance, the moodiness. She grabbed Tommy's shoulder.

"Tommy, I think she's pregnant. She might be miscarrying."

"What?" Peter took a cautious step forward.

Desi tugged down her daughter's ski pants and saw her underwear soaked through with blood. "Oh my God," she whispered.

Tommy took her pulse, checked her temperature and her blood pressure, and examined her abdomen again. He palpated for tenderness, rigidity, and sighed. "I have no way of checking the fetal heart rate. Do either of you know how far along she is?"

Peter and Desi shook their heads.

"Juliette, I need you to talk to me, okay? How far along are you?"

Jules was writhing in agony and wheezed between breaths. "Almost fourteen weeks," she stammered.

Fourteen weeks! Her daughter was over three months pregnant and she and Peter had no clue? She caught Peter's eye, but he looked away. Apparently, this time, they were both in the dark.

Desi eased forward and slipped Jules's hand in hers. "It's going to be okay, sweetheart. We're going to get you help." She tried to keep calm as Peter went outside.

A moment later, another flare went up. Desi kept talking. "You know, when I was almost four months along with you, I

started bleeding too," she recalled. "I thought I was losing you."
She hadn't thought of that day in so long. She'd been going
from one client meeting to the next and had felt something
dampen her skirt. She'd had to take a taxi to the hospital and
was hooked up to all sorts of machines. She thought it was her
punishment for pretending the baby was Peter's—that nature
was going to take its natural course and extinguish any chance
of her becoming a mother. "When I got to the hospital, I was
so scared, but you were such a fighter, Juliette. Even then." She
squeezed her hand. "I know your baby is going to be a fighter
too. Just like you." She glanced at Will. "Just like Will. You have
to stay strong, okay? For all of you."

She smoothed the damp hair from Jules's forehead and let
Tommy finish his examination. He sat back on his heels. "We've
got to get her to a hospital. There's nothing I can do for her here."

Desi glanced between her and Will. Desperation ricocheted
around the shelter. They both needed help.

Peter set out on foot to check the distance to the town Will
had mentioned and rushed back, saying it would be impossible
to get down there on foot. He paced outside, too antsy to stay
in the hut. Torturous thoughts pressed into her most vulnerable places. What if she lost her daughter? And if she survived,
what if Peter told Jules the truth? It seemed Desi had become
a destructive force in her own orbit. In the span of one day,
she might lose everything she had sacrificed so much for: her
family.

She huddled closer to Jules, stroking her hair, and hummed
quietly. There was so much she wanted to confess to her daughter, so much she wished she could undo. Instead, she remained
silent, the sticks sizzling and popping beneath the stoked flames.
Tommy fussed with his medical equipment, the tinkling of surgical tools lulling her into an almost meditative state as he

toggled between Will and Jules. Outside, a repetitive thudding thundered overhead. Tommy jumped to his feet just as Will surged awake. "Thank God."

He rushed outside. Desi kissed the back of Jules's hand, who was now sleeping, extricated her hand, and glanced at Will on her way out of the shelter.

"Help's here. It's going to be okay," she said.

Outside, the sky was bright, and she squinted until her eyes adjusted. Sure enough, there was a chopper headed their way. Everything in Desi's body relaxed as she jumped up and down and waved both arms.

Peter was already running toward it as it fought for space to land. The chopper blasted snow in every direction. The pilot hopped out, a burly, capable-looking man with a full beard and aviators. He marched toward them, careful to avoid the whip of the blades. "Only got one bodyboard," he shouted. Had they not sent a medical team too?

She quickly learned there was only one medical chopper in town, and it was small—too small for both Will and Jules.

How would they decide who to take?

If Will stayed, he risked not making it. But if Jules stayed, she could lose the baby. Tommy talked to the pilot, and they decided: they would take Will. When they broke the news to him, Will shook his head.

"No. I won't go." The words took effort to say, but they didn't have time to argue. "Take Jules."

"You're critical, bud," Tommy said. "They need to take you first."

"I won't go." He gritted his teeth.

Tommy sighed, knowing they were losing valuable minutes. "How fast can you get back?"

"Less than half an hour," the pilot said.

Did Will have half an hour?

They talked in hushed tones, then decidedly positioned Jules on the board. She moaned and gripped her stomach again.

Desi jogged after them toward the helicopter. Once they slid her into the back, Tommy turned. "Only room for one of you."

"What if Will doesn't make it?" she asked.

"They'll come back as quick as they can," Tommy said. "But one of you needs to go now."

Desi searched Peter's face. She wanted to be with her child more than anything, but she knew what she had to do. "You should go," she said.

Peter hesitated, but there was no time to argue. He gave a curt nod, tossed his pack to Tommy, and climbed into the chopper. She shuffled back as the pilot lifted the beast off the ground, the wind blowing fiercely around them. Tommy slung an arm around her shoulder as they walked back to the shelter.

"She's going to be fine," he assured her.

Inside the hut, Will screamed, and Tommy released her to duck inside.

"Shit." He lurched toward Will, who was convulsing and foaming at the mouth.

"What's happening?" Desi asked.

"He's seizing. Grab my bag. There's diazepam in there. It's labeled."

Desi's fingers fumbled with the small vial. She searched for the syringe, stuck the needle into the vial, and sucked up the medicine. She handed it to Tommy, who sunk it directly into Will's flesh. The seizing slowed, but his body continued to buck. "He's got to get that shrapnel out."

Desi attempted to process. "The chopper will circle right back, right?"

"He doesn't have time."

As if on cue, the wind picked up and a fresh round of snow began to fall. Desi felt paralyzed, trapped.

"This can't be happening," she said. "He can't die. Jules didn't even get to tell him goodbye."

"I know," Tommy said. He raked a hand through his disheveled hair. "I need more equipment. The lung decompression was just temporary, and if he's seizing . . ."

They fell into tortured silence, and Desi's brain whipped into a relentless loop of self-punishment, worry about Jules, and fear for Will. Every sound heard beyond the shelter, she prayed was the chopper coming back to save them.

"What did Peter say?" Tommy finally asked.

Desi wiped her nose and warmed her hands by the fire. "He said he'd never forgive me."

Tommy sighed. "Just give him time."

"No." She shook her head. "We're done. We've been done a long time. I should have never . . ." Her voice faded as she stared at the fire.

"Should never have what?"

"I should have chosen Carter." She'd never uttered those words out loud until now. She looked at her brother. "I love him."

"Don't say that." The flames flickered and cast a red hue over Tommy's face.

"Why? It's the truth. I'm so sick of secrets, of hiding things. When I get back to Chicago, I'm divorcing Peter. It's time we both lived our lives." She stared at Will, who lay so still. "I just hope it's not too late."

Tommy glanced over his shoulder at Will, fussed with his vitals, and then turned his attention back to the fire.

But the shelter started to close in. She couldn't breathe, couldn't think. She stumbled outside. The storm whipped furiously around her, stealing her breath and pounding her unzipped jacket and bare face. She searched for the helicopter in the bleached sky, practically willing it to come back.

She had to get out of here. Her daughter had to be okay. Will had to be okay.

They all just needed a second chance.

38

Desi

IT seemed like the chopper wasn't ever coming back.

After a while, Desi reentered the shelter. Even with the fire, the cold seeped into her bones, a steady ache. Will's pale face was eerily still, his chest barely rising and falling. Every second was critical. She searched Peter's bag for a bottle of water.

"I never meant to upset you," Tommy said. "If I said something . . ."

Wasn't that the theme of her entire life? She'd never meant to marry a soldier. She'd never meant to fall in love with another soldier. She'd never meant to have that soldier's baby and pass it off as someone else's. The type of mother and wife she'd become . . . How could she ever blame anyone but herself?

She addressed Tommy. "You didn't."

He blinked at her, then slid his gaze to Will. "I hope the baby is okay."

A lump rose in Desi's throat. She wanted to be with her daughter, but it was the right choice sending Peter. "Me too." She said a silent prayer that both Jules and the baby would be okay, that somehow, they'd all make it out of this.

"Jules?"

Tommy jumped to attention. Will's eyes opened and he stared between them, confused. He tried to speak, but couldn't. Desi pushed in beside him.

"The chopper took Jules to the hospital," Desi reminded him. "They're coming right back for you."

"Just hang on, bud," Tommy said.

Tears leaked down Will's cheeks, and he directed his slippery gaze toward Tommy. "The baby?"

Desi swallowed. "I'm sure they're doing everything they can."

Tommy administered an exam. Satisfied, he patted his leg and scribbled something down on a notepad.

"How bad is it?"

Desi shot Tommy a warning look, but she knew her brother. He wouldn't bullshit anyone or give them false hope. "Will, have you ever had seizures before?"

Desi waited for him to say no, but to her surprise, he nodded. "Only as a kid."

"Have you ever been checked for myocarditis?" Tommy asked.

Will shook his head no. "What is that?"

"Inflammation of the heart." He tossed his notebook to the side. "Look, your electrical system is shorting, bud. You also have a collapsed lung, a broken leg and ankle, and I'm almost positive you've broken your back."

Will emitted a low whimper.

"Hey," Desi said. She scooted closer. "We're going to get you to the hospital and they'll fix you right up. You're going to be fine."

He blinked again, his lids flapping double-time. "Am I going to die?" His voice was small, like a child's.

Panic lodged in Desi's throat. She looked at Tommy for re-assurance.

"I'm doing everything I can to keep that from happening,"

he said. "But you need to focus on taking deep breaths. Can you do that for me?"

Will glanced at the urn, devoid of his mother's ashes, then stared at the ceiling. "I can't feel my legs."

Tommy did another round of tests, but he was right—there were no reflexes.

"Just stay with me. Help is coming."

Desi felt like screaming. The chopper should have taken him up first. Yes, her daughter might have lost the baby, but Will was the one in critical condition.

"Will, look at me, okay?" She pushed in closer. "Jules needs you. You're going to be a father."

She waited for Tommy to say something positive, but he stayed silent.

She huddled in even closer, tugging his lifeless hand toward hers. "Think of the baby."

His eyes found hers. "I was there when my mother died," he gasped. "I don't want . . ." He was unable to finish, but Desi could surmise what he was trying to say.

Will wanted to be able to live a full, healthy life. He didn't want to die, but he also didn't want to suffer. He stared into space, tears dripping onto the blanket below in a series of soft taps.

"We just need to get you to the hospital," she reassured him. "You're going to be okay." The words tumbled from her mouth, but how could she promise him that?

"I can't . . ." He began to cry again and searched her eyes. "I'm in so much pain."

She looked to Tommy for help.

"I'm going to go check for the chopper. Hang tight."

Once he was gone, she struggled to think. "Remember your sister? How scary that was? And now look at her. She's better than ever." Even as she talked, she knew a severed arm wasn't the same as what Will was facing. If his back was broken, if he was paralyzed, if his condition worsened, if his heart gave out . . . She knew what a long road to recovery that would be. Especially with a new baby.

"I don't want to die," he said softly. His glassy eyes found hers.

Desi wanted to stay resolute for Will, but she began to cry too, so overcome with this young man's grief. She felt partly responsible for his position here, for talking to him that day last summer and convincing him to let Jules go.

"Will, you have to stay with me. Please."

Tommy reentered the shelter. He crouched down and examined Will's breathing again and sighed. "The needle decompression has reversed. He's losing oxygen."

Will's face was turning pale, and suddenly, he started gasping for breath.

"Isn't there something you can do?" she insisted. She smeared her tears away, the panic building in her chest.

"He needs a hospital, or he's going to suffocate."

Will's eyes were wild as he battled for breath. He began seizing again. Desi frantically searched for more medicine, but Tommy stopped her.

"I only had one vial." His eyes were anguished as Will began to make strange noises, like a wounded animal.

Tommy's jaw set into place as he rolled Will onto his side so he wouldn't choke. "He's not going to make it, Des." Even as he said it, he issued more oxygen, but it did little to help. He removed the mask. "Where the hell is that chopper?"

"Will." She squeezed his hand tighter. "Will, look at me. Just hang on. The helicopter will be here any minute. You can make it. Think of Jules. Think of the baby."

He opened his mouth again and said something that sounded

like *please*. Desi stared at him, heartbroken and scared. ***Please what?*** His body bucked again, his breath chaotic and uneven. He removed his hand from hers and tugged on the spare blanket beside him. He thrust it into her hands.

"Please," he said.

She looked at the blanket, understanding what he was asking, and shuddered. Tommy took it from her and automatically rolled it into the shape of a pillow.

"What are you doing?" She snatched the blanket from him.

"He's suffering, Des."

"So what? You're going to *smother* him?" Her hands trembled uncontrollably around the blanket. She felt sick.

Will gave the slightest nod and closed his eyes. "Do it."

With the blanket in hand, a guttural sob escaped her throat. She couldn't do this. She couldn't do what he was asking, and the fact that Tommy sat there, reticent, was unforgivable. She glimpsed the oxygen tank beside her, dropped the blanket, and secured it back into place instead, knowing this was a mere Band-Aid for the real problem, but after a few agonizing seconds, his body began to buck and tremble. His hand blindly searched beside him again, his wayward fingers closing around the blanket and thrusting it toward her.

She removed the oxygen mask and stared deeply into his eyes. "I can't."

"Please." The word was raspy and wrong. His lips opened and closed like an oxygen-starved fish on land.

Her fingers tightened on the blanket. She closed her eyes. "I'm so sorry, but I can't." She tossed the blanket away, imagining the horror of pressing the blanket over Will's face. The way her forearms would strain with effort. The surge of his body, and then the stillness.

No.

Outside, the thundering whoosh of the chopper's blades barreled closer. She scrambled to her knees, but Tommy was faster. He disappeared outside and Desi lightly tapped Will's face, trying to rouse him awake. "Will, the chopper is here. Hang on. Please hang on."

He was barely conscious.

She sprinted outside and wildly waved her hands. The chopper landed, once again blasting snow into the air, a mini tornado of ice.

The pilot hopped out, this time with the bodyboard and a medic. Tommy rushed forward to give him an update and the three ducked into the shelter. Desi waited outside, praying Will could hang on just a little longer.

She heard bags unzip and directions being barked into the unforgiving cold. His fate hung in the balance, but he couldn't end up like Lenore. Her daughter would not survive it.

A moment later, the medic and Tommy shuffled out, the slab of Will's body lifeless under the gray blanket. She couldn't tell if he was breathing. They took assured, practiced strides in the snow and deposited him into the helicopter. Tommy barked something over the roaring blades before tapping the door two times in a send-off. The helicopter swayed into the air and swerved back toward the hospital.

Once again, they were stranded.

She reentered the shelter, shell-shocked. She stared at the blood and the spare blanket she'd almost smothered her daughter's boyfriend with. She gripped it in her hands and then scuttled backward, dropping it when Tommy entered.

"They'll come back for us."

She turned toward him. "Is he . . . ?" She couldn't bring herself to the say the word *dead*.

"I'm just praying he makes it to the hospital."

"I really thought he was going to die."

Tommy tossed items back into his bag. "It's why I let Jules go up first. No point in two losses today." Tommy shoved the bag to the side and warmed his hands by the fire. Desi sat there, gazing at the makeshift bed where Will had just been. She closed her eyes, imagined herself lowering that blanket over his face.

What if she'd killed him?

The sorrow of the last few hours lashed her heart. She began to cry. Tommy stopped what he was doing and pulled her against his chest. She leaned into her big brother and sobbed until she was so congested, she could barely breathe.

"He can't die." Her voice was raw, emotions ravaged, until she was once again convulsing in sobs.

Tommy pressed his chin on the top of her head and held her firmly. "He still might, Des. You have to be willing to face that fact."

"He wanted me to end it," she whispered. She wavered between shock from the request and disgust about what her brother might have done if she hadn't been there to stop it. She sniffed and sat up. "He handed me that blanket. He wanted me to . . ." She couldn't finish the sentence.

He shook his head. "He was suffering. You have no idea what it's like to suffocate." He released her and stared gravely at the gangly branches that served as an exit, probably thinking of all the fallen men he'd seen, men who'd begged for their own end. But this wasn't war. This was the man her daughter loved, the father of her grandchild.

And one of them could have taken his life just because he'd said *please*.

"Jules." She said her name in a whisper and dropped her face into her hands. What if she lost both the baby and her boyfriend in a single day?

Tommy drew his knees to his chest. "Let's just wait until we get to the hospital to worry, okay?"

Yes, she had to figure out how to navigate the minefield of her daughter's emotions, but first she had to *get* to her daughter. How long would it take the chopper to circle back around this time?

She waited for Tommy to say something, but he tidied the space and gathered his equipment. She tended to the fire to give herself something to do while they waited, but her body convulsed from the shock and cold.

Finally, the familiar sound of the chopper roared overhead.

"You ready?" Tommy asked. He shouldered his bag and gazed around the shelter one last time.

She wasn't ready. She might not ever be ready. Before she followed Tommy, she spotted Lenore's urn in the corner. She clutched it to her chest and stepped outside into the wildly churning snow and mentally prepared for the emotional whirlwind ahead.

39

Jules

SHE opened her eyes.

Her lids were gritty and swollen. She slid her hands to her belly. The searing cramps had lessened, as had her rib pain. Her body was warm beneath the blanket, though she felt heavy and sore. A TV droned across from her. A tray with uneaten food perched beside her hospital bed. Her dad sat on a bench by the window, watching the snow.

Bits and pieces of the crash and its aftermath floated through her mind. Will. Lenore's ashes. The dismantled plane. The fear she might lose the baby.

"Dad?"

He whipped around and was at her bedside in a second. "Hey, sweetie." He kissed her forehead and stroked her hair.

"The baby?" She prepared herself for the news.

"The baby is doing just fine. Got you here just in time. You're lucky."

She sighed in relief.

"You've got some pretty significant injuries though. You're going to have to be on bedrest for a while."

She nodded. "Where's Will?"

"The chopper went back to get him."

Emotions swirled in her chest. He'd been in such bad shape when she'd left . . .

A sharp knock on the door made them both turn. The doctor entered. His salt-and-pepper hair was slicked back, as if he'd just gotten out of the shower. She could smell the musky bite of his cologne from across the room.

"How we doing?" He removed his stethoscope that dangled around his neck.

This was the second time she'd been in the hospital in a matter of months. She thought about making a joke, but was too exhausted. She let him check her vitals, then listened to the medical jargon about her injuries and how she'd need to rest for the baby and her rib. After what she'd been through, the thought didn't sound half-bad. She and Will could heal together.

Suddenly, her mother pushed into the room, her hair wild, her face flushed. Her eyes were swollen, as if she'd been crying.

"Oh, thank God." She jogged across the room and crushed Jules in a hug. "Is the baby okay?"

Jules nodded and struggled to sit up.

"I'll just give you three a moment."

The doctor slipped from the room, and Jules could hardly contain the question. "Is Will here? How bad is it?" She figured they would rush him right to surgery.

To her surprise, her mother began to cry.

"Des?" Peter looked at Desi, and she shook her head. Peter dropped his head and sighed. Jules lobbed between them, not understanding.

"What is it?"

Desi gathered herself and sat on the edge of her bed.

She slipped her hand in Jules's. "Right when they took you away, Will had a seizure. Tommy thinks he might suffer from myocarditis—which is a condition of the heart."

Jules tried to make sense of what she was saying. Will had never mentioned it.

"He had a collapsed lung, which Tommy temporarily treated, but he . . ." She trailed off and wiped her eyes. "He began to suffocate, Juliette."

Jules's body turned to ice. She stared at her mother, unmoving, unable to think.

"Is he okay?" It was a foolish question to ask, but she refused any answer other than yes. Of course Will was okay. They had finally found their way back to each other. They were going to live a long and happy life together. There could be no other choice.

"He's in critical condition. They rushed him to surgery, but I'm afraid the prognosis doesn't look good."

Jules held unnaturally still. "No," she finally said. He'd *promised* her. Her hands folded in a protective dome over her belly. His life was in her body. They had a baby to raise. "No!" She said it again, the shriek of her own voice surprising her. "No!" She began to scream so loudly, her father rushed to her side and tried to contain her, but Jules sat up, ripping the IV from her arm, fighting to get out of the bed. "I need to see him. I have to see him. He has to be okay!"

She attempted to stand, but her father firmly held her in place. She lashed out, her fingernails catching his forearm and drawing blood. He didn't flinch. He just held her tighter and kept whispering he was sorry. Her mother stood beside her bed, trembling violently. Her stomach ached and she screamed again, a piercing wail that sounded inhuman.

Nurses burst into the room joined by Tommy, who stood at the door.

"Tell them he's going to be okay!" she screamed at him. "You were with him. You were helping!"

Tommy took a step into the room. "I did everything I could."

"No!" Her entire world exploded, all of her hopes and dreams untangling and floating away. Her life would be *ruined* if he died. She couldn't do this without Will.

She cried until she got sick, dry heaving into a pink tray her mother held out for her. Her father gathered her hair, blood bubbling on the skin of his arm where she'd attacked him. The nurses reattached her IV and administered a sedative.

Before she knew it, she was going under, and she hoped all of this—the crash, Will, the news of his improbable survival—would be nothing more than a nightmare she would wake from.

40

Desi

THE hospital cafeteria smelled like cleaning products and burnt coffee.

Desi helped herself to a Styrofoam cup and slurped the watery brew. She traveled the halls, the linoleum dingy and yellow beneath her feet, the walls an offshoot of beige. She stopped outside the nursery, where babies curled inside their blankets, bucking new limbs, crying, or staring up into the harsh white lights. Desi's heart broke for Jules, but especially for Will.

She packed away the pain and weaved toward the waiting room, where a small cluster of people fanned out among the plastic chairs. A janitor enthusiastically mopped the halls, listening to music and mouthing words only he could hear. For the most part, the hospital was quiet, everyone tucked inside due to the snowstorm. But there was a collective buzz about the plane crash. News traveled fast in such a small town, and sure enough, all the local channels had splashed the wreckage of Will's plane on TV.

Ava and William Sr. had been notified of Will's condition and were trying to find a way to the hospital. Tommy dropped into a chair beside her, appearing as battered as she felt.

She stared at her brother's profile. She used to think he'd wasted so much of his life being reckless, but the way he'd taken action to try and save both Jules and Will was remarkable. She let go of her earlier judgments because he was right. She didn't know what it was like to suffocate. How did anyone know what they were truly capable of until put in that position?

"Still in surgery," he confirmed. "But even if he survives, he's going to have a long road ahead. We all need to be prepared for that." His words were wiped of emotion, and Desi wondered what reaction he expected. That she would somehow feel relieved?

Peter walked into the lobby, his boots loud on the linoleum floors. His coat was folded neatly in his arms, his ears still bright pink from hours in the cold. "She's going to be asleep for a while. One of us needs to get to the house to grab some belongings. They'll need to keep her for observation at least a few days."

Desi nodded. They had no car. It was the middle of a snowstorm. How would they even get home?

"Des and I will go. Just let me know what you need."

She glanced at her brother in surprise. "I'm not leaving." What if Will died while they were gone? What if something happened to the baby?

"I need your help picking out her stuff." There was something else behind his eyes she couldn't read, but she was too tired to ask, or fight.

She crept into Jules's room while Peter and Tommy made a list. Monitors beeped, all the machines hissing and calculating the metrics of a human life. She moved to the edge of the slim bed and smoothed some hair off Jules's forehead. She traced the bridge of her nose. Every summer, a spray of freckles emerged and then disappeared with the cold.

"I never meant for any of this to happen." The words leaked

out, reminding her of her earlier thoughts. Yet something else that shouldn't have happened. All because she'd refused her daughter's happiness. And now, Jules might have to live her life without the man she loved.

Desi really was the architect of all their lives.

She eased back the stiff blanket and crawled into the hospital bed, placing a hand lightly on Jules's belly. How unfair that Desi would get to watch this baby grow when Will might not. He could be wiped from the earth, just like Lenore.

The door opened and she sat up, the private moment dissolving between them. William Sr. and Ava stood at the entrance, their eyes red-rimmed. She rushed over and crushed them in hugs.

"I'm so sorry," she whispered. "Have you heard any updates from the doctor?"

"Still in surgery," William Sr. whispered. He squeezed her hand. "Thank you for taking care of my boy."

"Of course." Still, she couldn't shake the image of herself lowering that blanket over his face . . . of what she could have done.

William Sr. dabbed his eyes. "How is she?" He shuffled farther into the room.

"She's stable. The baby's okay." She sniffed.

Ava and William Sr. snapped their heads in her direction. "What baby?" Ava asked. She looked at her father. "Jules is pregnant?"

Desi nodded. "We just found out. Will knows too." She could barely say his name without crying.

William Sr. slung an arm around Ava. "At least we'll have that." There was a somberness to his words, a preparation of what might come. He, more than anyone, knew the cruel bite of the universe—how it could wipe away the people you loved.

"She's sedated, but take your time visiting. Let me know if you need anything."

In the lobby, Tommy jumped up when he saw her. "Got us a car."

She glanced outside the automatic doors. It looked like the snow had stopped.

"Plows have been out clearing the roads. We should be able to get there and back."

She hesitated. She really wanted to wait to hear the news about Will.

"He's going to be in surgery for at least another few hours," Tommy confirmed. "I promise we have time."

Placated, she followed him outside to find a rented Ford with four-wheel drive. The air bit her lungs as she took a full inhale. She buckled herself in and blasted the heat, instantly falling asleep before he'd even put the car into gear.

"Des. Desi, we're here."

Tommy shook her shoulder and she jolted awake, the skeleton of The Black House creeping into view. For a moment, she wondered if it was all a bad dream, but then reality came crashing in, and grief clawed at her heart once more.

He unlocked the front door and she walked straight to the master, ripping off her clothes and turning the shower as hot as it would go. She didn't know how long she stayed under the scalding spray, but when she emerged, she was still freezing. She dressed in layers and walked to the kitchen, where a fresh pot of coffee had been brewed.

Tommy had whipped up eggs and toast, and she gobbled both down, not even knowing what time of day it was, before taking a much-needed sip of coffee.

"Better?" he asked.

She ignored his question and went to sit by the fire, knowing they needed to get back to the hospital, but she was so fatigued, she could barely keep her eyes open. She just needed a second to sort through everything, to understand what she was supposed to do next.

Tommy joined her on the opposite end of the couch. "You okay?"

Her eyes found his and she skimmed his face. "I'm sorry I judged you earlier . . ." She trailed off.

"Look, the kid was on his deathbed." He sighed. "I'm trained to make fast decisions. In that moment, the inhumane thing would have been to let him suffer." He nodded once, as if convincing himself. "But he's still got a fighting chance, so you were right to ignore his request."

Did he really believe that? She thought about all the ways Will might suffer *if* he survived. Maybe that was a worse fate? She stretched her legs, which felt like lead. "I need to pack Jules and Peter a bag." She heaved herself off the couch and entered Jules's room, which was tidy and warm.

In her closet, Desi retrieved her white suitcase and unzipped it on the bed. She began pulling clothes from her dresser and closet, arranging them in tight rolls to save space. She packed some books and magazines, her sketch pad and charcoal pencils. She searched for anything else she might like and spotted a Polaroid of her and Will. She cradled it against her heart and forced away the tears. She slipped it into Jules's favorite book—*Arctic Dreams*—and wedged it carefully between her clothes.

All that pining, all that worrying, all that secret keeping. It seemed so small compared to this. Her daughter's grief was the biggest thing in the universe, and she didn't know how long it would take to contain it if Will died. Maybe forever. Desi might spend the second half of her life watching her daughter's misery unfold and doing everything in her power to stop it. And knowing, deep down, that she was the primary cause.

They packed the rest of the bags and hauled them into the car. Outside, the sun performed its last dance, the sky shifting from orange to lavender, then an instant, aching blackness shrouded her land. The temperature dropped. Their boots crunched in the snow, the only sounds between them. Her mind was a rampage.

Before they got into the car, Tommy turned to her. "Wait."

She shivered beneath her jacket and gloves. "What?"

He was obviously grappling with something. "Des, I never knew how unhappy you were," he finally said.

She sighed and shook her head. "I'm too tired to talk about this right now," she said. Her love life seemed so insignificant at this point.

"He wants to see you, Des."

She turned and found his face in the dark. "What?"

"He asked me to tell you that, but I didn't. I thought you needed time. I thought you and Peter could work it out, but . . . he really does care about you."

A small swell of hope rioted through her chest—a bright spot in an otherwise tragic day. "I care about him too. But this isn't about me. Right now, it's about Jules and Will." She climbed into the passenger seat and waited for him to start the car.

She gauged The Black House. She'd never forget the first time Peter and Jules had seen it. They'd traveled down their private road, murmuring about the greenery and the crisp mountain air. Jules had commented on the looming wrought-iron fence that outlined the entire property—that it seemed like something out of Harry Potter. Peter had punched in the code, then swerved beyond the gate and down the newly laid drive. She remembered the way their tires had popped over fallen branches and acorns. The cool air whipping through open windows. The shimmering pines bowing toward their car, diffusing the sunlight. And finally, The Black House that throttled into view, sprawling and ominous.

This place had brought so much pleasure and pain. She'd naively thought this house would save them, that it would bring them back to each other. Instead, it had brought them to the truth of who they were and what they all really wanted. Perhaps that was the point all along.

She composed herself as Tommy gunned the engine. They drove silently back to the hospital, careful on the slick turns and black ice. She tracked the full moon above, which bleached the sky silver.

"Please say something."

She glanced at him, at a face so familiar, then peered out the window. The landscape zoomed by in an icy blur. "Just tell him I miss him. And I'll reach out when I'm ready."

"Copy that." He nodded, then flipped on the radio to drown out the silence. Her thoughts played on a relentless loop, but she pushed her own feelings aside. She had to be strong for Jules and Will.

A half hour later, they arrived at the hospital. Tommy pulled out both luggage handles with a satisfying zip and rolled them to the entrance.

Inside, the hospital reeked of disinfectant. She bypassed the check-in and practically jogged to her daughter's room. Ava, William Sr., and Peter were gathered around Jules's bed, holding hands and sobbing. Tears streamed down Jules's face.

Oh God.

She steeled herself for the news.

"Mom." Jules and Desi locked eyes. Her daughter began to cry harder, and Desi rushed to her bed and took her in her arms. She searched for words of comfort but found none.

After a moment, Jules wiped her tears away and offered a painful smile. "He made it through surgery, Mom." She began crying and laughing at the same time. "He's got a long way to go, but he's going to make it. I know he is."

She looked at the others in disbelief, but everyone confirmed it.

"He might lose his leg, but they're trying to save it," Ava added. "They removed the shrapnel. His back is broken in three places, but the surgery was a success."

William Sr. swiped a handkerchief under his nose. "This family and their limbs. Your arm, his leg." He pointed to Ava then let out a sharp wail. "But I'll take it." He shook his fist at the ceiling and then pressed it to his heart. "I'll take you both in pieces and parts as long as I get to keep my children."

Ava hugged him, and Desi reached for his hand. She was so grateful for this unlikely bunch. In such a short time, they'd all been through so much.

Her eyes finally landed on Jules, and she kissed her cheek. "I love you, sweet girl."

"I love you too, Mom."

She glanced at Peter, who avoided her gaze, then looked back at Jules. "Are you allowed to see him yet?"

She shook her head. "Not yet."

She excused herself and found the doctor. She realized there was a protocol, but her daughter needed to see Will. They all did.

After what seemed like hours, the doctor okayed a short visit. William Sr. and Ava went first. Desi helped situate Jules in a wheelchair, and then Desi rolled her toward the intensive care unit. As they passed the quiet hall, she peered inside open doors, the sick and pale hooked up to machines. Will had too much life to live. He didn't belong here.

A nurse directed them to the right room, and outside of it, Jules stopped. "Do you mind if we have a minute alone first?"

"Of course."

Jules took a breath and then rolled herself inside, maneuvering to his bedside.

Desi watched through the window. Will's face was bandaged and swollen, much like the rest of his body. His leg was bloodied, bloated, and stapled, the metal scissoring up his leg from ankle to thigh. His lips parted into a smile when he saw her, and Jules practically leaped out of the wheelchair to get closer. She kissed his hand, crying, and brought it tenderly to her belly.

Jules caught her mother's eye through the window, and she said something to Will and pointed her way. Will craned his head a fraction and locked eyes with Desi.

She held her breath, unsure of what she would find waiting there. Resentment? Rage? Disappointment? Fear? Instead, he gave her the smallest nod—just like he'd done in the shelter—and mouthed *thank you*. She nodded back and blew them both a shaky kiss, her palm lingering against the window.

"You're welcome," she whispered.

Maybe she shouldn't focus on what could have happened in that shelter. Maybe she should focus on the fact that she'd actually given him hope to hang on.

Her daughter laughed, and Will emitted a short, painful laugh too. They threaded their hands together, her daughter's entire demeanor light and hopeful, despite what they'd both been through.

Desi took a few steps away from the window to give them privacy. She joined William Sr., Ava, Tommy, and Peter, who stood in a tight cluster a few feet away.

"So the lovers have reunited," Tommy declared. She could see the relief on his face—that perhaps not everything had such a horrible ending.

"Yes they have," she said.

She leaned against Tommy, who gave her a quick kiss on the head.

Her eyes roamed around the group. She memorized Ava's hopeful expression, William Sr.'s slack but grateful smile, Peter's stony, resolute silence, and Tommy's easygoing, talkative nature guiding everyone toward a much needed laugh.

She looped an arm around Tommy's waist and squeezed. They'd made it through this horrible tragedy, together. Despite all the odds. Despite all the heartbreak.

It would be a long road to recovery. They would need each other now, more than ever. But she would be here—no matter what came next.

SUMMER

Epilogue

THEY all sat around the dining room table.

It was the start of summer, and it was their first meal together at The Black House since that fateful winter day. Desi passed the mashed potatoes and arugula salad to the left.

"Thanks, Mom." Jules helped herself to extra potatoes and another piece of chicken, which sat on a platter of antique china in the middle of the walnut table. Jules was due any day now, and they'd all taken bets on when she'd give birth. Jules was having a girl—Willa Lenore Wright.

Even though six months had passed since the plane crash, the wounds ran deep. Desi had been with Jules almost every waking moment—taking her to therapy, to Will's, to her doctors' appointments—and getting her set up for life with an infant. Desi had decorated the nursery and loved organizing and shopping for every onesie, toy, and book.

She helped slide the giant chicken breast onto Jules's plate, who passed the dishes to Peter.

"Thanks, Mama-to-be."

Jules rolled her eyes at the affectionate nickname.

Desi and Peter had been officially divorced for a month, and with the dissolution of their marriage, some of the tension had eased between them. However, Peter didn't speak to her much beyond logistics. He'd moved out of the penthouse and built a separate guest house here in River Falls, in a cleared acre behind the house. He wanted Jules, Will, and the baby to have The Black House to themselves, and of course, she'd agreed.

"Dude, you're eating for two, not twelve!" Tommy jabbed his fork to fight for the last piece of sourdough bread. Jules laughed as he battled her in a tiny duel across the table.

Tommy had decided to move to River Falls to help with the baby while Jules took EMT classes next fall, which left Desi's life completely private back in Chicago. Once she'd filed for divorce, she'd finally asked Tommy to give her Carter's number. They'd talked a few times on the phone and were planning to see each other soon. She still grappled with whether to tell him the whole truth—that Jules was his daughter. She'd always wondered if he'd suspected it, but now that Peter knew, it seemed only fair to tell him too. However, she was so afraid of pushing him away again. She'd denied him the chance to be a father.

But it wasn't too late.

"Okay, kids. Enough," Peter joked. He'd gotten a haircut, was clean-shaven, and seemed so much emotionally lighter. She'd seen him smile more in the last few months than she had in years. Desi tried hard not to take that personally, as she too felt the slimmest possibility that she could find her own version of happiness someday. While he still hadn't forgiven Desi, she was mostly focused on forgiving herself. She needed time to heal, time to become her own person again. While the pull to see Carter was strong, she wasn't ready for any sort of relationship yet.

"How long are you staying once the baby is born?" Tommy

chewed with his mouth open and took a long swallow of water to wash it down.

"As long as this beautiful mama needs me," she said, winking at Jules.

Though Desi had stayed in The Black House for the last six months, traveling back to Chicago when needed, she'd ultimately decided the city was her home.

She wanted to give Jules space, to afford her a new life of her own choices. Jules had the support of William Sr. and Ava. She had River Falls, its community, Tommy, and Peter. Most importantly, she had the baby and Will. Jules was going to live a full, happy life here, in the safety of The Black House.

Will would be moving into the house once he was fully recovered. In the end, they'd saved his leg, and both that and his back were healing nicely, though he still couldn't walk. The doctors weren't overly confident that he'd be able to fly again, but Will was determined. Despite his initial grim diagnosis, his positive attitude, coupled with Jules's undying support, pushed him to improve every single day. He focused on one day at a time, like all of them.

Now, they all chatted about how lovely May was turning out to be, how gorgeous spring had been, and all the festivals that would soon unfold in River Falls.

Peter said something and Jules laughed. It had taken her daughter a while to smile again. After the initial relief of Will's survival, she'd been crippled with anxiety and nightmares for months—but now she was coming back to herself, understanding that she had a child to raise and a boyfriend to help. And that, like so many other hard lessons, life would go on whether she was ready or not.

Desi stared around the table at Peter, Jules, and Tommy. Her fractured little family. She'd kept secrets from all of them, locking away the darkest parts of herself *for* herself. But she was coming to terms with the secrets she'd kept and figuring out how to move forward without hurting anyone.

She swirled her wine and chimed in where appropriate, but her mind was somewhere else. Her eyes wandered to the cavernous living room, the banks of windows, the sparkling pool, and the pile of rainbow-colored towels heaped by the chairs from their earlier swim. And then beyond, to the woods. She couldn't have known when she built this house that it would become the container for all their hopes and sorrows.

Tommy offered her more wine and she lifted her glass appreciatively.

"To family," she said.

The crystal tinkled as everyone politely tipped their glasses to hers. She took a delicate sip and relaxed.

After dinner, they loaded the dishwasher and then all drifted to their separate spaces. She and Tommy shared a drink on the patio.

Desi leaned her head back. The last drops of humidity drained from the sky and left her slightly chilled.

"What a year, huh?" Tommy asked.

Desi couldn't even laugh. "That's putting it mildly." She took a sip of wine, that corkscrew of pain still driving inward whenever she was still with her thoughts. She'd lost so much this past year: her husband, Lenore, nearly her grandchild, her daughter, Will. It was too much to wrap her mind around. And at the same time, she was gaining the possibility of a more honest future. Through loss came clarity. Through tragedy came truth.

She yawned and closed her eyes as she and Tommy lapsed into a comfortable silence. The fountain gently lapped into the pool, practically lulling her to sleep. A few minutes later, Jules approached.

"I'm going for a walk," she announced.

Jules went for walks most nights, but the last few days, Desi was too nervous she'd go into labor alone in the woods.

"I'll come," she said.

Inside, she pulled on her sneakers and grabbed her phone. They pushed through the back gate and began walking, both lost in thought. Jules began to chat about Peter's recently launched survivalist courses and what a hit they were with the locals. Desi tuned in and out, a little buzzed from the wine, until she realized they'd veered slightly off path.

The sun faded until they were both submerged under the opalescent flush of the moon. Jules branched ahead, picking up speed. From the back, she could barely tell her daughter was pregnant. Still, Jules's steps were so assured, even as night approached. It was evident she belonged out here, in the wild.

"You coming, Mom?" She motioned for her to hurry.

Jules continued to chatter, her skin rosy and warm, her hair dark and wild, her smile honest and bright. Her supple belly strained against the fabric of her gray cotton dress, so full of unborn life.

Desi trotted to catch up and linked arms.

"I'm right here," she said.

Acknowledgments

This book started off as one thing and morphed into another (as I've learned most of my books do). As I was creating this world and these characters, it started with a house. The Black House, to be exact. In 2019, when I was doing a three-stop book tour, I was invited to the amazing Emily Carpenter's house in Georgia. I was so taken with her big, black house, that I immediately exclaimed upon arriving: "This is a great house for a murder!" (Thriller writers will totally understand what I mean.) While there is no murder in *Secrets of Our House*, there are plenty of secrets, lies, and betrayals. As we have all become more accustomed to being at home, I couldn't think of a more perfect setting than this house.

As this book began to take shape, it stuttered and started several times. This, more than any of my other books, was created in a vacuum. No writing groups to review it. No beta readers to give feedback. However, one person was with me for the entire ride. Joe Tower, your steadfast hand in helping me navigate this fictitious town of River Falls and all its secrets laid the foundation for a different type of story. You are my constant rock, my confidant, my business partner, my podcast co-host, and I love doing business (and life) together.

To my agent, Rachel Beck, who has been on this journey with me since 2016 . . . your patience, guidance, and enthusiasm have never waned, and that is one of your biggest superpowers. Thank you for staying the course. I'm looking forward to seeing what we do together next.

To my editor, Alex: if it weren't for you, I never would have accomplished my dream of becoming a published novelist. Your belief in me has been such a gift, and I will never forget it. Thank you for everything.

To the entire team at St. Martin's Press, who are the real unsung heroes of making any book come to life: the publicity team, the sales and marketing team, the distribution team, the audio team . . . so much goes into having a book published, and I appreciate every single one of you. To my copy editor, NaNá V. Stoelzle, you made my book better, line by line. Apparently, decades into my career, I still never know when to use "farther" versus "further." So, thank you for helping me take my manuscript farther. Or should it be further? Sigh.

To the incredible cover designer, Young Lim, who literally took my breath away when I glimpsed this cover. This is truly a cover I've been dreaming of, and you made it come to life. Thank you.

To all the book bloggers, Instagrammers, publicists, readers, and marketing wizards who helped this baby fly: thank you. You truly do make all the difference.

To my fellow author friends, of whom there are many: this past year has challenged us in more ways than one. Every post, text, or phone call went such a long way, and I appreciate your vast support during those trying times. You are all an inspiration.

Lastly, to my family and my husband, Alex, in particular:

You have stuck by me through every book, every success, every failure, and every uncertain moment. This past year, I really straddled the line between business owner, author, and mom, and it wasn't easy. But your support and belief in me helped push me along the way. Yes, I am an author, but I also run a business for writers. Yes, I write books, but I also help others write theirs too. I know I could simplify my life and just be an author (and trust me, some days, I'd love nothing more). But I'm passionate about sharing what I know with this community, and for every single person who picks up one of my books or takes the time to read and review, I say thank you.

Because you've made a difference in this writer's life . . . and for that, I am forever grateful.

Lastly, to my daughter, Sophie, who is just coming to understand what life is all about. The moment you asked "Can I be your editor?" I knew you were in this with me for the long haul. I know I am your mother, but you are truly my greatest teacher. Never lose that precious spirit, baby girl. I know it will change the world.

As I come to the close of one book and take steps to decide what comes next for me as an author, I just want everyone to know: being published is an absolute privilege, but it's also really hard. No longer are we in the days of writers just being writers. We have to do and be so much, and it can seem extremely overwhelming. So, if you are a reader, please share our books. And if you are a writer, please keep writing books. No matter what the industry says, we need your voices. *ALL* your voices. So be brave and tell the stories you want to tell.

I am beyond grateful that I get to tell mine.

Discussion Questions

1. Desi is a woman who is outwardly "perfect," inwardly living with a lot of pain and secrets. Did you identify with any of Desi's struggles?

2. Desi had to make a choice between two different men, and two different lives led. Do you think she made the "right" choice? Do you think she and Carter would have stayed together for life?

3. Explore the themes of keeping secrets, the weight they carry, and how that affects relationships over time. Do you think Desi and Peter's relationship would have been different had she told him about Carter, and Jules's true parentage, from the get-go? Do you think Jules would have made the choices she did had she told her parents, or Will, about the pregnancy earlier on?

4. Lenore is a mother figure to Jules in lots of ways. In what ways do you think Jules flourished under her nurturing, and how did she grow under Desi? Do you think it was inappropriate or unfair of Lenore to take on this kind of intimate role with Desi still present?

5. Why do you think Peter chose to deploy so soon after marrying Desi? Do you think their relationship was doomed from the start?

6. Put yourself in Desi's shoes. At what point do you decide the secrets are too many? After having an affair with Carter? After Jules is born? Would you keep the secret as long as she does?

7. The wilderness plays a huge role in this novel. How is nature both a place to retreat and be safe as well as a capricious place that can act like an enemy? Did this change or reinforce any feelings you have about the natural world and the people within it?

8. Do you think Jules was reckless with her safety, with her baby's safety, and with her future? Do you think she acted very much like an eighteen-year-old might?

9. Look at where all the characters are when the novel ends. Do you think everybody has ended up where they should be? Did you think the story would end differently for anyone?

10. Who was your favorite character? Why?

About the Author

© Vibe Tribe Creative

REA FREY is the author of *Not Her Daughter,*
Because You're Mine, and *Until I Find You,* as well
as several nonfiction books. She is also the CEO and
founder of Writeway, where aspiring writers become
published authors. To learn more, visit reafrey.com
or writewayco.com.